Gunn(

Hell's Ankhor: Book 2

Aiden Bates & Ali Lyda

© 2020

Disclaimer

This is a work of fiction. Names, places, characters, and events are all fictitious for the reader's pleasure. Any similarities to real people, places, events, living or dead are all coincidental.

This book contains sexually explicit content that is intended for ADULTS ONLY (+18).

Contents

Chapter 1 - Raven

I leaned closer to the center monitor on my desk. I'd been typing without pause through the past eight hours, and there was something wrong with the code I'd written. I scanned through the program for what felt like the hundredth time. When I got in the flow like this, the code became an extension of my mind—my own desires and goals reified into thousands of lines of sometimes inelegant but always functional programming.

Twelve hours ago I'd received an email: a picture of Dad's fatal bike crash with two words. NO ACCIDENT. The bug I was programming would latch onto the email and trace it backward to its point of origin. Or it would, if I could figure out why it wasn't compiling properly. After another few minutes, I finally identified the error—a misplaced semicolon—and adjusted it, and then began the compilation. It'd take a solid ten minutes to complete.

As soon as the timer began, and there was nothing I could do but wait, my wrists and fingers throbbed. I'd been so focused on the task at hand that I hadn't even noticed the pain.

The knuckles on my right hand were swollen and warm from the punch I'd landed on Gunnar just minutes after I'd gotten the email. With a grimace I stood up from my three-monitor desk. The room was dark despite the afternoon hour. My black light shades were drawn, and I worked under the blue light of the monitors and a single dim lamp. When I flicked the lights on in the bathroom, the brightness sent a spike of pain through my head.

Twelve hours. It'd only been twelve hours since everything changed.

I could see it in the dark circles under my eyes—Dad's eyes.

Why couldn't I look like my biological father, the man I'd never met, and never would? My mother and her brother—Ankh, who became my adopted Dad—shared the same dark hair and dark blue eyes. And so did I. When I looked in the mirror, I saw traces of Dad and had since I was young. When I'd thought his death was just an accident, seeing his gaze in the mirror was a comfort. I carried his memory in my heart and in my body as well.

But now it was a brutal reminder of what was taken away from me so unfairly. I clenched my fist, halfway wanting to shatter the mirror so I wouldn't have to see Dad looking back at me.

Instead, I ran cold water over my sore knuckles. Punching shit hadn't fixed anything. It'd felt good, though, clocking Gunnar on the jaw like that. I didn't remember the finer details of that moment, really—just the pain, anger, and satisfaction.

I had been standing at the edges of the club party with Siren last night, finishing up a game of pool and trying not to feel too jealous of Logan and Blade as they made out like teenagers in front of everybody. Then I had opened the anonymous email to see the familiar picture of Dad's crash—like I didn't see it enough in my nightmares. The words NO ACCIDENT had ripped through me like a bullet.

After that, it was a blur. All I had thought at that moment was that I needed to get to my computer and track the email. I had wanted what I always wanted in high-stakes situations: information. A plan. Something to do. Some way to help.

And Gunnar had put himself between me and my next steps.

Would I have punched just anyone who had done that, though? Logan? Coop?

Probably not.

But Gunnar had treated me like shit ever since our single night together last year. And he'd had the nerve to demand I talk to him like we were old friends. Normally I would've brushed him off, or, if I were in a particularly weak mood, I would've been grateful to have just a shred of his attention. But after seeing the email, I couldn't stand his entitled concern, and it had just enraged me more. So I'd cracked him across the face. I had half-expected him to punch me right back, but he'd been too stunned to do anything before I slammed my door in his face.

It had gotten him off my back, at least.

Then I had jumped immediately into writing the tracking program. Part of me had thought, in the back of my mind, that Gunnar would've burst into my room when he got sick of being kept in the dark. Now that he was sergeant-at-arms, he didn't take well to members keeping what he perceived as secrets. Or, at the very least, I'd thought Blade would knock on my door and ask in that annoyingly gentle voice of his if everything was okay. Handling me like a kid.

But no one had come. Gunnar had left me alone, thank fucking God.

I cracked my knuckles and winced at the loud pop in my right hand.

I was used to being alone. I'd been the only kid in the club growing up. The other members weren't exactly chomping at the bit to start families—the club *was* their family, and in that way, it felt like I had a shitload of uncles and a handful of aunts. I'd only interacted with other kids at school, and as soon as my friends' parents found out about my dads and the club, those friendships had come to an abrupt end.

I wasn't unhappy growing up, but I was lonely.

I operated in a no-man's land of maturity. When I was younger, I was a little bit smarter and a little more perceptive than my peers. Dad and Pops hadn't tried to hide anything from me—I knew my mother had died in labor with me. Growing up with that knowledge had made me different, and kids can tell when there's something off. My own eccentricities coupled with my club family had me putting up walls I hadn't even realized I was building. I'd wanted to connect with my peers, but no matter how much I reached out, no one my age was reaching back.

So I relied on the club for connection. But that, of course, had its own frustrations. I was smart, but I was still a kid. And everyone had *treated* me like a kid—but I had been desperate to be considered an adult. To be considered one of them.

Resentment built fast, especially in my teen years. When I was thirteen, I had asked Dad if I could attend a church meeting with him. He'd turned me down, using my least favorite words: "When you're older." I'd thrown a fit. Stole his bike during church and took it joyriding. I could barely handle the thing, but I'd managed to ride it to Elkin Lake.

Dad and Gunnar had followed me in a club pickup. As he had climbed onto his bike, Dad had said nothing—and his silence had been more terrifying than any discipline he could have doled out. Gunnar had driven me home in the pickup.

"Can I give you some advice?" Gunnar had asked, his gaze not veering from the road.

"No," I'd said sullenly.

So he hadn't said anything more. It had shocked me—that I'd refused his advice, so he hadn't given it. He hadn't just barreled ahead in an attempt to teach or mold me. The rest of the club guys— my dads especially—had good intentions, and everyone wanted to help me as I grew into adolescence.

But no one ever really wanted to listen to me.

In retrospect, I suppose that's when my crush on Gunnar started developing—though I didn't identify it as attraction until a few years later. But it was there, in the truck, when he had shrugged and went right on driving after I'd said no that I realized he was someone I could count on.

Of course, his respect for my refusal had been enough to change my mind.

"Okay, fine," I'd said. "What is it?"

"You gotta give respect to get it," Gunnar had said. "If you respect Ankh's choices about your involvement in the club, he's more likely to let you get more involved sooner. Club safety is our priority. If you show us you can take direction and respect boundaries, we'll feel a lot better about having you around the riskier shit."

I'd nodded and kept looking out the window.

"You know what I mean?" Gunnar'd asked.

"Yeah," I'd said. "It just makes me so mad. I'm not a kid anymore."

Obviously, I'd still very much been a kid, but Gunnar hadn't pointed that out.

"Next time, come to me," he'd said. "I've got some good remedies for anger."

That's how I'd started training with Gunnar, learning basic hand-to-hand techniques and, of course, hatchet-throwing at the trees out back. We were never super close the way he was with other club members, but he always looked out for me, and continued to offer me quiet advice. And as I grew up, I'd started noticing him differently. I'd started watching the muscles of his back moving under his t-shirts when he worked on his bike. The veins in his forearms when he held a cup of coffee in the morning. His smile when he laughed at something Blade said.

Things were fine until I turned eighteen. The training had started to have an effect on me: I'd started putting on muscle, filling out a little, looking less like a beanpole. A small part of me had hoped that one day, my new physique might attract some attention, but for the most part I hadn't thought much about it.

Meanwhile, Gunnar had been promising to show me some grappling techniques—it was supposed to be the next stage in my training. He'd wanted me to know safe, effective ways to take down guys bigger than me. Just in case, he'd said.

To demonstrate, Gunnar had gripped the front of my shirt in his hands and pulled me close. But before I could even process how close he was, he'd stepped to the side, and then swept both my feet out from under me. I'd fallen backward, landing with a thump on the soft grass of the backyard. Gunnar's grip hadn't left my shirt, and he'd dropped into a crouch at my side, hovering over me. His gaze had tracked rapidly over my face, and I'd dug my hands into the dirt so as to not reach for him.

For one crazy moment, I'd thought he might lean down and kiss me.

"So from here," he'd said, his voice a little tight, "You're in a good position to get your knife at your enemy's throat."

He placed two fingers against my throat, demonstrating. I swallowed, and he pulled his hand away.

Then he'd released me and stood up. With his back to me, he'd said, "Okay, that's it."

Almost overnight, our training sessions stopped. He'd started avoiding me when I sought him out for advice. I still didn't know what I did, or what happened that changed our relationship so drastically, but the easy, relaxed relationship we'd built as I'd grown up had disintegrated after that afternoon.

I'd caught him looking at me sometimes—not the way he'd look at club bunnies when he was trying to lure someone in. Differently, but there was still an attraction there. An intense look. But if I tried to look back, he'd close off. And he was confusing, too. Sometimes he'd be open and playful with me, like he'd been when I was younger, but then his hand would graze over my back and he'd leap back like he'd been electrocuted. And the easy demeanor would disappear.

And god forbid *I* tried to touch *him*, even a simple clap on the back or my hand on his forearm. He'd go to great lengths to ensure there was always distance between us. His moods were so fickle—one moment I'd be melting under his gaze, the next he'd be blowing me off and cracking jokes at my expense.

I'd thought my decision to go to college might snap him out of it. I'd hoped he'd realize I wouldn't be hanging around Elkin Lake forever, and maybe he'd start to value the time we had together a little more. I even tried to get him to train me again, but he refused. I'd shrugged it off at the time, but it'd stung—a lot. Then I went off to college, and I had my fair share of flings and boyfriends. And they were all tall, broad, blond, and older. Like a certain someone I'd left behind.

I'd decided that I'd come back with a hot man in tow, and it wouldn't matter what Gunnar thought of me anymore.

None of the flings lasted, though, and as my college career came to a close, I began to hope things might change between Gunnar and me. It was pathetic, but I had hoped that maybe I'd come back older, experienced, more mature—and Gunnar would finally see me as a man. Maybe even a man he could be with.

But I'd come back. And Gunnar hadn't changed.

And then Dad had died.

What was I thinking that night, after Dad's funeral, when I'd crawled pitifully into Gunnar's bed? I'd wanted comfort—the noncondescending comfort he'd always offered me when I was younger. I'd wanted him to know I looked at him the same way I'd seen him look at me.

I tried to push away the memory of that one night. It didn't do me any good to linger on it. Regardless of what I felt for Gunnar, he'd made it extremely clear he wanted nothing to do with me. And I wasn't going to waste my time pining over some asshole who treated me like dirt just because we used to be friends.

He was good at his job, so I dealt with him for the sake of the club, and because I knew Dad would want me to respect that. But I wasn't going to engage with him personally anymore. I wasn't going to stand around and let myself get hurt, over and over again.

I startled as my computer dinged. The program had finally compiled without errors. Soon I'd have the source of that email.

As the program ran, I opened the files I'd skimmed off the back end of the police database in between coding last night. It was laughable how lax their network security was. It hadn't taken me any time at all to find a back door and download all the reports I could find on Dad's accident.

I wouldn't take the email directly to the cops, though. Someone had targeted Dad specifically—and that made it club business. If the cops had missed a murder after their first investigation, there was no telling how they'd fuck it up if they reopened the case.

And I wasn't going to risk having the police standing between me and my revenge.

The police reports, the fire report, and the emergency medical reports all listed the cause as an accident. He lost control, the narrative said. He hit a wet patch, it said. Dead on arrival, it said.

But in the photos included with the report, another faint set of tracks were visible on the asphalt.

Dad had always handled his bike like an extension of his body. He could ride better than he could walk on his own two legs. He knew how to corner in rain, snow, sleet, ice, whatever. He wouldn't just lose control. It had taken me a long time to come to terms with the fact that he'd done what I thought was impossible, no matter how wrong it felt: he'd made a mistake while riding.

But what if I had been right initially? What if he hadn't lost control?

What if he'd been forced?

The email was right. It wasn't an accident.

Someone had murdered Dad.

Anger burned inside me with fresh fire. Whoever did this hadn't just taken Dad away from me. Whoever did this had killed a good man—a good *leader*. The backbone of the club. Whoever did this hadn't just hurt me and Pops, they'd hurt all of Hell's Ankhor.

Blade was a good President—a great one, even. The club would continue on and thrive. But Ankh had been taken from us too soon.

I wasn't going to pawn this job off on the enforcers—this was too personal, too important, and I knew that they'd try to keep me out of the investigation if they knew. They'd think I'm too sheltered, too soft, too young to be involved. But I'd find whoever did this. And I was ready to kill them myself.

Chapter 2 - Gunnar

"Fuckin' A," I grumbled at my own reflection. I leaned over the counter and examined the slightly swollen area over my left cheekbone. My eye above it was already beginning to swell, too, a familiar shade of purple. "You gotta be fuckin' kidding me."

Definitely a shiner. No way to hide it, either. Usually I was proud of the trophies I earned after a wild night—but they usually weren't from a pissed-off kid. I'd be getting shit from the rest of the brothers, that much was for sure. It was still pretty early, though. If I was lucky, most of the club would still be sleeping off the effects of last night's party.

As I slipped out of my room, I glanced down the hall toward Raven's room. His door was still locked, but the blue light shining under his door was a telltale sign that he was either awake and still messing around on his desktop, or he'd fallen asleep in the middle of some incomprehensible computer task, which was more likely. Not that I was going to check. I shouldn't have tried to talk to him last night, either. It was better for both of us if I kept my distance.

I'd let myself get too close in the past, and I wasn't going to make that mistake again. He'd always been a smart kid—too smart for his own good. He'd been more interested in club business than doing whatever normal kids did at school. I'd done my best to keep him safe and out of trouble—showing him the ropes of the club, I guess—but no more than Ankh or Priest would.

He was Ankh and Priest's only son. And by extension, pretty much the younger brother of the entire club. So it was only expected that I treated him as such, too. Right?

I hadn't been inappropriate. I'd had one moment of weakness—just one. I never should've told him I'd grapple with him. That'd been asking for trouble. I still remembered it, though. I'd just been trying to demonstrate an easy leg sweep, something quick and simple to add to Raven's self-defense repertoire.

But he'd gone to the ground so easily, and I hadn't pinned him, per se, but I'd kept my grip on his shirt and ended up close. Too close. His deep blue eyes had been wide with surprise—and something else, something darker. Then, as he'd looked up at me, he'd shifted slightly in the dirt and his tongue had darted out to wet his lips.

It would've been so easy for me to just lean down and close the distance between us.

And the fact that I'd even thought that was a sign I needed to back the fuck off. I'd seen the way he looked at me throughout his teen years, and I'd been careful to keep enough distance between us. It wasn't a big deal—shouldn't have been a big deal. He was just a kid, and it was just a teenage crush, and I wouldn't be dealing with those looks forever. He was smart as fuck, and he'd be leaving us all to run off to college before we knew it. That'd be good for him, I'd thought. I'd figured he'd meet someone there, someone as smart as him, someone worth his time.

Then he'd turned eighteen. And suddenly he wasn't a kid anymore.

He'd grown into himself fast. Handsome, quick-witted, and mature. And he still looked at me with obvious desire. And that—that couldn't happen. First off, it was insanely inappropriate for me to even *think* about Ankh and Priest's son in that way. And secondly, despite how mature he was, regardless of how old he was, he was still a kid.

I'd thought all I needed to do was to keep some distance between us, and that college would cure him of his crush on me, and we could both move on. My feelings didn't matter. I was older and had to be responsible. I'd be fine handling my attraction to Raven, and I'd never act on it. Even if I ended up alone, I'd be okay. I had the club, and that was enough.

He deserved more. He deserved better.

Part of me wished he hadn't come back after college. Those four years away had treated him well. He'd become even more gorgeous, lean and muscled and exhibiting a new, comfortable confidence. My attraction was supposed to have died down, but instead it came roaring back stronger than ever. His return had made my life a little more complicated—I was avoiding him as best I could. Trying to return our interactions to some baseline of normal. Pretending I wasn't thinking about him when I jerked off in the shower.

But a larger part of me was selfishly grateful he did come back. I'd missed his acerbic tongue and sharp intelligence in our club meetings. Even if I'd made it clear nothing could ever happen between us, especially after that night.

God, that night.

Nope. Stop thinking about it. Not now.

Even if something like that could never happen again, it was enough that he was around. Even if he hated me, at least I could be sure he was safe.

And just because I was glad he was around didn't mean I wanted to see him right this second. I inched down the stairs, listening for any sounds below. Hopefully I'd be able to get coffee and get gone before anyone else woke up and asked me about the shiner.

Just as I was about to round the corner into the kitchen, I heard Priest humming to himself. I jerked back before he saw me— Priest was the last person I wanted to explain this to. I waited as he fixed his coffee, and I heard the back door swing open and closed; he was likely having his coffee on the back porch, as he often did before the day got started.

I slunk into the kitchen and poured a cup of strong, black coffee from the carafe. Looking good so far—the common areas were abandoned. I'd slip out, hop on my bike, and go kill some time at the garage. Mav had some peas in the office freezer there, so that'd help with the swelling. I'd deal with explaining the shiner later. Excellent.

Then, a low whistle sounded behind me.

Fuck.

I turned around.

Blade was leaning against the front doorframe. He grinned at me, wide and lazy like a predatory cat. He always looked like that after a night with Logan. "Mean-looking shiner there. How's the other guy look?"

I grimaced. Lucky for me, Blade and Logan had left the party early, so Blade didn't know I'd spent the rest of the evening talking shit and drinking beer and not much else. If this conversation was happening a year ago—hell, a few months ago—he'd be right to ask. I got rowdy when I drank. I'd been known to knock some people around and get knocked around myself.

Part of the reason I fit in so well as an enforcer and now Blade's sergeant-at-arms: I wasn't afraid to dish violence out, and I had no problems taking it, either. I'd always had too much energy, and it built in me like a pressure valve. Only a good fight or a good fuck could take the edge off.

That was another perk of the club. We always had people hanging around, club bunnies, men and women interested in becoming prospects or just looking to have a good time. I'd never had any problems taking people home. I had fun with the girls, fun with the boys, and all parties left satisfied.

But recently, I'd been less interested. Really, I had to be pretty deep in the bottle to hook up at all. No one really interested me anymore, but I chalked it up to age. At thirty-nine, maybe my interest in frivolous sex was finally waning.

Yeah. Definitely that.

I still wanted sex. Just not meaningless sex. And not with a stranger.

But there was someone…

Nope. Couldn't open that door, not now, with Blade staring me down. I had real responsibilities now, more than I ever did as just a lowly enforcer. Blade was still my best friend, but he was my president now, too. We'd patched in together and climbed through the club ranks together; he was counting on me especially heavily during these early years of his presidency. And not just Blade—the whole club looked to me to ensure our safety. No exceptions. And no distractions.

I touched my swollen cheekbone.

That night, after Ankh died, Raven had come to me for comfort. I'd woken up to his silhouette in the doorway of my bedroom at the clubhouse. He'd looked so small, so hurt, his arms wrapped around his own body as if he were trying to ward off a chill. I should've turned him away. There wasn't any good that could've come from him seeking comfort from me like that.

But—I couldn't hurt him any further. Not when he had already been hurting so much from the loss of his Dad.

And honestly, I had been hurting, too. I had wanted another beating heart in my bed. So I had scooted over on the mattress and made space for Raven to crawl inside.

He'd pressed his body flush against mine, my chest against his back, and he'd just... fit. It had been so natural to wrap my arm around him and pull him close. It had been so long since we'd really touched at all. I'd kept myself from kissing the back of his neck, but just inhaling his scent of sweat and woodsy soap had ratcheted my desire up from a spark to a roaring flame. It'd been easy to fall asleep with Raven in my arms.

And then.

I'd woken up slow and lazy with a rich, warm pleasure already coursing through me. Raven. He'd been awake, between my legs, blowing me with those piercing blue eyes closed like it was the best thing he'd ever tasted. Still half-asleep, I'd wound his silky dark hair between my fingers, and when I'd pulled, he'd hummed around my cock like he loved it.

Then I'd woken up fully and reality had come crashing down. I'd stopped him before we could go any further. Sent him away.

It fucking haunted me, the way his face had crumpled as he'd left the room. I'd broken his heart.

I was such a fucking idiot. I never should've let him in my room in the first place. There were so many reasons no one could ever know how I felt, or what had happened between us. Not only was Raven way too young for me, but I'd watched him grow up. He'd grown into his long limbs and serious face, changing from an awkward, gangly teenager to a lean, elegant man. His brain moved fast—way faster than mine. He solved problems with his intellect; I solved problems with my fists. He didn't need to be around that any more than he had to be.

And of course, he was Priest's son. No fucking way Priest would ever approve.

Raven had a future ahead of him. With his smarts, and his looks, and his ambition—he could go anywhere. He had the education. He had the capabilities. He didn't need to get involved with a beat-up old lowlife like me.

"Yo, Gunnar, hello?" Blade waved a hand in front of my face. "Did whoever hit you give you brain damage?"

"Cool it, it's early." I took a slow sip of my coffee and tried to formulate an excuse. Blade didn't need to know Raven had socked me in the face. And not just to spare my pride. I'd been an enforcer for a long time, and I could tell when something was off—and something was off with Raven. I wasn't going to involve Blade, not yet, but if Raven thought he was going to get away with not explaining himself, he had another think coming. "It's not a big deal."

"Never is with you, is it?" Blade poured himself a cup of coffee.

"How was your night?"

Blade gave me a look. He knew I was deflecting, but let it slide. "Pretty good."

"Just pretty good? You carry Logan over the threshold and everything?"

"Why are you so eager for details? Didn't get any action of your own?"

"Maybe I got the shiner in the bedroom."

Blade laughed and clapped me on the shoulder. "Wouldn't surprise me. Listen, are you around today?"

"Sure," I said. "Probably heading over to the shop to help out Mav, unless you need something."

"Nah, just making sure. I might be out riding for a little while."

I raised an eyebrow. "What kind of riding?"

"Fuck off," Blade said, good-naturedly. "Just call me if you need anything. And for fuck's sake, ice that shiner, will you?"

I pressed my warm coffee mug to the throbbing shiner instead. Raven had a mean right hook. He might be a bookworm, but he could throw a punch. Despite the pain, I couldn't help but feel a small swell of pride that my lessons had stuck. He was still a Hell's Ankhor member through and through.

And I was his sergeant-at-arms. I had to get my personal feelings back under control and talk to him enforcer to member, figure out what was going on.

I'd talk to Raven. Like adults. As soon as this shiner didn't look quite so gnarly.

Chapter 3 - Raven

I'd been shut up in my room for what felt like a week, but in reality it'd only been thirty-six hours since I'd received the email, the night before last. I'd been awake nearly the whole time, trawling through my research and trying to improve my tracking program. The initial program I'd written was still running, trying to hone in on the email's source, and in the meantime, I was trying to improve a new version to speed it up, or make it more accurate.

Anything to keep me busy, to make me feel like I was making progress. I needed to feel like I was moving toward something, even if I was just running on a treadmill. The activity kept me sane.

But the sheer amount of time I'd stayed awake was starting to weigh on me. I wasn't ready to crash yet, though. Coffee was necessary.

I opened my bedroom door as quietly as I could and listened hard for Pops' voice. I couldn't tell him what was going on—not yet. Not until I knew more. If this was just a false alarm, I didn't want to cause him any undue stress.

It wasn't a false alarm, though. That much I'd figured out by now.

But if Pops knew Dad had been murdered, he'd blame himself. He'd wonder how he hadn't seen it coming, or how he didn't figure it out sooner. He knew Dad better than anyone. If Pops had even an inkling of the thought that he could've prevented this—that if he had done something different, Ankh would still be here with us—he'd break. Pops' road to healing had been brutal. I wasn't going to send him back down that path.

After Mom had died bearing me, things could've gone a lot differently in my life. I could've bounced around foster care and ended up alone at eighteen. But instead, Mom's brother—Dad—adopted me. Because of that, I got stability. I got two parents who loved me. And I got an entire family of bikers who'd lay down their lives for each other, no questions asked.

Pops didn't need me to throw another wrench into his life. Not yet.

The common area of the clubhouse was empty, so I slipped downstairs. Thankfully there was coffee on, as per usual, hot and strong. Just the smell of it sent a new rush of energy through me. My research thus far hadn't revealed anything beyond the fact that the police report was bullshit. There was nothing in the narratives that suggested foul play.

I'd have to take my sniffing around off the internet and into the real world soon. There had to be something that would lead me toward the killer—something that hadn't gotten written down. There were plenty of people involved in the aftermath: first responders, cops, witnesses. Someone had to have seen *something*. I just had to start methodically questioning people. Cast a wide net, and you'll eventually snag something.

I had to believe that.

"Hey, morning," Logan said as he stepped into the clubhouse. He looked flushed and happy in his new club leathers. "Any coffee left?"

I poured him a mug. "Don't you have coffee at home?"

"Me too, please," Blade said, entering the clubhouse on Logan's heels.

They were both still basking in the afterglow of Logan's recent patching-in. Blade followed Logan into the kitchen like he was magnetized to him and slid one hand under Logan's jacket across his lower back. Logan leaned into the touch just the barest amount.

Something pinched hard in my chest. I was happy for them both—Logan especially. Blade was my president, and Logan my brother. They deserved to be happy, maybe more than anyone else I knew. So why was it so hard for me to see them like this?

But I knew the answer, even if it made me feel petty and small: No one ever touched me like Blade touched Logan.

Gunnar barged in the front door a moment later, shuffling through a stack of papers in his hands.

"Yo, Blade, I got the paperwork from the new prospect. Not much there, should be a quick background check." Then he glanced up and started like he wasn't expecting to see me there. "Morning."

I didn't say anything. I moved a few paces away from the coffeemaker and sat at the island. Gunnar could fix his own coffee.

"Thanks." Blade took the papers from Gunnar's outstretched hand. "Yeah, looks pretty rudimentary. Raven, can you run a background check on this guy? He might be prospecting."

"Can't today, sorry. I've got some personal business to attend to."

"Personal business?" Blade looked up from the papers with his brow furrowed. "What kind of personal business?"

I crossed my arms over my chest. Blade had a right to pry, sure. He was the president. It was his job to be in everyone's business. But between the lack of sleep, the failed research, the slow tracking program, Gunnar's presence, and the fact that my

Dad had been fucking murdered—I wasn't exactly in the most giving mood.

Three pairs of eyes honed in on me. I said nothing. I was so tired of being treated like a kid still, like someone needed to check in on me to make sure everything was okay. I didn't need Blade or Gunnar to step in and save me, and I didn't want to involve them. So I said nothing.

"Right," Blade said. "Okay then. Whatever you're handling, take some back-up, will you?" He nodded toward Gunnar.

Gunnar pressed his lips together. He wouldn't meet my eyes.

I did not need the sergeant-at-arms around while I was looking into Dad's death. That was a guarantee that whatever I found would get funneled directly to Blade, and by extension, Pops. And if I was being one hundred percent honest with myself, having Gunnar around would distract me from my investigation more than I wanted to admit. Even though Gunnar clearly wanted nothing to do with me, that didn't stop me from staring at his broad shoulders and tight ass whenever he wasn't looking. Lust and frustration would mix poorly with the anger and nausea I already felt about Dad's death.

Besides, I wasn't a kid anymore—I didn't need to be fucking babysat. I'd sparred with most of the guys in the club. Gunnar had trained me himself. Hell, I'd even laid Blade out with a judo throw once or twice.

"Didn't I just say it was personal?" I snapped. I clenched my fist unconsciously, which sent a dull throb of pain through my arm. Without thinking I rubbed my swollen knuckles to ease the ache.

Blade's gaze followed the motion, and then flicked to Gunnar's unmistakable shiner. Realization dawned on his face. "Take Coop with you, then."

I started to fight back, but Blade lifted a hand to stop me. "That's an order."

I slumped back into my seat. "Fine. Even though it'll set me behind schedule."

Coop was a notoriously late sleeper, and a real bitch before he had about five cups of coffee. Coop was one of the club's enforcers, and even though he technically had to defer to Gunnar, he wasn't afraid to ask tough questions and push for what he thought was right. But when he wasn't working, he was lighthearted and hilarious.

I liked having him around. Even though I didn't want backup for this investigation, maybe Coop's jokes would take the edge off the pain. And anyone was better than Gunnar.

I stood up, giving a lazy wave to Blade and Logan. "If I want to leave within the hour, I better wake him up now."

***

Gunnar

Raven disappeared up the stairs to shout Coop awake. I couldn't tear my gaze away from the pert shape of his ass in his snug jeans. Sure, he was off-limits, but that didn't mean I couldn't look now and then.

Once Raven was upstairs and beating on Coop's door, Logan whirled toward me, his green eyes flashing furiously. "What did you do to him?"

I raised my arms up in a sign of surrender. "What the fuck? Why is it my fault? I didn't do anything."

Blade glanced between us, brow furrowed seriously. He really wasn't going to take my side on this?

Logan jammed his finger into my chest. "Do I really need to say it? I think that shiner on your face says it all."

Upon first impression, Logan and Blade seemed like polar opposites. And when Logan had first stumbled into Ballast off the side of the road, I hadn't trusted him. He'd been cagey about his past—and with good reason, because he'd stumbled into Hell's Ankhor while on the run from his father, the president of the Viper's Nest.

But he'd grown on me over the past few months that he'd been with the club. He'd been good for Blade. With Logan at his side, Blade was a little calmer, a little more grounded, a little happier; less of the in-your-face guy always looking for a fight. Logan made him a better president. And Logan was funny, a little bitchy, and not afraid to speak his mind… A lot like Blade.

And now I remembered they both had that same protective streak running through them. If Logan thought I'd hurt Raven, he'd at least attempt to kick my ass.

"I don't know what you're talking about," I said.

"Don't play dumb." Logan glanced toward the stairs, and then lowered his voice. "You know Raven's carrying a torch for you. What did you do?"

"I didn't fucking do anything!" I said again, harsh but quiet. When he'd first shown up here, my tone of voice would've scared Logan off. But now he just sneered back at me.

"You need to talk to him," Logan said. "Whatever you did to make him hit you? Make it right. He's clearly fucked up about something."

"Yeah, he's fucked up about something," I said. "Too bad I don't know what it is! I tried to talk to him night before last, and this is what I got for it!"

"For fuck's sake, Gunnar," Logan said. "Are you being stupid on purpose? He's probably fucked up over *you*!"

"I'm not being stupid!" I said. "Of course, I fucking know how he feels—I watch him just as much as he watches me! But if you haven't figured it out yet, he's off-limits. I'm not going to fuck around with Priest's son, especially since I practically watched him grow up."

Blade and Logan both gaped at me, stunned silent.

"And anyway," I crossed my arms over my chest and fidgeted under their twin stares, "that's not what he was upset about."

Panic churned in my stomach. I shouldn't have had that little outburst. Whatever was going on, I just made it worse, because now both Blade and Logan would be in my business. I'd never admitted my feelings for Raven out loud to anyone, even in a roundabout way.

Logan took a step back. "So that means you…"

"You're into him," Blade said. "Well. Shit."

The front door opened again and Priest ambled in, but stopped as soon as he crossed the threshold. He glanced between the three of us in the kitchen.

"Hi, boys," he said curiously. "Everything all right this morning? You're all looking a little tense."

I turned back to the coffeemaker and poured myself a much-needed cup of coffee. If Priest weren't standing there looking suspicious, I might've added a shot or two of something harder to take off the edge.

Priest had been vice president for as long as I'd been in the club, and even though Blade was technically the president, it was Priest that I didn't want to disappoint. Priest was the foundation of Hell's Ankhor, especially now with Ankh gone. No matter what I wanted, no matter how I felt about Raven, it wasn't worth any pain or stress it'd cause Priest. He'd been through enough.

"All good, Priest," Blade said easily.

Priest rubbed his salt-and-pepper beard thoughtfully as he moved into the kitchen. I poured him a mug of coffee and handed it over. Priest accepted it, but his knowing gray eyes bored right through me. He knew something was up. Lucky for me, he didn't press, just took his coffee with a grateful nod and stepped onto the back porch to enjoy it in the brisk morning air.

All three of us stared at the back door, waiting for it to latch closed. Then Blade fixed me with his stern, most presidential glare. "You keep an eye on Raven. I don't care what kind of bullshit excuses you have to make—you're my sergeant-at-arms, and if something sketchy is going on, club safety is your first priority. Over whatever personal issues you have. Got it?"

"You really think you have to tell me that?" I asked.

Blade softened slightly. "No. I know you wouldn't let anything get in the way of the club."

"Damn right," I said. If I cared less about the club, I would've made a move on Raven ages ago.

"Just watch his back." Blade looked to Logan, and Logan nodded his approval. "I trust the other enforcers to do their jobs. But I trust your intuition most."

I nodded. I couldn't act on my feelings, and it was my responsibility to ensure Raven didn't act on his again. But that didn't mean I didn't care about him. I'd always have his back no matter what. That's what Hell's Ankhor was about. The brotherhood came first.

Chapter 4 - Raven

"Why are *you* being so pissy?" Coop groused as he followed me outside the clubhouse. He was not dressed for a day out in town; his long, dark hair was loose, and he was wearing sweatpants with his club leather slung carelessly over a threadbare t-shirt. He still looked good, though—he looked good in most things. Perks of being tall and muscular. If he had a different personality, he'd be intimidating, but he almost always had a bright, toothy grin and a joke or five. "Aren't you the one who just woke me up and demanded I come with you?"

"Actually, Blade demanded you come with me," I said. I had to take Coop with me if I didn't want Blade and, by extension, Gunnar, to be on my ass about what I was doing. And anyway, it was a brisk, gorgeous morning. Perfect riding weather. Coop didn't have too much reason to complain. "So you better keep up."

I hopped on my bike and peeled out of the clubhouse parking lot, my back wheel kicking up a cloud of gravel dust. I heard Coop shout my name before his engine roared to life as he hurried to follow me. I loved my bike: a sleek, low-profile Roadster that couldn't match the roar of the enforcers' bikes but could leave them in the dust if necessary.

Without my club leathers on, I didn't look like much of a biker, but I'd been riding even longer than I'd been driving. Dad had stuck me on the back of his bike before I could pedal a bicycle, spending full days riding around, just the two of us.

I shook off the memories. If I was going to pull off this plan, I needed a clear head—I couldn't afford to get lost in grief. I rode fast down the narrow, winding roads that led from the clubhouse to Elkin Lake proper. The chill in the air felt good slicing across my face, refreshing, and it woke me up better than the coffee had.

I needed to dig into this investigation on my own. If Coop found out what I was looking into, he'd definitely tell the other enforcers, and involving Blade or Gunnar at this stage would just complicate things.

Luckily, I knew just where to start to get Coop off my back.

I turned onto Elkin Lake's main drag, riding slow and relaxed down the strip. There were people out getting breakfast and coffee, but it was still quiet. The citizens of Elkin Lake were used to seeing club guys ride through, and we got a few friendly waves, but most people didn't pay us any attention. We were simply part of the fabric of the community.

I parked my bike outside of the police station and climbed off it. I pulled my helmet off and shook out my hair as Coop parked beside me.

"Okay, want to explain what we're doing here?" Coop said.

I gave Coop a pointed look.

"You in trouble?" he asked.

I rolled my eyes. "No, I'm not. I'm just going to ask some questions. You coming in?"

"You fucking kidding me? You think I'd ever walk into a pig pen willingly?" He spit at the curb. "The fuck you think they're going to do except try to dig up some dirt they can use against you later?"

"I don't know what your problem is. We've been communicating with the Elkin Lake cops for as long as I've been patched in. What have they ever done to you?"

"Doesn't matter," Coop says. "Pig's a pig. No matter what game they're playing, they're not on our side. Never will be. As soon as they decide we're not useful, they'll be at our throats, same as they are any other club."

"You're paranoid," I said. Coop hated cops worse than any other member of the club. He always had, long as I'd known him. He never really explained why, not beyond the standard arguments he was parroting now, the same ones I'd heard him spout over and over. I couldn't help but think there must be something deeper behind it—Coop was one of the least presumptuous, least prejudiced guys I knew—but I didn't have time to get into it now. I needed my pan to work. "Look, I'm going to deal with some shit. It'll probably take all day. Come on."

He took the bait. "Hell, no. I'll wait with the bikes."

A twinge of guilt twisted in my chest. It was almost too easy to manipulate Coop into staying away.

"Suit yourself," I said and walked inside.

The police station was quiet. Inside, the receptionist greeted me blandly. After some back and forth, she agreed to call up one of their officers. A short wait later, a muscular man with buzzed black hair walked out of the back and introduced himself as Officer Tam.

"You asked to speak to someone about an old case?" He glanced at my club leathers. "You're with Hell's Ankhor?"

"Yeah," I said. "My father was killed in a motorcycle accident last year."

"Ah, yeah, I remember that case. Come on, kid. Coffee?"

I bristled at the diminutive—this guy couldn't be more than a few years older than me—but I accepted the offer. Tam led me to a small interrogation room and stepped out for a moment, and then returned with two Styrofoam cups.

"This about that case?" he asked.

I nodded. "Look, I have the photos you all provided of the scene." I pulled the photo up on my phone and zoomed in. "There's an additional set of tire tracks on the asphalt. This case has been closed for a while, I know, but this is weird, right?"

Officer Tam sighed and rubbed his hand across his forehead. "Look, this case was what, a year ago? Year and a half?"

"Fifteen months," I said.

"Our forensics teams looked into the tracks when we were on-scene," he said. "We determined they were there before the accident occurred."

"How can you be sure?" I pressed. "You don't think it's weird? The placement? There are no tracks anywhere else on that stretch of road."

"Kid, I'm going to pretend I don't understand what you're implying," Officer Tam said. "That's a tough corner, and there are a lot of tracks from club guys like you taking it a little too recklessly. We conducted a thorough investigation at the time of the incident, and I don't see any reason to reopen it."

"You saying we're reckless, Officer?"

"Let this go," Officer Tam said. "It was a terrible accident. Nothing more."

I snatched my phone off the table and stuffed it back into my pocket. Showing the cops the email had never really been in the plan, and now I knew I *definitely* couldn't, since Officer Tam clearly didn't see any possible foul play. He wouldn't take it seriously—he'd probably just chalk it up to *us biker types* playing sick jokes on a rival club.

Really, all I'd needed here was to cover my bases and ensure they didn't have any information that wasn't in the report. Once my tracking program found the source of the email, I'd handle it on my own.

But for a moment, I agreed with Coop—cops were useless.

I left my coffee untouched in the interrogation room. Officer Tam shook my hand and disappeared into the break room, and then I was alone in the back hallway of the police station.

So I'd gotten nothing from the cops. Frustration still chewed at me, and the fluorescent lights made my sleep-deprived head pound. I hadn't planned on ditching Coop entirely—I'd just wanted privacy during my questioning—but now I couldn't stand the thought of babysitting Coop and trying to keep him out of my business all day.

I slipped out the back door of the police station and got my bearings. I hated leaving my bike behind, but it'd only be for the day. Ankhor Works was within walking distance, so I could grab one of the club's cages—I knew one of the club cars was being serviced there. But the emergency medical station was just around the corner. I'd poke around there first.

I knocked on the emergency medical station door and an exhausted-looking man in a blue polo answered. I had barely finished explaining who I was before the man, who introduced himself as the district chief, waved me inside and led me to the kitchen.

"Wait here, son," he said. "Mike's on shift today; if memory serves, he worked that call."

The paramedic, Mike, shook my hand before he sat down at the kitchen table with me. He was short but broad-shouldered, probably in his mid-thirties but with deep crow's feet at the corners of his eyes. "Hey, man. Chief said you're family of one of the motorcycle calls we ran?"

"Yeah," I said. "I'm Raven. This would've been just over a year ago?"

I knew the reports backward and forward. At this point I could pack away my emotions, at least temporarily, and explain the accident like it had happened to someone else. "A man in his early sixties riding a Harley Davidson motorcycle lost control of his bike as it went around a corner on Route 56 heading north. The driver collided with a tree head-on and was thrown. He suffered head and spinal trauma and was declared dead at the hospital."

Mike grimaced with recognition. "Yeah, I worked that call. That was a rough one." He sighed. "What can I help you with?"

I had come here for the details I didn't already have. But the details—the details would hurt. Whatever this medic had to add to the story, however he fleshed it out, I wouldn't be able to box *those* feelings away. I took a deep breath before asking, "Was he conscious? Did he say anything?"

"Listen," Mike said. "I'll tell you whatever you want to know. I've been doing this job a long time—I know talking to people who were there can help you find closure. But… Are you sure you want to hear all this?"

I steeled myself and met Mike's concerned gaze. "I'm sure."

He sighed and scrubbed one hand over his buzzed hair. "All right. If you're sure." He paused, gathering his thoughts. "I've got nothing against you boys in the club, but motorcycle accidents are no fuckin' joke. Most of our bike calls are riders laying down the bike to prevent something worse—the road rash is unpleasant, but it's not life-threatening. The bad ones are when riders are hit, or hit something themselves. Like your dad. He was thrown from his bike. Most people who are thrown don't survive."

My gut twisted with nausea. That moment must've felt like forever to Dad—the collision, and then sailing through the air toward the asphalt. Knowing the impact was coming. Dad knew about the risks of riding. He must've known what would happen when he struck the road.

"He'd been lying there a while before we got there. At least twenty minutes. We didn't get a call until another motorist drove by and saw him. He was unresponsive when we arrived. He had a bad head injury—helmet didn't prevent it. Cerebrospinal fluid coming from his ears and nose. That would've been bad enough, but it looked like the force of the accident had made him bounce across the asphalt a few times. Lot of musculoskeletal damage."

"Twenty minutes?" I could see it so vividly in my mind. Dad thrown from his bike, the bike he loved so much, tossed like a rag doll over the roads he'd ridden thousands of times. Lying there dying for twenty minutes. All alone.

Dad had dedicated his life to building the club into a family, creating a support group for the rejects and outcasts, building a brotherhood. And in return, he'd died alone and in pain on the side of the road.

I thought I might throw up.

"Yeah." Mike reached across the table and patted the back of my hand awkwardly. "You look a little pale. You don't need to hear the rest."

"Yes, I do," I said. "I'm fine. Did the head injury kill him?"

"No," Mike said. "His pelvis was shattered. By the time we arrived, he'd lost too much blood. He went into traumatic cardiac arrest before we could transport. Couldn't get him back."

Grief clawed at me. "What if someone had found him earlier?"

Mike shook his head hard. "Can't think like that, especially in my line of business."

But that didn't help. I still couldn't help but wonder—what if someone had driven by sooner? What if someone else had been riding with him? Dad's death was part of the reason Blade was so insistent on members taking backup on rides. But why did this have to be the way we learned that?

"Was anyone else there?" I asked. "Another biker? Or anyone strange poking around?"

"Honestly, I couldn't tell you," Mike said. "That's the police's job. If they're on-scene, I'm just focused on my patient."

I stared at my hands on the table, blinking away the tears threatening to fall.

"We did everything we could," Mike said. "We talked to him. He wasn't alone when he passed."

The radio on his hip sounded and the dispatcher's staticky voice cut through the tense silence between us. "That's my cue."

"Thanks," I said. "For talking to me. And for being there. With Dad."

Mike nodded and shook my hand firmly before jogging out of the kitchen and into the ambulance bay. I sat for a long moment, alone in the empty kitchen with the buzz of the fluorescent light overhead.

So that was it. He'd hit the tree. He'd shattered his pelvis. The medics had tried to keep his heart beating, but there wasn't enough blood in his body to keep him alive. I leaned forward, putting my head between my knees, and stayed like that until I didn't feel like puking anymore.

I called a cab and stood outside the station with my club leather zipped up against the chill. Was it better or worse that I knew all the details of Dad's death now? The image of his broken body lying in a pool of dark blood was burned into my mind. He had to have suffered, and that only made my determination harden.

Whoever did this would pay.

I couldn't summon enough anger, though, not with the deep wound of grief freshly reopened. Of course the mystery hadn't been solved by asking the first responders the same rudimentary questions that they'd answered in their incident reports—I hadn't expected it to. Still, part of me had hoped that someone had seen something they hadn't recorded. Something that they'd maybe forgotten about until now. Something minor even, but enough to give me a lead. I needed forward momentum. I needed something to chase to outrun my grief.

The cab arrived, and I directed it to Ankhor Works. Since my bike was still with Coop, and I was *not* dealing with that, I needed a car to get to the site of the accident.

I had the cab pull around the back of the shop, and I bypassed the warehouse building entirely, opting to go in through the gate to the back parking lot instead. I didn't want to run into Maverick or anyone else. Just needed to grab the car and go.

The car was one of Dad's old rides—a 1979 Pontiac Trans Am, not quite a classic muscle car, but not unimpressive either. If I had to be in a cage, the Pontiac was my preferred choice: it handled nicely, the transmission was smooth, and I could still feel the road beneath the tires.

I took a moment and ran my hand over the car's gleaming black roof.

I remembered riding in the passenger seat with Dad behind the wheel. I was probably twelve or thirteen, and we'd been driving through the winding mountain roads. Dad had been wearing his club leathers and a pair of aviator sunglasses. He had looked so cool. Like a movie star. I had wanted to be just like him.

"Okay, Raven," he'd said as we idled at a scenic overlook. "We're going up this mountain, and I want you to tell me when to shift gears, okay? Before you can drive a car like this, you've got to understand the engine. You've got to be able to feel it."

I had nodded, hanging on to every word, even though anxiety had been coursing through me. What if I did it wrong and told him to shift at the wrong time? What if I fucked up the engine?

In retrospect, of course Dad wouldn't have let that happen. He was amazing in that way—he always knew how to make me feel capable, without putting me over the edge into overwhelming responsibility.

"All right," he had said. "Let's do this."

He'd grinned and pulled the Pontiac out of the overlook.

The engine had roared.

"Don't look at the RPMs," Dad had shouted over the noise. "Feel it?"

I had closed my eyes and felt the Pontiac's vibrations beneath me and had heard the engine roar—then, the tone had shifted a little higher. "Shift!"

"Good!"

"Shift again!"

"Very good!"

The road had flattened out and the Pontiac had picked up speed, moving smoothly across the asphalt. With the windows rolled down and the wind whipping my hair, I had called out "Shift!" one last time, and had watched in awe as Dad easily hit the clutch hard and shifted the Pontiac into fourth.

"Good boy!" Dad had laughed, his voice warm with pride. He'd reached across the bench seating and tousled my hair roughly, and then pushed it out of my eyes. "We'll have you driving this thing before your next birthday!"

Sometimes I half-expected to hear his voice in the clubhouse still, or his loud, raucous laugh. As a teenager, it used to annoy me, how he was always cracking jokes or calling me stupid nicknames or pulling club members into headlocks. Now I'd give anything to hear that laugh one more time. But Dad was gone.

Taking a deep breath, I unlocked the car, but before I could open the door, I heard a shout behind me.

"Hey! You'd better not!" Gunnar stalked furiously across the parking lot, leaving the back door of the shop wide open behind him. He'd left his club leathers inside and his navy waffle-knit Henley was snug with the sleeves pushed halfway to his elbows. His fists were clenched, the muscles tensed all the way up his muscular forearms.

With the top few buttons of his shirt undone, I couldn't help but stare at the immense tattoo of the club logo on the side of his neck. Though it was slightly faded from age, it was still intimidating: an anchor in a bed of flames, with the top bar of the anchor culminating in the rounded shape of an ankh. The tattoo was impossible to hide. That alone showed his unwavering commitment to the club.

And sure, I respected his dedication.

I even liked the way his Henley clung tight to his arms and waist.

And his deep, rumbling voice made my stomach do a somersault while his unwavering stare sent a small thrill down my spine. Which immediately pissed me off. I hated that he still had this effect on me—that one shred of his attention could reduce me to my teenage self, desperately pining for him.

I did not want to deal with him. Not now. From his purposeful gait and pointed gaze, he was clearly in sergeant mode, and he was going to be a real fucking pain in my ass.

I grabbed the car door handle, hoping to jump in and drive off before Gunnar could get into my business. But he closed the distance between us and grabbed my wrist, yanking me away from the door and then shoving my back up against it.

"Sorry, you don't get to run away from this conversation," Gunnar said.

The swelling around his shiner had gone down, but it was still an impressive shade of purple. His voice was rough with frustration, and his furious gaze bored into me. But even when he was looking at me with disdain and annoyance—he was at least looking at me. My stomach flipped, which felt like a betrayal. The closeness between us drove my body crazy with the desire for just a little more—another touch, another look—but logically, I wanted him gone.

He didn't want me. He didn't care about me as anything but a club member. Why couldn't I just accept that and move on?

"What the fuck is going on with you?" Gunnar asked. "First you freaked out when I tried to talk to you after Logan's patching in, and now Coop calls me to tell me you ditched him? He had to call Tex to come out and ride your bike back to the clubhouse! You know how he feels about parking tickets."

"It's none of your business." I was too used to hearing Gunnar talk to me in that strict holier-than-thou tone of voice, when he bothered to talk to me at all. I tried to shove him away. He didn't budge at all.

"Nope," he said. "Not good enough. Are you in trouble? Why were you at the cop shop?"

"It's not anything that involves you."

"Bullshit!" Gunnar braced his hands on the roof of the car, boxing me in with his arms.

We were way too close together. I couldn't meet his eyes.

"It involves me," Gunnar said, "because I'm the sergeant-at-arms of this club, and member safety is my responsibility. That's *everyone's* safety. Including your uncooperative punk ass."

"Not everything is about you." I steeled myself and finally met his gaze, tilting my chin up to stare him down. Anger twisted inside me—anger and desire. I hated that. I hated that even when he was talking down to me, prying into my life, I still wanted him. "Since when do you care so much? You've been perfectly content ignoring me since that night"—Gunnar pressed his lips together and finally looked away at the mention of our night together—"but the second I try to have a little privacy, suddenly you're entitled to know everything?"

Gunnar said nothing, but didn't back off.

"Whatever," I said. "I'm over it. I've never gotten any complaints before, but I must've done something really wrong for you to treat me like that afterward."

"I don't want to fucking hear it," Gunnar said.

"Hear what? You can't even acknowledge that night happened?"

"I don't want to hear about other guys." He gripped the front of my shirt in his hand and pulled me closer to him, his dark eyes boring into mine.

My breath caught in my chest. I was trapped between him and the car, our bodies so close they were nearly flush. His face was inches from mine. I clenched my fists helplessly at my side. We hadn't been this close since that night, and the heat from his body made me breathless.

Part of me wanted to reach out and touch him, to feel the hard muscle of his chest and the angle of his hips again, but the majority of me wanted him gone. He didn't get to treat me like shit, walk around picking up men and women alike at parties right in front of me, and then act all possessive when I had the audacity to suggest I had a life that didn't include him. I wasn't going to give him the satisfaction of a response.

But at the same time, I knew he wouldn't let this go. He took his job seriously. And for as much as it annoyed me to admit, he was good at it. He trusted his intuition, and he took every precaution necessary to ensure members' safety.

"You done?" My voice sounded a lot more collected than I felt.

Gunnar deflated at the quiet words. He let go of my shirt, stepped back, and then crossed his arms over his chest. I sniffed and rubbed at my nose, and then looked away. I still felt exposed under his unrelenting gaze.

"Raven, please."

I hadn't heard him speak to me so quietly in a long time. Like he used to, before I screwed it all up.

"Will you tell me what's going on?" he asked. "I'm not trying to invade your privacy. I'm just trying to do my job."

I couldn't tell him everything, not until I had all the pieces of the puzzle. But I could tell him a little bit, just enough to distract him, like giving a bloodhound a bone.

"I've been thinking about Dad," I said. I pulled the car keys out of my pocket and tossed them from hand to hand. "You know this was his car."

"Yeah, I know," Gunnar said. "That's why no one drives it but you."

"I'm fine with other people driving it."

"Sure, everyone knows that, too. But it's yours now. Didn't he teach you to drive stick in it?"

I toed at the dirt. "It used to smell like him. Like his jacket. But it finally wore off—now it's just a cage."

"Raven…"

I sniffed hard and scrubbed at my eyes, once, just to get my bearings. "I just wanted to talk to the police who dealt with the crash."

"What were you trying to find?"

"Nothing. I don't know. It just thought it would make me feel better. I'm going to visit the crash site."

"Yeah?" Gunnar asked. He stepped forward, quick as a flash, and snatched the keys from my hand. "I'm coming with you."

Before I could say anything as a retort, he leaped over the hood of the Pontiac, sliding over it smooth like he'd done it hundreds of times, and then jumped into the passenger seat. It was a stupid, show-off move, but it still brought a small smile to my face. He jangled the keys at me from inside the car.

Fine. This was not how this was supposed to go, but I guess Gunnar was along for the ride—and I definitely didn't have a choice about it. Hopefully this would be enough to sate his curiosity. If I could just get through this afternoon, he'd lose interest soon enough, and I'd be able to continue investigating in peace.

Hopefully.

Chapter 5 - Gunnar

Gunnar

I shouldn't have been so pushy with Raven. If I had known it was Ankh's death that was chewing at him, making him so tetchy, I wouldn't have been so aggressive. Raven wasn't open with his grief. He had always been a little reclusive, a little private, and Ankh's death had only amplified that. But we all knew he was struggling.

Raven drove the Pontiac with practiced ease up the mountain toward the site of Ankh's crash. He kept his gaze fixed on the road, pointedly not looking at me. I couldn't help but watch him drive, though. The late afternoon sun caught his dark, mussed hair and set it shining.

As soon as he'd sat in the driver's seat, an ease had washed over him, like he was exactly where he needed to be. His body just relaxed into the driver's seat, same as it did when he climbed onto his bike. He kept his right hand on the gear shifter, casually resting it there, his fingers drumming to whatever rock song was playing low on the radio.

I could forgive him for his pissy attitude the past few days, since he was still wrestling with grief from Ankh's loss. We all were, but it was worse for Raven. Ankh was our president, but he was Raven's *dad*.

My kindness didn't extend quite far enough to forgive the punch, though. The shiner would last a while.

There wasn't really a reason for me to come with Raven to the crash site. I mean—it was within my line of duty to ensure member safety. So it's not like there wasn't a reason at all, but he'd've been fine on his own. It'd been instinctive, really, to insist I come with him.

I guess I didn't want him to be at the crash site alone.

When he'd said it was Ankh's death that was bothering him, he'd looked different—vulnerable. Honest. Like he'd dropped the badass façade he felt he had to wear to fit in. It had set something aflame in me: a desire to protect him that was definitely not part of my duty as sergeant. And it was something I needed to tamp out, fast.

We drove deep into the mountains outside Elkin Lake, onto narrow, winding side roads far from the routes we usually rode on our bikes. Finally, Raven pulled the Pontiac onto the shoulder. He climbed out of the car without saying anything. I followed him.

An immense tree grew on the side of the road, just beyond a narrow, hairpin turn. Raven walked directly toward it.

The view from the side of the mountain was gorgeous. The valley below was lush with trees, vibrant green against the clear blue sky.

I hated it for being beautiful. A crazy, grieving part of me couldn't believe that Ankh's death hadn't changed the landscape. His death was so sudden, and cruel, and profound, the mountain itself should've transformed in some way. There should've been a rockslide. The tree should've died. The world couldn't just go on being beautiful after his death.

The realization hit me like a punch in the chest, knocking the breath out of me. I was standing where Ankh had died.

I missed him in a bone-deep, aching way. Ankh had been the first person to believe I was more than just an attack dog.

The military had been my initial escape route—a path away from the life my father had wanted for me before he'd died, working the same spot on the same factory line for decades. I needed more than that. God, I'd been easy fodder for the Marines recruiter. Young, restless, and desperate. All he'd done was wave the idea of good pay, good benefits, and even free education, and I was in. And maybe if I'd had a different CO, things could've gone differently. I was supposed to follow orders, and I did, even when I didn't know why those orders were being given. But eventually that didn't sit right with me.

I still had nightmares about Afghanistan—about that one day that changed everything.

But after four years, I was out, and back in California where I started. I'd thought the Marines would be the beginning of a career—of my life. But there I was, a twenty-two-year-old veteran who felt like he'd done nothing worthy of pride over there, feeling like damaged goods, like I'd never be worth a damn again. The things I'd done that day, back in the desert heat—I'd done them on someone else's orders. But I'd still done them. The blood was still on my hands.

I'd first decided to prospect with Hell's Ankhor because I misunderstood it. I thought the club would be violent, bloodthirsty, and lawbreaking. I was ready to trade one militia for another, because that's all I thought I was good for, and I felt like I had something to prove. I definitely had plenty of anger to burn. What else was I supposed to do—go crawling back to the factory?

In my first prospecting meeting with Ankh, I told him what I'd done overseas. And he hadn't flinched, or ignored it, or pretended it wasn't as hard as it was. He was always able to do that: to look the truth straight in the eyes. And he'd thought there was more to me than my past. He had faith in me. I still didn't know why.

His death had cut me to my bones. It wasn't just grief. It was like death had visited me, too, and scooped out all the best parts of me, leaving just a gaping chasm behind. It'd taken me a long time to recover. I couldn't imagine what Ankh's death had done to his son.

After all Raven had been through, he deserved someone good in his life. Someone who would make him happy—and I had no business wanting to be that person. My service, so far in my rearview mirror, still haunted me. Raven deserved someone better—someone who could keep up with his sharp wit and ambition. Someone who hadn't had the joy wrung out of their life in the sands of the Middle East. Someone who hadn't taken lives before they could legally drink. Someone he could trust, someone who could keep up with him, someone he could grow old with.

Someone nothing like me.

Here, on the side of the mountain, Raven stood stoic and unmoving in front of the tree, save for a slight twitching in his right hand.

I walked the short distance between us and stood at his side. "Have you been up here before?"

Raven shook his head.

"Good," I said.

He finally looked away from the tree and furrowed his brow in confusion at me. "Why do you say that?"

"Well, I... I just think you shouldn't be here alone. Without a friend."

Raven crossed his arms over his chest. "Is that what we are? Friends?"

My heart sank. I had always assumed that despite the tension between us, there was still an undercurrent of a bond. And there was, sure, but maybe it was more like… coworkers. I didn't have the same friendship with Raven that I did with the other members of Hell's Ankhor, not anymore. We didn't laugh together, or shoot the shit, or share meals, or any of the everyday things I did with the other guys. We were just occasionally in the same room. And he was right. Proximity didn't constitute a friendship.

That was good, though. Distance between us. Boundaries.

Shame flooded me regardless.

"Well, fuck," I muttered. "I must be a pretty shitty person if you don't even think we're friends."

Raven blinked and studied me for a long moment. His dark blue eyes, deep and thoughtful, always made him look like he was holding something back. What was going on in that rapid-fire mind of his?

He finally curved his lips into a small smile. "You're not that bad."

"You think?"

"Yeah, Sarge. You're middling." He bit back a smile. "Mediocre."

"A mediocre friend?"

"Sure," Raven said. "That's what we'll call it."

"I'll take it."

We both looked back at the immense tree directly ahead of us. Its huge trunk was fully unblemished. The accident hadn't harmed the tree at all. Raven's focus zeroed in on it as if I no longer existed. He chewed thoughtfully on his lower lip, brow furrowed in the same way it did when I saw him in the clubhouse, fixated on some unknown problem on his laptop.

He looked from the tree to a few narrow driveways splitting off the highway. Only one of the houses, a small one-story cabin, was visible from where we stood on the road. Raven's hand twitched again.

"You all right?" I asked.

"Yeah," Raven said distractedly. "Just got a lot on my mind."

Raven always had a lot on his mind. This, though—this wasn't his pensive face. This was his problem-solving face. But what problem was there to solve up here?

"That all?" I asked. "What did you expect to gain from coming up here?"

"Just closure," Raven said. "That's all."

It didn't sound like he'd found it.

Chapter 6 - Raven

For two weeks I'd been digging nonstop, turning up only breadcrumbs that led nowhere. I'd spent most of my time away from the clubhouse, dodging members as best as I could. If I was home, I was locked in my room with my computer, just like I was now. I'd been sleeping poorly since the emails arrived, but tonight was especially bad. I tossed and turned until midnight, and then I gave up and climbed out of bed. The clubhouse was quiet—most of the guys were still at Ballast.

I'd finally made time to get back up to the accident site, alone this time, and knocked on the door of the cabin near it. I couldn't have asked questions with Gunnar there. If Gunnar knew I thought Ankh had been murdered, he'd absolutely blow his top. He wouldn't investigate—he'd go on a rampage. He'd immediately make his interest known to everyone, and whoever did this would have a chance to cut and run. I wasn't going to risk that level of exposure. I had to investigate as subtly and quietly as possible. Gunnar was about as far from "subtle" and "quiet" as a man could get.

The owners of the cabin had been friendly, but only offered more breadcrumbs that piqued my interest yet ultimately led me nowhere. They hadn't seen anything—they hadn't even realized anyone had crashed until the police arrived. But they remembered hearing the familiar sound of bike engines.

Plural, they said. Engines.

Interesting, but circumstantial. It could've just been a different group riding before Dad.

But what if it wasn't? What if they'd heard his killer?

This was the information I was reviewing when my tracking program finally—finally!—pinged.

I jumped up from where I was lying on my bed and immediately unlocked my computer. I opened my geographic information software and imported the coordinates the program had provided.

The server was in San Francisco.

I double-checked the coordinates. Not just San Francisco—El Acantilado, the town just southeast of the city. The home of the Viper's Nest.

Hell's Ankhor had only just recovered from the Vipers' attempt to take over Elkin Lake. They'd funneled bath salts into our clubs, turned one of our own against us, and tried to send one of *their* own in as a mole. Unfortunately for them, the Vipers had underestimated Logan. Instead of acting as a mole for the Vipers, he'd helped us drive them out of our territory. Blade was lucky to call Logan his Old Man. And I was lucky to call him my best friend.

Logan's deadbeat dad—Crave, the Viper's Nest president—was still breathing, though. That pissed Blade off something fierce.

If the Vipers were somehow involved in Ankh's death... I didn't know what Blade would do. And Logan—I knew he'd blame himself. I wouldn't put that weight on Logan's shoulders, either. Not until I knew more.

Thankful for the silence of the clubhouse, I bolted down the stairs, hopped on my bike, and tore out of the parking lot. I shaved thirty minutes off the three-hour ride between our territories.

As I finally arrived in El Acantilado, I paused at city limits to pull off my club leather and stuffed it in my oversized saddlebag. I wore just a flannel instead. The air was chilly, but it was better to be cold than attacked by Vipers. Then I rode quietly, smoothly into town, as if I were just another casual rider checking out the sights. I double-checked the location on my phone.

Snakebite Lounge. A Viper hangout.

I left my bike on a side street and ducked behind the bar near the dumpsters. It was freezing cold, dark, and dirty, but I needed to get my bearings and decide how to proceed.

My phone vibrated in my pocket. I fished it out of my pocket and saw the caller ID: Blade. I winced and considered blowing him off—but that would only make him more worried.

"Hey," I answered quietly.

"Where the fuck are you?" Blade barked over the phone. "We just got back to the clubhouse from Ballast, and Gunnar went looking for you. You're not in your room, and Priest says he hasn't seen you at home, either."

"I checked in with Priest," I said.

"Sure, hours ago," Blade said. "Before you apparently disappeared into thin air."

"Sorry," I said, though I wasn't really. And why was Gunnar checking up on me? Why couldn't he and Blade accept that I was capable of handling myself? "I'm not trying to make you worry. That's why I'm keeping in touch with Priest."

"That is not how this club is run," Blade said. "I'm your president, not Priest. You don't get to disappear without telling me. If you can't stand for that, you can find another president to follow."

"That's not what— I'm not trying to create a rift."

"I know you're not trying to," Blade said. "But your actions *are*."

I sighed and leaned my head back against the cold brick of the alley. Blade was the best successor to Ankh I could've hoped for. The thought of disappointing him made me nauseous. Blade was doing his part to uphold Ankh's legacy—how could I explain that I was just trying to do my part, too?

"I'd never follow another president," I said firmly. "Ankh chose you. And you've more than proven he made the right choice. That's why—that's why I'm doing this, okay? I know what I'm doing. Can you just trust me? For a little while longer?"

I could practically hear Blade frowning into the phone. "Fine. You'd better have a good explanation for all this."

"I'll tell you everything as soon as I can," I said.

As I hung up the phone, I hoped I could fulfill that promise. I had to get something from this excursion. Some bit of information— some further bit of proof. I was running out of leads. If this went nowhere, I wasn't sure where I'd go next.

I sighed and leaned back against the brick wall heavily.

It had been getting harder and harder to keep Gunnar off my mind ever since that first trip to the crash site. Whenever I wasn't thinking about finding new leads, my thoughts always seemed to end up back on him. What would I have done if I had been in my room at the clubhouse and Gunnar knocked on my door tonight? Would I have let him in? Talked to him?

Tried something more in a moment of frustration and bad judgment?

I let myself imagine it, in the cold darkness of the alley. Just a little—I couldn't get too distracted. I was in enemy territory, after all. But having Gunnar at my side up on that mountain road had been grounding in a way I hadn't expected, and it made the truth a little less painful to face. The difference was especially apparent now that I was investigating so far from home, and all alone.

Gunnar wouldn't have wanted anything from me if he had found me—not like I would want from him. He was just worried now. Worried and nosy.

But if he did...

What if I had opened the door to my room to find Gunnar standing on the other side of it? Would he have grabbed me by the front of my shirt like he did that day at Ankhor Works and hauled me close to him? He'd been so deliciously close that afternoon. All I'd have to do to close the distance between us was lift up on my toes.

Ugh. No point lingering on it. I'd given him multiple openings at the shop—I'd let him get close. I'd even brought up our night together. If he wanted things to be any different between us, he would've said something then. And even if he claimed we were friends, one nice moment at Dad's crash site didn't make up for how he'd treated me all year since I'd come home. All the times he'd ignored me, or blown me off, or belittled me. I'd been too obvious with my feelings, and I'd been a pest. Just the club kid he couldn't get off his back.

And I never should've given him that blowjob. Not when he was asleep. I'd read something into our relationship that clearly wasn't there. When he invited me into his bed, it was because he saw me as a pitiful, sad kid—not someone who he wanted to fuck.

He *always* treated me like a kid, someone to be careful with. I guess the blowjob had been a crazy hail Mary attempt to make him see me differently. Like he'd suddenly open his eyes and realize how badly I wanted him—and maybe he'd realize he wanted me, too.

So fucking stupid. The wish of a reckless, naïve kid.

And this is why I had started avoiding Gunnar back just as much as he was avoiding me—letting him get close was just too distracting. I had to stop chasing my thoughts in circles if I wanted to focus on what was really important. The reason I was here.

After another minute, the back door swung open.

I pressed myself back against the wall and stood still in the shadows, mostly hidden by the beer-stinking dumpster. A tall, solidly built man stepped into the alley and fished a pack of cigarettes from the pocket of his Viper's Nest jacket. As he lit his smoke, the dim light from the flame illuminated his angular features and hazel eyes.

Rebel. Logan's brother. The resemblance between them was uncanny—they had the same build, though Rebel was a little broader, and they had the same sharp nose, same expressive mouth. I wasn't sure what to think about Rebel. He'd help save Logan's life, but he was still here in El Acantilado working with the Vipers. When Logan had been kidnapped by Crave, and then shot in the warehouse, Rebel had stepped out from the shadows after all the other Vipers had left, forgoing his loyalty to Crave just long enough to help save Logan's life.

My gut twisted. Maybe he loved his brother deep down, but he was still a Viper.

I remained in the shadows and watched as Rebel sucked his cigarette down in deep, rushed breaths, as if smoking was a chore. He smashed the butt underfoot before ducking back into the club.

If Rebel was there, it was likely the other Vipers were there as well. But that shouldn't be too much of a problem. I didn't often go on runs with Hell's Ankhor, so it was unlikely they'd know who I was. I could still slip inside and observe. Or—even better idea—I could check out their clubhouse while they were all at the bar drinking and drop some surveillance bugs.

That was a plan. A half-decent one, I thought, for having driven out here so spontaneously. Step one, I'd duck into the bar and see who all was there to gauge whether I could get into the clubhouse unnoticed.

Before I could get to step two in my head, though, my phone buzzed again.

An email alert.

From the same address that sent the photo.

I sucked in a breath; part of me wanted to delete it without opening it. If it was anything like the first email, it might break me completely. But at the same time, if it included more information about Dad's death... I couldn't ignore it.

"THEY KNOW," the email read. "KEEP QUIET. MEET TMRW. 11P." Coordinates included.

In the chill of the night, I snapped to attention and scanned the alleyway for any sign of surveillance: cameras, mirrors, even the odd window. But nothing looked out of place. Still, it had to have been my presence in El Acantilado that sparked the email. I'd gotten too close.

What if the Vipers had been watching me—following my online activity the same way I'd pinged their email to its source? I was good at covering my tracks. But what if they had their own tech guy?

All at once, this had gotten too big for me to handle alone. If the Vipers were on to me, I needed club backup. If the Vipers had the capabilities to murder *Dad* and cover it up, I didn't want to think about what they'd be willing to do to *me*.

I wasn't afraid for my own safety—but I *was* afraid for my Pops. Losing Dad had nearly killed him. He wouldn't survive if he lost me, too.

I drove out of El Acantilado as quickly as I could without drawing any more attention to myself. It was so late, it was nearly dawn; exhaustion weighed heavily on me. I pulled into a roadside motel to crash for a few hours. Once I got into my room, I flopped heavily onto the bed, fully clothed, and stared at the email once more.

Who would be waiting for me tomorrow night? What did they want?

Despite my exhaustion, sleep seemed far, far away. I stared at the water-stained ceiling. My thoughts raced nonstop, circular and out of control. In the darkness, alone in the dingy motel on top of its cheap, scratchy comforter, I sighed and admitted the truth to myself.

I *needed* the club's backup... But I *wanted* Gunnar's backup. I trusted him the most in situations like this. I trusted his leadership and his intuition. He always seemed to know when it was worth an attempt to de-escalate, and when it was a better idea to start kicking ass. As sergeant, he wasn't afraid to get his hands dirty.

Still, I wished he hadn't pushed me up against my car and gotten so close. I wished he hadn't said what he said—that he didn't want to hear about other guys. That show of strength and aggression and... jealousy?... had brought my attraction to him roaring back after I'd spent so long trying to drown it.

What I needed was to clear my head before going back. Slow everything down. Get my attraction to Gunnar out of my system, and relax myself enough to fall asleep.

That's what I told myself it was, anyway. That was the only reason I was letting myself do this.

I closed my eyes and let myself drift into a fantasy, just this once.

I imagined Gunnar pushing me up against the car again. His hands would be fisted in my shirt, forcing me close to him. Instead of looking away this time, like I had in reality, I imagined myself turning my head slightly and lifting up onto my toes to kiss him.

Our lips would meet. Gunnar would inhale slightly in surprise.

And then he'd devour me. He'd kiss me like it meant something.

I rolled onto my stomach on the bed and shifted my hips against the mattress. My cock was hardening fast at the images of Gunnar's lips on mine.

Gunnar would let go of my shirt and grab my hips instead, stepping closer to me. He'd pin me against the car and slide his thigh between my legs. The pressure would be intoxicating.

I shifted my hips harder against the mattress beneath me, chasing the feeling.

He'd kiss like he did everything else: with focus. Intention. He didn't half-ass anything, and a kiss would be no different. It'd be deep and hot, and he'd take control. God, the closeness would be delicious—I'd finally get to feel his muscled torso press against mine. I'd loop my arms around his neck to keep him close. We'd kiss until he could feel the hardness of my cock against his thigh.

"Not thinking about other guys now, are you?" he'd ask in that low, rumbling voice.

"Never was," I would admit. "It's always you."

That'd make his eyes flash with possessive heat again. He'd kiss my neck before sliding his hands under my shirt, and his callus-roughened hand would skate gently over my skin.

Then he'd drop suddenly to his knees and look up at me with a wicked grin.

In my motel room, I pulled my jeans open just enough to shove my hands into my shorts and gripped my cock. I gasped into the pillow at the sudden pleasure of it, and then focused back on the fantasy, eager to unravel what happened next.

Gunnar would notice my immediate reaction: I'd suck in a breath and reach for him to run my fingers through his short blond hair. He'd press his face into my crotch and mouth at the shape of my cock through my jeans. Just the hot wet pressure of his mouth, even with layers of fabric between us, would be enough to make me moan.

Then, slowly, cruelly slowly, Gunnar would unbutton my jeans and slide the zipper down.

Moaning at the image sparking behind my eyelids, I fisted my cock hard and shifted my hips, thrusting against my hand and the mattress beneath me. Pleasure built like heat inside me, and I was sweating in my club leather. More, I needed more…

Gunnar would draw my cock out of my shorts. He'd tease me a little, making me wait, jerking me off slowly while pressing kisses to my abs, until I was squirming under him and begging for it. He'd make me say his name.

Wanting it to feel as real as possible, I murmured his name into my pillow, and it devolved into a low moan.

Once I'd given him what he wanted, Gunnar would finally, finally suck my cock into his mouth. It'd be hot, and sloppy, passionate—like he couldn't get enough of me. Like he'd been waiting for it. Like he longed for me like I did for him.

I imagined Gunnar swallowing my cock to the base, the intensity of it causing spit to drip from the corners of his mouth. He'd be unrelenting, his hands on my hips keeping me pinned to the car as he blew me.

I came with Gunnar's name in my mouth, in my fantasy and in the motel room. My orgasm hit me like a punch to the gut; I shuddered through it, and then lay on the bed, breathing heavily as my heart rate slowed. I slowly withdrew my hand from my shorts and cringed at the stickiness.

And I did feel better: a little calmer, and sleep was definitely in my future. But I needed to get a grip—I had to be careful. This attraction was only going to make it hurt more when Gunnar pushed me away again. I had to remember that's all this was, and all it would stay—a fantasy.

Well, no way in hell was I climbing into these dingy sheets. I pulled my leather tight around me, a comforting blanket that smelled of leather and sweat and bike exhaust. As I drifted toward sleep, I wasn't haunted by worries about Vipers, nor distracted by the fantasy I'd concocted.

No—I thought of the softness in Gunnar's eyes when he'd asked me what was wrong.

Chapter 7 - Gunnar

After my third attempt to guess Raven's password, his desktop computer locked me out.

"Fuck!" I slammed my fist hard on his desk.

Raven hadn't been in his room when I'd returned to the clubhouse after a night at Ballast. I hadn't slept much; I'd been straining all night to hear the sound of the clubhouse door opening and Raven sneaking up the stairs. It never came.

But as soon as my alarm had gone off, I was awake. I pulled on sweatpants, not even bothering with a shirt, and pounded on Raven's door again.

Still absent. For nearly two weeks now he'd barely been home, and no one had any real idea of what he was doing—not even Priest. He checked in with Priest, but only to confirm that he was okay. No details. No timelines. No real information.

It made me furious. Not only was it dangerous, it was disrespectful to the club. We had rules for a reason. He couldn't just disappear and think I'd let it slide.

I'd tried to do some recon of my own. Blade had asked me to do it, but he hadn't needed to. It was my duty as sergeant and as Raven's friend to keep an eye on him, especially when he was being so cagey. But my attempts to follow him, or at least figure out *why* he was sneaking off, hadn't turned up anything. Same way he'd ditched Coop, he ditched me.

I turned away from the computer. If I were Raven, where else would I keep information?

That was the problem at the heart of all this, wasn't it? I couldn't keep up with Raven. He was smart enough to set up his computer to lock out prying eyes, smart enough to ditch any tails, smart enough to run some sort of investigation with no help from the club. This was a doomed endeavor.

I couldn't just give up, though.

I'd thought we had connected a little bit that day at Ankh's crash site—or at least that the walls he kept up had started to crack. But maybe he was just telling me what I wanted to hear so I'd lay off him. He'd been so weird after that, and I'd started to wonder if whatever he was digging into had something to do with Ankh's death. But what was there to investigate? We'd done all the verification we'd needed at his time of death.

Grief was funny like that, though. Definitely wasn't linear. Maybe going to the crash site had irritated that barely healed wound. Maybe he was just diving into random research to distract himself.

Maybe I'd been too hard on him.

It had been the only way I'd known how to put distance between us, though. The first time he'd really caught my eye was—Jesus, seven years ago. He'd just turned eighteen, and I'd been thirty-two.

It had been summertime, and we were spending a few hours at the lake—Blade, Priest, Ankh, Raven, and me. It had felt like an idyllic family trip. A few other members had planned to join us after taking care of some club business, but for a short while, it was just us.

As soon as we'd parked our bikes, Raven had made his way to the end of the Elkin Lake dock and set up his towel and his cooler. He'd tilted his face up to the sun and sighed with pleasure at the warmth.

Then he'd stripped off his t-shirt and jeans like it was nothing. His swim trunks underneath had been barely long enough to graze his mid-thigh. His legs were long and muscular—when had that happened? And why couldn't I stop thinking about running my hands up his legs from ankle to hip?

"Help me out, please," he'd ordered me as he tossed me a bottle of sunscreen. I fumbled with the bottle as I caught it.

"Hope this is SPF one hundred," I'd grumbled in faux-protest. I'd stood behind him and smoothed sunscreen over the lean, muscled planes of his back. All that smooth white skin. My hands had looked so rough and tan in comparison. And he'd shivered slightly under my touch—from the chill of the sunscreen or something else, I didn't know.

I'd done a thorough job, smoothing my hands over his shoulders and nape, working methodically down his back. Finally I'd reached his lower back, dimpled just over the small, pert curve of his ass. I'd rubbed the sunscreen in carefully, across his back, around his hips, and then, because I was apparently insane, I'd dipped my fingertips under the waistband of his shorts and spread sunscreen delicately over the very top of his ass.

Raven had shuddered beneath my touch.

"All done," I'd said, and my voice had sounded rough to my ears.

"Thanks." He'd turned around to take the bottle of sunscreen from my hands. Our gazes had met, but I couldn't parse what emotions ran in those deep blue eyes. I'd just straightened up and turned away to spread out my own towel on the dock.

Raven had dove gracefully into the lake. When he re-emerged, dripping wet and his jet black hair slicked back, accentuating the angular structure of his face, the spark in my gut had burst suddenly into a roaring flame.

But he was a kid, even at eighteen. And I was a grown fucking man! He was perceptive, though—he'd probably known I'd been attracted to him since that day at the lake, and it had only gotten worse after my poorly thought-out grappling lesson. But that didn't make my desire any more appropriate. If anything, it just made me feel worse. The older he got, the more I wanted him, and the more I had to push that down. Ankh had given me a second chance with this club. He'd given me a home. And if I abused that trust by fucking his only child, I'd never be able to forgive myself.

Raven was still young. He had so much life ahead of him, and so much ambition. I was just a fucked-up old man with my best years behind me. I'd only hold him back.

But that didn't mean I was going to abandon my duties as sergeant. It was my responsibility to figure out what was going on.

There was nothing on his bedside table or in his dresser, though. Nothing that would indicate any sort of research—no hand-scribbled notes, no books, no maps, nothing. Everything must be on his laptop or his phone. I rubbed my hand across my forehead. I was wasting my time. I turned back to his desktop, wondering if I could try to plug in another password yet.

Suddenly the door opened.

Raven stood in the doorway and gaped at me. He looked awful—dark bags under his eyes, shoulders hunched, his hair dull and mussed. His jeans and t-shirt were wrinkled like he'd slept in them.

All at once, my frustration beat out my concern, and I couldn't hold back. "What the fuck is going on, Raven?"

Raven blinked. His gaze darted over me, lingering on my bare chest and the too-low waistband of my sweatpants. I'd barely slept—I was sure I didn't look any better than he did.

"Excuse me?" he asked.

"Where have you been all night? Where the fuck do you keep going?"

He huffed a disbelieving laugh. "I should be asking *you* what the fuck is going on. You're the one standing shirtless in the middle of my fucking room!"

"Because I'm trying to figure out what the fuck you're doing!" I barked. "In case you forgot, it's my job to be in the loop. If you won't loop me in, I have to resort to other methods."

"Or you could just *trust* me!" Raven stepped fully into the room and slammed the door behind him. "Like Priest does. Like apparently everyone in this club does except *you*!"

"Of course I trust you," I said. "But you're acting like you know everything! Risk assessment is my job. You can't do everything on your own!"

"Everything is going fine," Raven said coldly. "I don't need your help."

He didn't need my help? It sure as hell seemed like he needed *someone's* help. Why the hell was he so resistant to accepting it?

"Is this about your crush on me?" I nearly shouted. "Is that why you're being so fucking difficult?"

Raven went completely still.

Oh, shit. I'd really fucked it up now.

Raven was scarily calm as he lifted his gaze to meet mine. I was used to handling a myriad of Raven's emotions: frustration, irritation, caginess, and occasionally, warmth. But this stoic, calm reaction was new. And I didn't like it.

"First off, a *crush*? Like I'm some fucking *kid*?" He rolled his eyes. "You think all my decisions revolve around how I feel about you? Which, for the record, is *nothing*. I don't feel a fucking thing for you."

My stomach clenched, and I stepped back like he'd struck me.

"You are such a fucking narcissist," he said. "The world doesn't revolve around you. My world certainly doesn't."

I was used to Raven's sarcasm. He could dish it out, and I could take it and even throw a little back. But this wasn't one of the half-serious, half-teasing verbal tussles we'd had when he was still a teenager. The tenuous bond we had was disintegrating in front of me. Because of what I'd said.

"Wait," I said. Fear rose in my throat like bile. "That's not what I meant—Raven—"

Raven threw his hands up. "You know what? Fuck you. Maybe you're right. Maybe I just need to grow up." He spat that sentence out like it left a bad taste in his mouth. "Or even better—if I'm not willing to play by your rules, maybe I should just leave the club colors behind."

"That's not what I meant and you know it." I closed the distance between us and Raven backed up against the door. A slight tinge of color rose in his cheeks. "We're family. This club is your family. I know you know that. Don't say shit you don't mean."

"You don't get to decide what I say," Raven said. "I'm not your property."

My heart jumped. Is that what I wanted? Not just to protect him—but to claim him?

"Stop acting like this," I pleaded. "Just let me help you."

Raven scoffed. He shoved me away, hard, but even as he was rejecting me, his slim hands on my chest sent a spark of desire down my spine.

"Fuck. You." He threw a pointed look at his desktop computer. "Keep trying to hack into my shit and see how far it gets you. If I needed help, I'd get it. And it wouldn't be from the club slut."

My mouth dropped open. Was that really what he thought of me?

Sure, I had fun every now and then, but—

I felt sick.

"Don't worry about my 'crush.'" Raven opened the door. "If I ever felt anything for you, I don't anymore."

He left, slamming the door behind him.

I stood in the middle of Raven's bedroom, surrounded by his things: his humming computer, his unmade bed, his laundry on the floor. It was a snapshot of his life—a life I apparently knew nothing about. I'd meant to put distance between us to keep my feelings under control, but I didn't want him to *hate* me. I didn't want him to be a stranger.

His words had left me aching, but something else still had to be going on. Raven had Hell's Ankhor in his blood. He'd never leave us behind.

Would he?

Had I pushed him to that brink? Had I made him feel so isolated, so alone, that he didn't even think he could turn to the club for help?

Not a great achievement for a sergeant-at-arms. Shit—I couldn't let him leave, not in this state of mind. Who knew where he'd go? Or when—if?—he'd come back.

I rushed out of his bedroom. "Raven! Wait!"

Coop was sitting in the clubhouse's kitchen with a coffee and a bowl of cereal. He stared wide-eyed at me. "Uh, Gunnar? Everything cool?"

"Where'd he go?"

Outside, an engine roared to life. By the time I got to the front door of the clubhouse, Raven's bike had already disappeared around the corner.

"He left," Coop said.

I slammed my fist hard against the drywall. "Fuck!"

Coop stood up and chugged the rest of his coffee. "I'll go after him."

"Don't." I took a deep breath and rubbed my temples. "He'll just ditch you again, like last time. I'll give him some time to cool down."

Coop gave me an odd look. "Seriously. Is everything okay?"

"Honestly?" I joined him in the kitchen and leaned heavily against the counter. "I don't think so."

Chapter 8 - Raven

I jumped on my bike and revved my engine hard. Gunnar called my name from the clubhouse, but I didn't acknowledge it—just revved my engine again and took off.

I gunned my bike, as if I could outrun the frustration and fear chewing at me. I'd covered the distance between El Acantilado and Elkin Lake this morning in the chilly dawn, after my fitful night at the motel. I'd been ready to shower, get a little sleep in my own bed, and then loop the club into everything I'd discovered so far.

I'd finally made some progress, but not in the way I'd wanted. I'd effectively been chasing my own tail until I'd received the second email. How had the Vipers known I was watching? Who warned me? There were too many unknown factors. Too much danger. I had wanted to keep things to myself until I knew more, to protect Pops and to ensure the whole thing wasn't bullshit, but I wasn't an idiot. Despite what everyone seemed to think, I had boundaries, and I'd felt in over my head.

I'd planned to ask for backup for the meeting with the informant tonight. But now, stupid or not, that plan was out the window.

Gunnar had been in my room.

In my fucking room! He was apparently incapable of respecting my privacy.

The worst part was—it was like a scene from one of my fantasies. Even better than the one I'd come up with last night.

Gunnar had been in my room, shirtless, in a pair of gray sweatpants so thin they were nearly translucent. He'd been leaning over my desk when I walked in, trying to break the lock on my desktop. As if he ever had a chance.

I had stared at the muscled curve of his ass and the broad planes of his back, his skin a shade paler on his bare back than his arms. When he'd turned around to face me, I could hardly meet his eyes, instead staring at his chest and the definition of his abs and the blond trail of hair leading into his sweatpants. He'd been tense with anger. He was so burly, so strong, even when he'd clearly just woken up. It would've been so easy for him to just grab me and throw me onto the bed.

For a moment, I'd thought that's why he was there. Not because he was concerned about the club, but because he was worried about *me*. Because he cared about me... And *wanted* me.

Pathetic. He'd told me to my face that he didn't trust me, that he considered me a silly, naïve kid. Even worse, he'd thrown my feelings for him directly in my face, like they meant nothing.

Maybe I was stupid. I'd spent so much time growing up, waiting for Gunnar to notice me. There were moments—just moments—when I thought maybe he felt something for me, too. Especially before I left for college, I'd catch his eyes lingering on me when he thought I wasn't looking. It had happened enough that I thought he just needed a push. To know for real that I wanted him, too.

Even after everything, I'd thought it was something else holding him back—my parents, or the age gap, or simply the idea of hooking up with another club member.

But apparently it was just *me* he didn't want.

The freeway stretched open and inviting ahead of me. I was headed north again, back to El Acantilado. I'd find my father's killer. I didn't need the club to help me. This wasn't about politics. This was about Dad, and as his son, it was up to me to find a resolution for this.

I was used to being alone, anyway.

It was early afternoon when I reached San Francisco. I wouldn't ride into El Acantilado yet—definitely didn't need to spend any more time there than necessary. Not if the Vipers were looking for me. Instead, I rode into San Francisco proper for a meal and to do a little research. Better to work from a public computer than my own until I'd scanned it for any bugs after that last email had come in.

In the library, I typed the coordinates from the second email into Google Maps.

The location looked to be another bar. It was east of El Acantilado, the inland side, about an hour's ride from the center of San Francisco. Even though there wasn't much surrounding the bar, the fact that it was at least a public business put me at ease. None of this abandoned warehouse mess like we'd dealt with when Logan was kidnapped. Business meant there'd be other people around, so whoever I was meeting couldn't pull anything too sketchy.

I spent the rest of the afternoon in San Francisco, eating, researching, and trying not to think about Gunnar. I had to be sharp when I met the informer, not distracted by a man who would only ever see me as an annoying, precocious kid he was obligated to look after.

When night finally rolled around, I rode the distance to El Acantilado, wearing a plain jacket against the chill instead of my Hell's Ankhor leather.

The Hideaway Bar was less a bar and more a shack on the side of the highway. The sign was barely visible, and there were a few bikes already parked out front.

I parked my bike next to them and walked inside. The few patrons inside glanced at me, but no one made any moves. I checked my phone—I was right on time. This was the right location. My informant should've been here by now.

I got a beer and sat near the door.

Nursing my drink patiently, I started to get nervous. The bar itself was bizarrely quiet—the jukebox in the corner appeared to be broken, and the patrons inside were more concerned with their drinks than anything else. The bartender, a middle-aged woman with deep lines in her face, was engrossed in the muted horror movie on the ancient television.

Then, a man walked into the bar. Tall, unremarkable, and sallow-skinned, and I knew he was a Viper from the dramatic patch on the front of his jacket. He glanced around the bar until his gaze landed on me. He suppressed a smirk.

"You waiting on someone?"

I didn't see any obvious weapons on him, but something still felt... off.

"Think so," I said. "You?"

"Think so," he parroted. "Grab a smoke?" He pulled a packet of cigarettes from his pocket and waved me towards the back door.

Going against my gut instinct, I followed him.

The parking lot behind the building was empty, save for two bikes and two other patch-wearing Viper's Nest members.

"You know," the first one said as he lit a cigarette. "We were hoping to find whoever was feeding you information."

He stood in front of the back door. His two lackeys stepped closer, effectively trapping me.

Fuck. Fear rose like bile in my throat. This wasn't my informant… This was someone *looking* for the informant. I had to get out of here, and fast.

"I don't know what you're talking about," I said.

"We Vipers are a pretty tight-knit group," he said. "We don't take kindly to members leaking our personal business. Especially not to the Hell's Ankhor whiz kid. So" —he took a long inhale of smoke, and then exhaled it into my face— "we planned on handling this internally. But since you showed, all by your lonesome, and your source didn't, we'll have to send that message another way."

Fuck, fuck, fuck. I reached for the pocketknife I kept tucked in my back pocket, but the Viper behind me kicked me in the back of the knees hard, and I buckled onto the gravel.

"Don't even think about it." The Viper grabbed my chin roughly and turned my face towards him. "You're lucky you're pretty, kid."

He jerked my head roughly to the side. With a cold smirk on his face he pressed the lit butt of the cigarette to the skin of my neck.

Pain coursed through me. I bit into my lip hard, holding back any sounds—I wouldn't give them the satisfaction. I could barely process the awful hiss and stomach-turning smell of my own burning skin.

"Don't go sniffing into our business," the Viper said. "Ever again."

He withdrew the cigarette, and I sucked in a few desperate, heaving breaths. "What'd you sickos do to my father?"

"Your father?" The Viper looked over my head at his two companions. "He's already lost it, boys. Talking nonsense."

"Don't fucking play dumb." I spit a wad of blood at his feet from the gash I'd opened in my lower lip. "I know you fuckers are behind it."

"You really think you should be making demands right now?" The Viper flicked his cigarette into the gravel. He released his grip on my chin and jerked my face up by my hair instead. "When you're the one on your knees?"

"All fucking talk," I said. "Can't even own up to your own schemes. *Cowards*."

"All right," the Viper said. "Enough with your smart fucking mouth. I've got a message for your little buddy feeding you information: You tell them we know about them. We're going to find out who they are. And they're fucking dead for what they've done."

"You're bluffing."

He backhanded me hard across the face, and a bright flash of pain exploded in my head. My ears rang and blood filled my mouth.

The Vipers were laughing, but the sound was distant, as if it were miles away.

I lurched forward hard and headbutted my forehead into the lead Viper's groin. He groaned in pain, doubling over slightly, enough that all I had to do was shove myself upward in order to slam the top of my head into the Viper's chin. A few teeth in his mouth broke with a sick clacking sound. I scrambled to my feet.

Blood poured from the Viper's mouth. "*You're* fucking dead now." His eyes cut to the two Vipers behind me, standing stunned. "Don't just fucking *stand there*."

I caught one of the Vipers behind me with an elbow to the face, and the other with a hard kick to the shin. They both wailed, but I couldn't keep them both off me—one of them managed to get my arms trapped behind my back. I kicked my heel hard into his shin, and he hissed, but didn't let go.

The lead Viper wiped the blood from his chin. "Not so tough now, huh?"

He threw two sharp punches into my gut. I gasped and tried to double over, but the Viper behind me kept me standing. The pain was dull, throbbing, and my breaths came short, like my lungs were in shock.

Two more punches. One, two.

Maybe I'd puke on his shoes.

The lead Viper was saying something, but I couldn't hear it over my own pulse pounding in my ears.

"Hey!" A woman's voice cut through. The bartender was standing in the back doorway, looking furiously at the Viper.

"I told you a hundred times, no fights on my property!" She frowned. "But this ain't much of a fight, is it? Three-on-one?"

"This ain't your business, Lyn."

"As long as you want to bring your people around my bar, it is! No fucking fights, that's the agreement!"

The Vipers released me. Laughing and catcalling me, they shoved past the bartender and back into the bar. I collapsed into the gravel, breathing heavily. The pinprick stars in the sky seemed to rotate and spin.

"Go home, kid," the bartender said. "And best not come back."

I was in no shape to ride my bike—dizzy, hurting, and potentially concussed. But what choice did I have? Pass out behind the Hideaway and get gutted by the Vipers at closing time? Or get as far away as I could while I was still conscious?

I didn't make it far. Just a few miles south, my vision went spotty. I pulled off onto a scenic overlook, parked my bike halfway-hidden behind a bush, and sat down on the curb.

If the Vipers followed me and found me here, it was over. No kindly bartender to save me now.

I fished my phone from my pocket. I needed help. Needed someone to pick me up. My entire body throbbed and ached. Even in the cold night air with the freezing ground beneath me, I wouldn't be able to stay conscious. And sleep sounded really fucking good right now.

So I called Gunnar. He was the sergeant. He'd come and get me. It was his job.

Hot tears stung my eyes. I knew I didn't just want the sergeant to help me—I wanted *Gunnar* here. I wanted his arms around me. I wanted to hear his low voice and feel it vibrate in his chest when he held me.

I didn't want to be alone.

"Raven? It's the middle of the night! What the fuck is going on? Where have you been?"

My breath caught, and I began to cry freely then, choking on it. How could I explain what had happened? How huge of a mistake I'd made? How he'd been right about my naivete?

I couldn't. I tried to say his name, but it stuck in my throat. The dizziness worsened.

I pulled my phone away from my ear. Thank fucking God I had GPS out here. I sent Gunnar my location, and then let myself fall back onto the curb and slip into a cold, miserable sleep.

Chapter 9 - Gunnar

I sat at the far end of the bar in Ballast with a few fingers of Jack in a glass in front of me. Since Ballast was the club-owned bar, it was typically where we all ended up at the end of the day. I wasn't here to socialize tonight, though. I'd made that clear without needing to say a word, and the other Hell's Ankhor members had steered clear of me. I was only here because I knew if I was alone, I'd get so wrapped up in my head that I'd pace through the floor or punch a hole in the wall. I'd thought a drink would take the edge off, but the whiskey had done nothing to numb the anger coursing through me.

I wasn't angry at Raven. I couldn't blame him for reacting the way he did. He was right—it was fucking narcissistic of me to think that whatever was going on with him was somehow related to me. We didn't have anything between us. I'd pushed him too far away, and he didn't owe me any friendship, especially not when I'd treated him the way I had out of some misguided attempt to reset the boundaries between us. It was probably for the best, since I could never really be with him, not the way either of us might want—or might have wanted, at some point. It'd be easier for both of us if we just stayed away from each other.

That thought nearly cleaved me in two, though.

I couldn't imagine a life without Raven in it. Even the relationship we'd had before all this had been better than no relationship at all. I needed him in some capacity, even if he was just on the periphery of my life: his quiet, breathy laugh, his biting sarcasm, his untamed hair. Even just coming downstairs in the morning and seeing him already posted up at the island on his third cup of coffee, fingers already flying across the keyboard of his laptop, not even lifting his gaze to grunt a hello.

Even *that* was better than nothing.

My phone rang in my pocket. I pulled it from my jacket, intending to shut it off so whoever the fuck was calling would leave me alone.

But it was Raven's name on the caller ID. After he'd found me snooping, and then stormed out of the clubhouse without looking back, I'd expected that I wouldn't hear from him for ages. That I'd be relegated to getting updates from Priest, if I was to get any updates at all.

I picked up immediately. "Raven? It's the middle of the night!"

He didn't answer. His ragged breathing echoed on the other end of the line.

"What the fuck is going on? Where have you been?" I asked. Terror cut through me, ice-cold.

Raven's breath stuttered. Like he was crying. "Gunnar," he choked.

I stood up so quickly my chair behind me clattered to the floor. I caught Blade's eye. He rushed over, and Priest, Coop, and Logan followed on his heels.

"What is it?" Blade asked.

"It's Raven," I said.

Priest pursed his lips and furrowed his brow deeply. "Where is he? Is he okay?"

"Where are you?" I asked again.

Raven didn't answer. His breathing was fast and shallow, like he was hurting.

"You gotta talk to me, baby." I closed my eyes like if I listened hard enough, I could deduce where he was. "I'll come get you. It's all gonna be okay. You just gotta tell me where you are, okay?"

Raven murmured something, but I couldn't make out the words. His voice sounded far away.

"You're gonna be fine. Come on, Raven, stay with me. I'm coming, okay?"

My phone beeped in my ear, and then the line went dead.

"Fuck!" I slammed my phone on the table.

Blade already had his club leather on and his bike helmet under his arm. "Where are we going?"

At his side, Priest was ready to ride as well, and Coop was gathering the rest of the enforcers.

"He didn't say." I clenched my fist hard. "He sounded bad. Sounded hurt. We have to find him."

"Give me that." Logan grabbed my phone off the table and opened my texts. "Raven's not stupid. There."

He turned the phone toward me, and in the empty text thread was a pair of coordinates, imported from Raven's phone's GPS. Logan shook his head in a strange mix of worry and admiration. "He couldn't talk to us, so he had his phone talk for him."

I grabbed Logan roughly by the shoulder and squeezed. "Thanks."

Logan nodded. "I'll get my medical bag. Let's go."

We headed north. Blade led the group on his bike, riding fast with Priest riding at his side, and the enforcers following. Tex, Maverick, and Coop rode their bikes. I brought up the rear in a cage: an SUV with a comfortable backseat. Logan sat shotgun with his medical bag at his feet, and Siren rode in the backseat, anxiously fiddling with a pocketknife.

Whatever condition he was in, Raven wouldn't be on his bike. He'd be in the backseat, and Siren would ride his bike home.

I drove with one hand on the steering wheel, and the other at my mouth, my knuckles worrying against my lips.

"Gunnar." Logan fixed me with a steady look. "He's gonna be okay."

"He's a smart kid," Siren said.

"Is he? He's almost two hours away. He couldn't even speak on the phone!" I smacked the steering wheel hard. "I never should've let him leave. I shouldn't have let him get into whatever this is by himself."

"You couldn't have stopped him," Logan said. "No one could've. He's bullheaded—like you."

"But it's my fucking job," I said. "It's my fucking job to protect him."

"He called you, didn't he?"

I blinked away the tears suddenly blurring my vision and refocused on the bikes in front of me. He had called *me*—not Priest, not Logan, not Blade. Even after our fight. Was it just because I was the sergeant-at-arms?

Or was it something else?

According to the location he'd sent my phone, he was in the middle of nowhere, pulled off the side of some rarely used highway. Lying alone in the dark and the cold. He'd barely been able to form words on the phone—his voice had come in gasps. I'd heard him sob weakly.

It was like a terrible dream.

When I had heard his voice on the phone, a very simple truth had been revealed to me, something that overshadowed all the details that seemed so insignificant now: I would walk through fire for Raven. I would find whoever did this and I would destroy them.

As sergeant-at-arms of the club, I was willing to do whatever it took to ensure the safety of its members and its territory. But this was different. This wasn't the determination I felt as sergeant, and it wasn't the blind loyalty I'd prescribed to in the military. It was rage. Rage and a brutal thirst for justice. No one who was capable of hurting someone like Raven deserved to walk this earth.

The depth of this feeling—I couldn't put a name to it, I wouldn't—really fucking scared me. It was more than infatuation or lust. And I was even more terrified that Raven would find out. But one thing I knew for sure, things couldn't stay the same as they were.

His well-being came first, always. We'd get through this. I'd find him, and then I'd find whoever did this. And then—and then it was a mystery. But even if he wanted to never talk to me again, I'd be fine, as long as he was okay.

"Here's the turn-off," Siren said.

I followed the bikes onto the scenic overlook. In the darkness the view was gorgeous, all silhouetted mountains and the speckled headlights of cars driving through the valley below. I didn't look at it at all. I threw the SUV into park and jumped out, jogging to the dark shape of Raven's bike, which was haphazardly parked near a bush. Like he'd wanted to hide it. Even when he was about to pass out, he was thinking two steps ahead.

A narrow sidewalk was paved in front of the short wall that protected overlook viewers from the drop-off. Raven was lying on his back on the sidewalk, his legs in the road like he'd been sitting on the curb before he passed out.

I crouched by his side. He was breathing, thank God. I brushed the hair from his forehead; his skin was cool from the chill outside, and an enormous bruise was forming on the side of his face.

"Raven," I said. "Raven, wake up. We gotta get up."

His dark blue eyes blinked open wearily, and his chapped lips parted, caked with drying blood. "You came."

"Course I did." I placed a hand gingerly on his face. "You thought I wouldn't?"

He closed his eyes again. "S'cold."

"Don't go back to sleep. Can you get up?"

"Nope," Logan said. "Don't move, Raven. We'll carry you."

Logan gave me a look and I reluctantly stepped back, giving Logan space to drop his medical bag next to Raven. Without any hesitation, Logan snapped immediately into nurse-mode. "Blade, make sure the area's secure, will you? Don't want to get surprised by anyone."

Blade nodded. Even in the midst of a terrible situation, seeing Logan jump into action always made Blade's eyes warm with pride and love. "Got it. You're with me, Tex."

Logan nodded. "Siren, make sure his bike's okay. Gunnar, Coop, Priest—help me move him."

Priest's face was twisted with grief as he approached. With the four of us working on Logan's count, we lifted Raven gingerly and slid him into the backseat of the SUV. After the all-clear from Blade and Siren, we drove back toward Elkin Lake. Logan rode in the backseat with Raven, and I heard them murmuring as I chewed up the miles as fast as I could.

Chapter 10 - Raven

I was dragged back into consciousness like someone had pulled me from deep underwater. My body hurt—a pounding ache concentrated in my gut, a brutal throb that prevented me from taking any deep breaths. My head pounded, too, like my heartbeat itself was an instrument of torture. But it was warm inside, and the couch beneath me was soft, at least.

"Raven? Can you hear me?"

I blinked my eyes open reluctantly. God, it was too fucking bright. The light sent a sharp bolt of pain through my head alongside the standard ache.

"Hey," the voice said. The person connected to the voice waved at somebody, and the overhead lights dimmed. I relaxed minutely.

"Can you hear me?" It was Logan's voice, I finally realized. "You awake?"

I nodded.

"Can you tell me your name?" he asked.

"Don't be annoying," I grumbled.

"Humor me, please."

"Raven," I said.

"Do you know where you are? And what day it is?"

"Fuck you," I said. "The clubhouse. I think it's Sunday."

Logan managed a slight smile. "Thanks. Do you remember what happened?"

I closed my eyes again.

It came rushing back, pummeling me like a wave. The bar. The informant that didn't show. The Viper—his hand on my face and in my hair. I turned my face away from Logan and into the back of the couch to hide the tears threatening to spill.

"I just wanted—I was trying—" I choked back a sob. "Dad—"

Grief chewed at my insides, and I curled into myself. My breath came in shallow gasps as I tried not to lose myself in the sobs clawing at my throat to escape. My investigation, if I could even call it that, had been the dam holding back my grief since I'd gotten that first email. As long as I was pushing forward, doing something meaningful, I could keep outrunning the despair that snapped at my heels.

But I had no new information about the truth of Dad's death. I'd done everything wrong: I had no leads, no ideas, no proof. I'd *failed* him. I'd turned my back on the club trying to avenge Dad, and all I'd done was put the club in danger.

"Hey, hey now," my Pops said soothingly. He knelt next to the couch and placed one hand gently on my shoulder. "You're okay now. You're safe."

I clutched at Pops' arms where he held me the same way he had when I was still a kid who'd had a nightmare.

But this reality was worse than any nightmare I'd ever had.

"Everything's gonna be okay, son." Pops rubbed my back in gentle circles.

"It's not. It won't." My tears stained his shirt.

Pops hummed, but didn't press. He held me like that, rocking me slightly, muttering nonsense, until the worst of it passed.

I pulled away slightly and rubbed hard at my eyes. "Sorry."

Pops' face fell. He touched the purpling bruise on the side of my face, and then the bandage on the side of my neck covering the cigarette burn there. I grimaced.

"Let's let Logan finish checking you out. You up to that?"

I nodded and sat up on the couch, leaning up against the armrest with no small amount of effort.

Blade and Logan stood a few paces away, watching with concern. Blade had his arms wrapped around Logan, so Logan's back was to Blade's chest. Logan lifted one of Blade's hands to his lips and kissed his knuckles before pulling out of Blade's grasp to get his medical bag.

I glanced around the room. No one else was present. Certainly not Gunnar. And why would he be? Why even look? He'd basically told me something like this would happen. He was probably at Ballast with the rest of the enforcers, cursing me over a beer for being stupid, and for not listening to him. For all the extra trouble I'd caused.

And yet I still sunk back into the pillows and had to blink hard to keep the tears from returning. I wanted Gunnar at my side.

I wanted him to care.

Blade tucked his hands into the pockets of his jacket. His dark gaze bore into me. "He came for you."

I blinked. "What?"

"Gunnar," Blade said. As if he could read my mind. "He came for you. We all did, the moment you called."

"Called?" I asked. "I called Gunnar?"

Logan started. "You don't remember? Look at me, please." He shined a penlight in my eyes. "Hey, do you remember hitting your head at any point last night? Maybe when you passed out on the curb?"

"No, I lay down," I said. "I just got hit in the face."

Pops winced.

Logan didn't look convinced. "Yeah, you called him, but you weren't really speaking. You sent him your location through your GPS."

I nodded slowly.

"Though I don't know why you would send that to Gunnar," Logan grumbled. "Can't hardly work his phone. Should've sent it to me."

The memory returned, slow and hazy. I'd been cold and hurting. I'd called Gunnar because—because—

Because I trusted him. As much as I didn't want to. As much as I tried to back off, pull away, forget the way I felt about him. I knew if I asked him to come for me, he would. Which meant he'd seen me all loopy and miserable on the side of the road. I winced at the thought.

"Yeah, he's not happy," Priest said. "And neither am I. We're going to have to have a chat about these lone ranger antics."

"Damn right we are," Blade said. "No more secrets. What the fuck is going on? Who did this? And why?"

"Blade." Logan's voice was stern. "Not now. Go fix some coffee, please."

It still surprised me every time Blade listened to Logan, but even I wanted to listen to Logan when he was in his snappy nurse-mode.

"Fine," Blade said. "But once you feel a little better, Raven, we're coming back to this."

I nodded.

"You want something harder in the coffee? Take the edge off?" Blade asked.

"Yes, please," I said.

"It's not for you," Logan said. "Not while you potentially have a concussion."

I pouted.

Logan was unmoved. He lifted the hem of my shirt and examined the bruises purpling nastily across my abs. He poked around, pressing at my belly and feeling the expansion of my ribs.

"Nothing's broken, far as I can tell," he determined. "No internal bleeding. Lucky bastard. You should still go to the ER, though, get a CT scan, make sure it's all okay." His defeated tone made it clear he already knew my answer.

"No, I'm okay," I said.

Logan glanced at Priest. "I really think he should go."

He packed up his medical supplies and joined Blade in the kitchen without waiting for a response.

Pops crouched by the couch again. "Logan's right, you know."

"I'm fine, Pops." I closed my eyes. "I just need to rest. Please."

Pops sighed. He patted my arm, gently, like he wasn't sure where to touch me without hurting me. "I'm about out of good will, son," he said, not unkindly.

"Just need to rest," I murmured, and I let sleep overtake me.

Chapter 11 - Gunnar

I hurled a hatchet at the bullseye posted on the immense oak in the backyard for the fifth or sixth time. It flew true and embedded itself deeply into the wooden target. I threw another, and another, each throw harder than the last until I was grunting with the effort, like there was a Viper in front of me instead of a tree.

It would've been easy to blame the Vipers for it all. But I was culpable, too. I'd let Raven walk into their territory without backup. Worse than that—he'd done it because he felt he couldn't trust me to provide the necessary backup. It wasn't just a breach of duty as sergeant-at-arms, but a failure of friendship.

All I'd wanted was to ensure Raven could live the life he deserved, with someone who deserved him back. I wasn't right for him. I hadn't want any feelings he had for me to keep him from meeting people who would be better for him, who would be *good* for him. To keep him from building his own life. But instead, I'd driven him away from the club, and into a situation that'd nearly gotten him killed.

I stalked across the yard and wrenched the hatchets out of the target. I'd throw them until I was exhausted or I cut the damn tree down.

I turned around to walk to the back porch again. Priest slipped out the back door and joined me.

"He'll be fine," Priest said, before I could ask. "Nothing's broken. Mild concussion, maybe. Mostly he's just bruised."

"He shouldn't fucking be hurt at all." I chucked the hatchet hard. It went wide and sailed past the tree. "He shouldn't be going into enemy territory without any goddamned backup!"

Priest nodded and said nothing.

Anger bubbled within me, and once I started, it was as if a floodgate had opened, and I couldn't stop.

"He was raised in this club! If there's anyone who should know the rules—basic shit like territory rules—it should be him. We don't do lone wolf bullshit, right? That's the whole point of the structure! The club doesn't fucking exist if we just ignore the rules!" I hurled another hatchet. "He shouldn't be keeping secrets. He knew it was dangerous, but he still went. Alone. What if I hadn't picked up the phone?"

The thought sent a fresh rush of fear through me. I met Priest's soft gaze.

"What about that, huh? What if I hadn't had my phone on me? What if we'd been too drunk to ride? What then? He could've just been lying on that curb for hours. Or the Vipers could've found him again. He didn't get far."

"But that didn't happen," Priest said. "Don't waste energy beating yourself up over the what-ifs."

"The what-ifs are my *job*! I have to plan for these kinds of things! What if he runs off again?"

"He won't," Priest said.

"You don't know that."

"Sometimes I think I don't know a damn thing," Priest admitted. "But I know my son. And he knows he fucked up."

"Does he?" I tossed the remaining hatchet in my hand, spinning it in the air and catching it by the handle. "Or does he just regret that it went wrong?"

"Give me that," Priest said.

I tossed him the hatchet. He caught it easily, and then stood beside me and threw it gracefully into the bullseye.

"Show-off," I said.

Priest continued as if I hadn't spoken. "Raven's always had a stubborn streak. Just like his dad." He paused and rubbed at his beard. "God, I miss him."

I knocked my shoulder against Priest's but said nothing.

"He ever tell you how we met?"

"No, he didn't."

"In a bar, of course. I had just moved to LA a few weeks before we met—this was years and years ago, I wasn't even twenty yet. Now, this wasn't a gay bar, but it wasn't *not* a gay bar, you know. One of the bars in Hollywood that catered to everyone. One of those places that'd let in the eighteen-year-olds, and then you'd run into the bathroom and wash the pen off your hands and get hammered.

"Got a lot of people who were curious, you know. This was right before the AIDS crisis, so people weren't afraid yet. Lots of wild stuff going on in those clubs." He shook his head. "Just a year or two later, well... I'll spare you that part.

"Anyway, he was at the bar by himself. Completely gorgeous guy. This thick, dark hair, short and coiffed. He always had a Brando thing going on. He had a tattoo on his bicep of a raven. I had a similar one." He pointed to the faded tattoo on his forearm. "Shockingly, it does predate my son. I struck up a conversation. He was cordial, but quickly let me know he was straight."

"Then why was he at the bar?"

"That's what I said! I think I said something ridiculous and corny like, 'What's a guy like you doing in a place like this?' He thought it was funny. You know when Raven thinks something is stupid, but funny at the same time, and he shakes his head and smiles at his feet like he's embarrassed he thinks it's funny?"

I knew exactly what he was talking about. "Yeah, every time he talks to me."

"His dad did the same thing. Same reaction to my terrible pick-up lines. But I was completely smitten from the second I saw him. It was his laugh, you know. And the way he always focused on me like there wasn't anyone else in the room. He let me down easy… But he kept coming back to the bar. And so did I.

"Same time, one or twice a week, we'd have a drink and shoot the shit. He was a good straight kid from the rich side of town. Wasn't supposed to spend time in the dives I hung out in. I was broke, alone, and publicly out when that wasn't the easiest thing to do. You know he was in law school?"

"Ankh? Law school?"

"Yeah. He was supposed to take over his dad's firm. He denied the feelings growing between us for a long time. We'd been talking for months before he finally got drunk enough to kiss me. After that he went fully one-eighty. Pushed me away, tried to fight me a few times, and then disappeared from the bar. I thought I'd never see him again. He was in denial for a long time. But eventually he came back. Lucky for him, I still carried a torch."

"You forgave him? After he treated you like that?"

"He was trying to figure out who he was," Priest said. "He thought he was protecting me. Thought he was too messed up and confused to get involved with me—that he'd do me more harm than good. But staying away from the person your heart wants to be with—that's how you do real harm. He did finish law school, though. That's why our club charter is so good."

"Why are you telling me this?" I asked suddenly. Why did this matter when Raven was beaten halfway to death and the Vipers were in our business yet again?

Priest raised his eyebrows. "You play a lot dumber than you are, Gunnar."

I said nothing. I rarely doubted Priest's read on things. But if he knew how I really felt about Raven, he'd keep his son far away from me. No father would want their son to be involved with someone so much older, someone with so much baggage and so much blood on their hands. I couldn't even blame him.

"Listen," Priest said. "Until we figure out what's going on, I want you to act as Raven's protective detail. Siren will act as the enforcers' road captain while you do. If Raven is on the Vipers' list, he needs security around the clock."

He pressed his lips together. "We saw what the Vipers are capable of with Logan. If they get their hands on Raven, I don't—I can't think about what might happen."

"Nothing's going to happen, sir," I said. The formality just slipped out, as it often did when Priest went full vice president and started dropping orders. You could take the dog out of the military, but not the military out of the dog. "Not on my watch. But Raven's not going to like having me around."

"This isn't about Raven's personal preferences. He gave up that luxury when he ran off."

"Can't say I disagree with you there."

"And you're the best man for the job." Priest gripped my shoulder. "I can count on you, yeah?"

I met his steady gaze. "Always, sir."

"Good man." He smiled wearily. "Don't take the tree down with the hatchet-throwing."

Priest left me alone in the backyard. I paced through the grass to recover the rogue hatchet.

Protective detail. I turned the order over in my head. Part of me was deeply relieved—now Raven couldn't ditch me, claiming I was being nosy or paranoid. Now I had a direct order from Priest to back me up, and Raven, for all his stubbornness, was rarely willing to go blatantly against Priest or Blade.

But another part of me dreaded the closeness. This meant I'd never get a reprieve from Raven. Would I be able to keep it professional? Could I keep my desire leashed? I had to be his sergeant right now, not his—

His what?

His friend?

Lover?

Something else?

Something more?

And why had Priest taken the time to tell me about the intricacies of his and Ankh's early relationship? If I thought too hard about it, I was worried he might have been doing more than just reminiscing. I knew he wanted Raven to be happy, but Priest had to know Raven couldn't ever truly be happy with me. I was too old, too jaded, too fucked up. I'd killed people—not for the club, not people who had wronged us. I'd killed innocent people. Under the beating hot sun in Afghanistan. Sure, I'd been under orders, but I hadn't questioned them. I hadn't even thought it was wrong.

I'd just pointed my gun where I was told to and watched the blood stain the sand. My superior officer hadn't realized our intel was incorrect until it was too late.

Most people weren't capable of the things I could do. The things I'd already done. The things I'd do again, if it meant keeping my people safe. Raven deserved to be with someone... clean. Someone as smart, sharp, and ambitious as Raven, without a heavy past weighing them down.

But there was no denying that I was the best option for his protective detail. The skills that had been a barrier to a romantic relationship with Raven in the past were the same skills that could potentially save his life now. In order to do that, though, I needed to keep Raven close, where I could actually *keep him safe*. And clearly, how I'd been trying to navigate my relationship with Raven before wasn't going to cut it.

I'd have to change tactics. I had to make Raven feel comfortable again. I had to show him he belonged in this club, and that he could come to any of us for what he needed—that he could come to *me* for what he needed, without fear of being pushed away or condescended to.

This was more than an order or a job. This felt almost like a calling—a chance for redemption.

Determination steadied me. I'd keep Raven safe and get to the bottom of who hurt him—and why the Vipers were after him—no matter what it took.

Chapter 12 - Raven

When I woke up, my bedroom was shrouded in darkness, lit only by the moonlight shining through the window. I ached all over, a full-body soreness that reminded me of the aches and pains I'd gotten when I first started going on long-haul rides with the club. Not the powerful, dizzying pain I'd first experienced at the hands of the Vipers... whenever that was. I had no concept of how long I'd been asleep. But it felt like a long time.

I was lying slightly propped up on a mound of pillows in my own bed. A cannula had been inserted into my left arm, attached to a slow-dripping saline bag. Logan's handiwork. We were lucky to have him—his connections with the clinic in town meant I could recover at home instead of in the hospital. I coughed and cleared my throat—dry as sandpaper. I'd definitely been out a while.

"Here, drink this."

I startled hard, whipping my head around to the source of the voice.

"Sorry. Didn't mean to scare you."

Gunnar was sitting in my desk chair, which he'd scooted close to my bedside. I hadn't even noticed him there. He was wearing those thin gray sweatpants that drove me crazy, and a white undershirt that clung tight to his chest. Ridiculous. I'd gotten the shit beaten out of me and still the first thing I noticed were Gunnar's tense muscles and the concerned downward tilt of his mouth.

I took the glass gratefully and drank it down. "What time is it?"

"Nearly midnight. On Tuesday."

"Tuesday?" I dropped my head back down onto the pillows. "That means—"

"Yeah, you've been out almost two days." He pinned me with his intense gaze. It was like a physical weight on me. I drew my lower lip in between my teeth.

I remembered bits and pieces. I remembered being woken up a lot, pestered into checkups. I still felt a little loopy, like I was teetering on the edge of a bad hangover. But if Gunnar was here, that meant I was in for a lecture or a late-night shouting match. And I really didn't want that. I was so tired. I wanted him to crawl into the bed next to me and lull me to sleep with the warmth of his body, but I'd already made the mistake of asking for that once before.

"How are you feeling?" His voice was so warm and gentle it shocked me.

"Sore," I admitted. "Stiff. But my head doesn't feel like it's going to burst anymore."

"That's an improvement," Gunnar said.

"Yeah."

We sat in silence for a moment. Gunnar rested his elbows on his knees, leaning his body toward me, his fingers pressed together against his lips. I was struck by the sudden, intense desire to reach out and skate my hand over the curve of his upper back. To soothe him.

"You're really not going to harass me?" I asked. "About what happened?"

"I'm not," Gunnar said.

I looked away. "Then why are you here?"

Gunnar seemed confused, like he wasn't sure exactly how to answer. Finally, he stood up, and moved toward the door. "I should get Logan, now that you're awake."

"Don't," I said without thinking. As grateful as I was to Logan, I didn't want him at my beside prodding me.

I wanted Gunnar.

"Don't what?" He turned and faced me. Standing at the foot of my bed, he tilted his chin down to look at me properly. With his thumbs tucked into the waistband of his sweatpants, the moonlight illuminated the muscles in arms in gorgeous chiaroscuro.

"Don't leave."

A multitude of emotions ran across Gunnar's face, so quickly I couldn't track them, until his gaze settled into something soft and concerned. He placed one hand on my ankle and squeezed gently. A reassuring touch. But even with a blanket between us, his touch was enough to spark desire deep inside me. Despite the aches and bruises that my brush with the Vipers had left on me, my cock twitched hard and began to harden.

I shifted my hips slightly. My face flushed hot with embarrassment. My body was betraying me, reacting like I was a teenager again, but even this small touch from Gunnar was so intoxicating that I couldn't tamp down how badly I wanted more.

Gunnar didn't move his hand. His attention was like a physical weight on me, pinning me to the bed.

"Raven." Gunnar's voice deepened. His gaze moved down my body and lingered at my crotch, where the shape of my hardening cock was visible through the thin blanket. His hand didn't move from my ankle, and his grip felt like a brand. "What do you want?"

There was an almost dangerous stillness to Gunnar, like a predatory cat waiting to pounce on its prey.

"Nothing." I turned my head into the pillow, too mortified to meet his eyes. "Forget it. You can leave. I won't break into your room and molest you again, promise."

I already knew Gunnar didn't want me. Especially now that I'd proven myself to be a complete idiot, running into enemy territory and getting my ass kicked, and I didn't even have any information to show for it. I was useless. The fact that he was there right now didn't change anything.

"I know you're only here because you have to be," I said. "You don't have to pretend to care. I know I'm basically dead weight in the club."

"What?" Gunnar furrowed his brow deeply. "That's not even close to true. Don't talk about yourself like that."

I huffed a laugh. "That's rich, coming from you, since that's all you make me feel."

His touch finally left my ankle. I waited to hear the door open and close. But it didn't. Instead, the bed shifted as Gunnar sat down at the foot of the bed.

"That's not..." He trailed off, sliding his hand over my shin and up to my thigh.

I shuddered under his touch.

"I never wanted you to feel that way," Gunnar said. "I think you're the best Hell's Ankhor has to offer. Smarter than the rest of us combined, I'm pretty sure. Funny. Observant—maybe too observant. Right hook like a guy twice your size."

"Maybe that last part's true." I tried to suppress a small smile. A faint hope bloomed in my chest, but I tried to ignore it. Just because Gunnar was being nice to me now didn't mean anything. He probably just felt guilty because he hadn't been able to follow me effectively. He'd made it extremely clear, over and over, that he wanted nothing to do with me sexually or romantically. Even with his hand gripping at my thigh and his gaze fixed on my mouth, I had to remember that. I couldn't get my hopes up just to get let down again. "But the rest isn't. You don't have to patronize me just because I'm a little banged up."

"I'm not patronizing you," Gunnar said. "I'm trying to be honest here."

"Then be honest," I said. "I know you think I'm just a dumb kid with a crush."

"Oh, yeah?" He paused, leveling me with his gaze for a long moment of hesitation before a smile spread slowly on his face, and he pulled his lower lip in between his teeth. Predatory but teasing at the same time. It sent a hot thrill down my spine. "You want me to be honest? You want to know what I think?"

I met his gaze steadily. If this was a challenge, I wasn't backing down.

Gunnar hopped onto the bed, on his knees, with my legs pinned between them. My breath caught in my chest. The weight of his body on my legs was nearly overwhelming.

"I think you need to stay very, very still," he said.

I gripped the sheet beneath me. My eyes widened. He pulled the thin blanket down around my thighs. Without hesitation Gunnar reached out and gripped my hard cock through my briefs. I gasped. His grip was rough, unselfconscious—he didn't move his hand at all, but the pressure was enough to send my mind reeling.

Was this really happening? Things had changed so suddenly—this was like something from my fantasies. I half-expected to wake up at any moment—this *had* to be a vivid dream. I'd blame the pain medications.

Gunnar was watching me with something like awe on his face.

"God, you're reactive," he murmured. "Stay still. And quiet."

Then he slid my briefs down just enough to free my cock. My hands twitched at my sides. Remaining motionless felt nearly impossible—I itched to touch him. Wherever he'd let me.

He skated one callused hand gently over my bruised abs. His face twisted slightly as he touched them, but the pained expression didn't linger. Then he ducked down and, without preamble, sucked the head of my cock into his mouth.

If my legs hadn't been pinned underneath him, and his hands hadn't moved to my hips, I would've arched off the bed. He sucked me down slowly, taking his time, like he was savoring it.

He'd told me to stay still, but if this was a one-time opportunity, I was taking advantage of it. I touched his head gently, and when he didn't pull away, I dragged my fingers through his close-cut blond hair. When I ran my nails over his scalp, he groaned around my length, and the vibration sent a bolt of pleasure through me.

"Gunnar," I whispered. "I can't—I won't last."

He slid his mouth off my cock with an obscene wet sound. He licked his lips as he jacked me slowly with one hand, the motion smooth and easy, lubricated by his saliva.

"Don't hold back," he said. "Let me return the favor."

Did that mean—he couldn't mean that.

And then he winked at me.

I didn't understand a fucking thing about this man.

He ran the flat of his tongue up the length of my cock, and then sucked me back down again, taking the full length of my cock all the way into his throat easy as anything. I melted into the mattress beneath him, letting his weight pin me down and the slow, luxurious pace of the blowjob create a slow build of pleasure in my gut like a tide rising.

I still had my hands in his hair, and I slid one hand around the back of his head, scraping my nails across the soft hair of his nape. He moaned deeply and quietly, like a purr.

He kept his pace slow and steady. Heat coursed through me. My skin flushed with it. My toes curled in the sheets. I tried to wiggle beneath him, but it was impossible to move under his bulk, and somehow that made the blowjob even more delicious.

"I'm close," I whispered.

Gunnar hummed around me then slid one hand up my torso, under my shirt. He slid his palm over my pec, and then pinched my nipple hard between his thumb and forefinger.

The quick, sharp flare of pain was enough to send me over the edge. My orgasm rolled over me like a wave. I closed my eyes and tried to arch up, to get even deeper into his mouth, and Gunnar let me, taking me as deep as he could.

He swallowed it all, sucking me down like he couldn't get enough.

I panted through the aftershocks, almost dizzy from how hard I'd come. Gunnar grinned at me, and then fixed my briefs and pulled the blanket back up. Like this was just a rudimentary thing rather than something earth-shattering. He was still kneeling on the bed, and his cock tented his sweatpants, a small wet stain formed where he'd spurted precum. It made my mouth water—and it was reassuring, in a way, to see physical evidence that sucking me off had turned him on.

"Let me," I said. "I wanna get you off."

Gunnar chewed his lower lip like he was thinking about it. Then he shook his head and stood up. He adjusted his cock with a grunt, a sound that sent another thrill of desire through me. I couldn't get enough of him.

"Not about me," he said. "You need to rest."

As if he'd cast a spell, exhaustion crashed over me. I tried to blink it away.

"See?" he said. "You're falling asleep just talking to me."

"Getting you off will wake me up," I argued half-heartedly.

"Nice try."

"Gunnar, I…" My eyes flickered closed. Because I was tired, and because I couldn't stand to look him in the eyes when I was halfway to begging. "Don't leave, though."

He didn't respond, but his touch grazed over my forehead as he brushed my hair away from my eyes. I had a vague memory of a similar gesture when I was in-and-out of consciousness.

Had he touched me so tenderly before?

It didn't seem possible.

"I'm not going anywhere," he said. "Get some sleep."

I didn't say: Stay here. In my bed. Like we did that night.

I knew he wouldn't, and I wasn't going to push my luck. If this was all I ever got, I wanted the memory to end like this, with Gunnar's strong hands gentle on my forehead as I fell into sleep.

Chapter 13 - Raven

Gunnar was true to his word. When I awoke, he was there, leaning against the wall by the door with his arms crossed over his chest. But before I could say anything, he slipped out the door. Logan stormed in moments later, his green eyes blazing.

"I can't believe you." Logan's words were sharp and fast, like he'd been waiting to chew me out—and he probably *had* been waiting for the go-ahead to dress me down. "You saw what the Vipers are capable of. You saw what they did to me."

He pulled my shirt up perfunctorily, without even waiting for my agreement, and examined the bruising. He poked and prodded at my ribs.

"That hurts!"

"You are really fucking lucky," Logan said. "You should have broken ribs, or worse."

I said nothing. No way I was telling Logan it was genuinely pure luck that saved me.

Logan's hands shook the barest amount. "You scared us. Me especially."

Shame flooded me suddenly, overwhelming the sting of pain as Logan pressed on my ribs again. I hadn't considered how Logan might react to having to grapple with the Vipers again. His kidnapping was still fresh. He'd only been in Hell's Ankhor a few months, but he'd slotted in like he was filling a hole in the club I hadn't realized existed. He was a brother to me.

"I never meant—"

"I know. Just—don't do it again, okay? If you hadn't gotten away..." He paused and took a deep breath, pressing gauze to one of my wounds. "They like to send messages. What happened to me could've happened to you. They don't fuck around."

"Yeah," I said. "I really get that now."

"Do you?"

"Trust me," I grumbled. "I'm not keen on getting my ass beat again."

"I do trust you," Logan said warmly. "I just think you're a bit of a moron."

"Well, it's part of my charm."

Logan rolled his eyes and taped the gauze down.

"That's gonna linger for a week or so," he said, nodding towards the bruise on my cheek.

"Figures. Karma, I guess."

"No, karma would be Gunnar pushing you into the lake, or something. Not a Viper beatdown." Logan hummed thoughtfully as he gathered his medical equipment. "You know he's your detail now, right?"

"Excuse me?" That shocked me into full wakefulness. I was annoyed, and then relieved, and then both, all in the space of a breath.

"Yeah, Priest told me he assigned him to you. Though if you ask me, Priest didn't need to make it official. Gunnar would've been doing it anyway." He raised his eyebrows. "Is that cool with you?"

"Guess it has to be," I said. "I feel like I've already taken a few years off Pops' life. I can't push back on this."

"Not really what I was asking," Logan said. "But good."

I said nothing, and Logan didn't push. He always knew when to push and when to back off. I was especially grateful for that now.

"Listen," Logan said. "Everyone wants to bother you. You want me to keep them away for a few hours, or are you good to receive your adoring public?"

"Gimme a half-hour to clean up," I said.

Then Logan left me alone, and I took a long, much-needed shower.

So Gunnar had spent the night because he had to. Priest's orders. But would he have stayed otherwise? The blowjob he'd given me—the fucking best blowjob of my life, so lingering and luxurious, my cock stirred with interest at just the memory— was definitely not part of his duties as sergeant, and he could have spent the night stationed outside the door if he'd really wanted to. But he'd stayed, because I asked.

And I had to admit to myself there was no small amount of relief that Gunnar was at my back. Even though I hadn't involved the club the way I planned to, I was grateful I had backup now. I couldn't continue on this path alone. Especially now that the Vipers knew who I was and what I looked like— and what I was after. They'd be waiting for me to show back up.

After my shower, in the dense steam in my bathroom, I wiped the mirror clear and examined my reflection. All things considered, I didn't look too bad. My eye was definitely on its way to swollen, and the bruises on my torso made me appear even paler than usual.

I was a mess.

And Gunnar had still wanted me.

But for how long?

* * *

I spent the next three days recovering. I slept for hours and hours, ate immense amounts of food, and tried not to linger too much on my investigation. The bruises along my ribs and abdomen where the Vipers had pummeled me were fading into sickening shades of yellow and green. The worse they looked, the less they hurt.

Logan had me off booze and on more ibuprofen than I thought necessary, but it seemed to be working. The bruise on my face where the Viper had backhanded me had coalesced into a lovely shiner. That was karma, I guessed, for my earlier pigheadedness—and for the shiner I'd given Gunnar when all of this started. But for as much time as I spent in my room, I didn't spend a whole lot of it alone. Every member had spent time with me, bringing me food or books or in Siren's case, a few hands of poker.

Siren examined the cards in her hand thoughtfully. "I call." She added a few chips to the pile growing on the edge of my bed.

I'd always resented the extra attention the rest of the club members showed me; the way they would single me out to spend time with me was not something they seemed to do with other members, and felt like a holdover from the days when I'd been a kid they'd been awkwardly trying to bond with. I hated feeling coddled, or like I was receiving special treatment because I was the leadership's son.

But something in my perception had changed in the last few days. Maybe it was getting so close to the Vipers and seeing not only how they treated me, but how they treated each other, but

I realized I'd been taking Hell's Ankhor for granted. The way I was being cared for now—not just Logan's physical care, but the near-constant barrage of visits—wasn't coddling or babying.

It was just love. I saw that now. Everyone in this club loved me like they loved every other member. I wasn't a drain on the club, or the annoying kid they put up with because they didn't have a choice. I was one of them. We'd fight to the death for each other, if need be. Not every club was like that. And I'd wasted so much time rejecting them and wallowing in my own insecurities, feeling like I had to handle things on my own.

No wonder Gunnar had pushed me away. He'd treated me like a kid because I'd acted like one. Petulant and insecure.

"Fold," Gunnar said gruffly, and dropped his cards face-down at the foot of the bed.

Gunnar was taking his duty seriously, and he had remained posted in my room like a sentinel. He'd either loomed in the corner, or perched in a chair, or stood silently outside the door. But he hadn't spoken to me directly. Not since that night. Technically we'd spent the entirety of the past three days together, but we hadn't had a single private moment together.

I felt like an idiot for thinking the blowjob changed anything. It must have been a fluke. Temporary insanity. He'd probably just felt bad for me and wanted to give me a little gift to make me feel better. Why had I thought that meant we'd have anything real together?

But… He was sticking around. He could've had the other enforcers help keep watch. But it was only him, the whole time.

I tried to quash these little bursts of hope whenever they appeared. What Gunnar felt for me was the same thing he felt for the other members. We were a brotherhood. It wasn't anything more than that. I wouldn't make the same mistakes as last time and chase after him, thinking his small gestures meant something more than they did. This was at least better than it had been since I'd gotten home from college.

"All right, show 'em," Siren said.

"Full house." I dropped my cards face-up.

"Ooh, almost." Siren grinned, catlike. "Four of a kind."

"Every fuckin' time," I grumbled as Siren gathered the chips.

"Sorry," she said in a decidedly unapologetic tone. "Consider it revenge for all the pool games. All right, I gotta get ready for church. You're coming?"

I nodded. I was dreading it, but I was going.

Siren left with a jaunty salute. Gunnar stood up to follow her.

"Gunnar—"

"I'll be right outside if you need me." Gunnar followed her out the door and closed it behind him.

I huffed in frustration. Gunnar had been so warm and kind to me—for Gunnar, at least—as I'd recovered, making sure I always had what I needed, or that someone was with me. I'd started to see glimmers of our old relationship, and I'd started to hope that maybe we could be cordial again. Friends, even.

But then he'd do something like this—walk out and ignore me—and leave me feeling hurt and confused about where we stood. I climbed out of bed and got dressed slowly. I still had to take care with my bruising, so I sat at the edge of the bed to pull on my boots. Gunnar's cards from the poker game still lay face-down at my side. I flipped them over.

Straight flush. The winning hand.

"What an ass," I muttered.

Someone rapped on the door. "Hope you're talking about yourself there, boy."

"Hey, Pops."

Pops stepped into my room and closed the door behind him. Maybe I was just imagining it, seeing things as a way to cope with my guilt, but it looked like he'd aged a lot in the past weeks. The crow's feet around his eyes looked deeper, and I thought the silver streaks at his temples were more defined.

And he walked with a little more heaviness to him, like it was a little bit more challenging to move under the weight of the world. Pops had spent more time at my side this week than anyone other than Gunnar—and he was the only other member of the club who hadn't chewed me out for what I'd done.

Pops' lack of anger hurt worse than any of the arguments I'd gotten from the other members. He hadn't been angry at me— he'd been afraid. And the fear I'd seen in Pops' eyes when he first saw my wounds had sent shame coursing through me.

So I'd told him. Everything. Last night, when Gunnar had taken a break to shower and Pops had been alone in my room with me, I'd told him about the emails, the cops, the medics, the witnesses—everything. I'd watched as the color had drained from his face.

It was well within his rights to demand action immediately. But Pops believed in the club, and he'd called for a church meeting instead.

"Our brothers deserve to know," he'd said. "I won't make any decisions without them."

And now he was here, ensuring that I wouldn't be late. Did he think I'd bitch out? That I'd try to hide instead of showing up at church?

Pops sat down on the foot of the bed next to me and sighed.

No. Of course not. He wanted to be here with me—so we could support each other. I leaned against him, and he wrapped his arm around my shoulders.

"How you feeling, son?"

"Tired," I admitted. "But better."

"You know this won't be easy."

"I know." I ran my hand through my hair. "I'm sorry. I'm sorry I waited so long."

"I am, too, son," Pops said. "I wish—I wish I understood why you thought you needed to hide this from us. From me."

My heart twisted at the pain in Pops' voice. "I thought I was protecting the club. I didn't want to sound the alarm before I knew I had something. And... I wanted to figure it out. I wanted to avenge Dad's death myself."

"You have nothing to prove to the club. We're a family, Raven. We help each other. We don't face things like this alone." He squeezed my shoulder hard. "Your Dad wouldn't have wanted you to face this alone."

I pressed my lips together, fighting back the sob that threatened to escape.

"When you're hurting, or confused, or lost, that's when you need the club most," Pops said. "Don't turn your back on us, okay? Because we'll never turn our backs on you."

"I know, Pops." My voice was choked. "I'm sorry."

"I don't need you to be sorry," Pops said kindly. "I need you to understand. You understand you scared us? You won't do anything like this again?"

"I won't, Pops." I blinked my eyes clear of the tears and met his gaze steadily. "I won't."

"Good." He pulled me into a tight hug. "Let's go to church so you can confess your sins."

***

I didn't have to go far. Church was held in the clubhouse kitchen, with all senior members of the Hell's Ankhor inner circle sitting around the kitchen island with coffee mugs and frosty beers. Blade had a highball glass of bourbon in front of him and a scowl on his face. Gunnar sat to his left and Pops on his right. I sat where Blade pointed me—the seat directly across from him. The enforcers, Tex, Coop, and Siren, were all there, as well as Maverick and Logan.

I sat with my laptop closed on the island in front of me. Blade glowered at me, irritated, like I was a petty criminal caught at the edges of the territory.

"All right, everyone," Blade said. "We all know why Pops called this meeting. Raven." He fixed his gaze on me. "You've kept secrets from the club and engaged in a rogue investigation into enemy territory, bypassing the official channels and avoiding the required backup. Your actions risked our relationship with the local citizen law enforcement as well as endangering your own life."

I didn't often hear Blade speak so sternly and formally, and when I did, it usually wasn't directed at me. I felt exposed under his assessment, like he could see every flaw I had, every mistake I'd made. But it wasn't unkind—it was thorough. I had to face head-on what I'd done, with all the senior members there to see it.

"This behavior is not like you," Blade said. "In a disciplinary hearing, I'm not typically interested in excuses or complaints. But in this case, since this behavior is so out-of-character, I want to give you a chance to explain your side of the story."

He leaned back in his chair and crossed his arms over his chest. His gaze never left my face.

This was a test. I wanted to pass. I wanted to make Blade proud. I wanted to make *Dad* proud.

"I made a mistake," I said. A lump rose in my throat, like my grief was trying to claw its way out of my body.

Everyone watched me intently. Even Gunnar.

"I... haven't been in my right mind."

I met Gunnar's gaze. He narrowed his eyes and looked away.

"I received an email." I took a deep, steadying breath. I tried to stay professional. I fixed my gaze on the ceiling, because if I saw any of the members' reactions, I'd break. "The night Logan was patched in. It came through an encrypted account—the security was beyond me. And I couldn't let it go. I didn't want to bring this issue to everyone's attention until I had something more concrete, like the source of the email, at least. But I got in too deep. I let my personal feelings dictate my behavior, and I turned my back when I should've asked for help."

I risked a look around the table. Gunnar wouldn't meet my eyes now. But this wasn't about him—even though it was our fight in my bedroom that had pushed me to ride back to El Acantilado, this was all on me. I looked to my Pops, and he nodded his approval.

I opened my laptop. I didn't want to see that goddamned photo ever again. I'd spent so much time studying it I could nearly draw it from memory. And what had I gained from all the work and investigation?

An ass-beating. Pops' disappointment. And this chasm of grief, reopened.

I turned the laptop around, revealing the email to the club with the email's text beneath it.

A beat.

Then the room exploded in activity. Everyone began shouting at once, asking questions, trying to get closer to the laptop.

"Fuck does that mean, 'no accident'?"

"How did they get this photo?"

"Did they send anything else?"

"Settle!" Blade roared, and slammed his fist hard on the kitchen island. "Settle the fuck down, everyone!"

Everyone fell still, but the room seemed to vibrate with unasked questions.

Blade motioned for the laptop, and through the hands of the other members it made its way toward him. He and Gunnar examined the email. Pops looked away.

"This is what you were doing?" Blade asked. "Investigating the source of this email?"

I nodded. I felt like I was teetering on the edge of a cliff, just barely hanging on to my composure. And Blade was about to push me over.

"And you didn't bring this to the club sooner?" Blade said coolly. "Why?"

Rage shot through me, sudden and hot like an internal flame.

"Because it's my fucking Dad!" I shouted. I pushed the heels of my hands into my eyes and took a deep breath. "I was so angry. I wasn't thinking long-term, I just started acting. I couldn't even—" I had to stop to clear my throat. "If I told everyone else, that made it real. If his death was a murder... How am I supposed to live in a world where my dad's killer walks free?"

"You think there's merit to this, then?" Gunnar asked.

His gaze was soft when it landed on me. His mouth was twisted in concern.

"Yeah," I said. "There's more."

I showed them the second email and explained why I was in Viper territory. "There's a turncoat in their ranks. Someone close to the Vipers wants me to have this information."

"Priest," Blade said. "Your take?"

Priest nodded at Blade, and then addressed the rest of the senior club members. "My son came to me with this information last night. I've been just as in the dark as the rest of you. I think we all know how grief clouds the mind." Nods all around. "Raven handled this improperly. But that doesn't mean the Vipers can get away with assaulting him."

"Damn fucking right," Logan said.

"And what Raven has dug up suggests the Vipers are involved with my old man's death. And in this club" —he beat his fist on the patch on his club leather—"we protect our own, and we avenge our own. I say let's go to war."

Blade mirrored Priest's motion. "War it is."

The rest of the club shouted their agreements. The energy in the room was oddly high, a mix of anger and determination and club solidarity.

The roar of the club, like one immense voice, relieved some of the pain I'd felt. Despite my mistakes, my family still had my back—and Dad's back. As long as Dad was avenged, I didn't care what punishments I had to endure.

From across the island, Gunnar stared me down. "We better start making a plan."

On his face I saw an odd combination of disappointment and admiration, but I couldn't fully read him. When I met his gaze, he nodded, and the small acknowledgement was enough to ease my fears.

For a moment, the room seemed to move in slow motion, with Gunnar's gaze on mine as the club rioted around us. Whatever was going on between us, I knew this much: the Vipers would pay. And for now, that could be enough.

Chapter 14 - Gunnar

Over many more coffees and a few more beers, my enforcers and I began to hammer out a plan to deal with the Viper's Nest.

Raven's confession had stunned me into silence. It'd pissed me off that he was hiding something, but I'd had no idea it was something of this magnitude. If Ankh had been murdered... That changed everything. It changed the club.

Raven was usually so stoic and controlled. He had a guarded demeanor, and always had a snarky joke or rebuttal if things got too serious, or if someone got too close. He'd never broken down in front of the club members before, let alone in church. But when he'd tried to explain how receiving the email had affected him, he could hardly get the words out. Tears had shone in his eyes. He'd had to pause and compose himself.

I wanted to fucking kill every last Viper in California.

And until we had this under control, I wasn't letting Raven out of my sight. Not again. If the Vipers got another shot at him, they wouldn't leave the job half-finished.

The majority of the club filtered out of the clubhouse to start preparations, leaving Blade and me alone with Raven.

"Okay, let me explain the tracking program." Raven had his laptop open in front of him with Blade peering over his shoulder. I stood on Raven's other side. I wanted suddenly, crazily, to touch the back of his neck. To comfort him in some way.

"So, I pulled the header from the email to find the IP address of the sending location—but the header was forged, so I had to crack the encryption on the email to get the actual header. The IP address was somewhere in Sweden, which is a super obvious

VPN locale—that clued me in to the fact that they were using a VPN, maybe multiple, to bounce it between servers and throw me off the scent."

Raven opened the tracking program he'd written and walked us through it piece by piece, explaining how he'd pinged the various servers the email had bounced around, looking for a certain response. It was all completely over my head.

This was the future of the club. Soon our territorial scuffles wouldn't be solved by fistfights at the border or intimidation rides through enemy areas. It'd all be online. Surveillance, hacking, all this shit I didn't fully understand. Maybe the next big issue we had with the Vipers wouldn't be their presence in our territory, but their noses in our servers.

The old guard like me was going out of style.

Raven had written this insanely complicated code while in the throes of grief and anger. He'd barely been able to think straight, and he'd pulled this off? He was so smart—how could I ever hope to measure up?

Leaning over his shoulder, the faint floral scent of his shampoo filled my senses.

This was the kind of intimacy I didn't deserve from Raven. I shouldn't know the smell of his shampoo, or the way his face scrunched up when he first woke up in the morning, or the low murmur of his voice in sleep.

The blowjob was supposed to have been just that—a blowjob. Nothing more. A brief loss of control. A blowjob didn't have to mean anything. I'd given tons of guys blowjobs.

None of them had been as gorgeously responsive as Raven, though, the way he'd fidgeted against the mattress, trying to stay still as I'd instructed. None of the other guys had known how much I liked nails raking across my scalp. No one tasted like Raven, felt like Raven.

And I'd felt so fucking guilty about him getting jumped. I should've been there. It was my job to protect him, and I'd let him run off alone to seek out the Vipers—I'd all but pushed him into their arms.

Then, on top of all of that, he'd started talking down on himself, like he'd deserved to be jumped.

I'd just wanted him to know that I didn't think of him like a dumb kid. I'd wanted to make him feel good, even if only for a moment, and show him I didn't feel the way he thought I did.

Words weren't my strong suit—and neither were relationships. In the moment, I'd stupidly thought it'd be the perfect solution to boost Raven's self-esteem a little bit, and cut the tension between us, so we could talk about this Viper problem without our own issues getting in the way. Maybe even repair our friendship a little, so that disastrous night I'd pushed him away wouldn't be breathing down our necks.

Of course, things couldn't be so simple. Because instead of making it easier for me to be around Raven, now I only wanted him more. I'd finally experienced how he tasted, how he moved and gasped and sighed my name, and I wanted that again. I wanted it all the time.

"Thanks, Raven. This is good info, even if you went about it the wrong way. Good work." Blade squeezed Raven's shoulder warmly, and then he straightened up and met my eyes. "I need to go talk to Logan, hash out some details."

Raven nodded seriously, and then Blade left the clubhouse.

And Raven and I were alone in the kitchen.

Raven sighed and closed his laptop with a definitive click. He turned, leaning against the kitchen island, and faced me with his arms crossed over his chest. Not a defensive position, but resigned. There wasn't a whole lot of distance between us, and I remembered that day at Ankhor Works, when he'd let me box him up against his car.

I cleared my throat.

Raven met my eyes, eyebrows raised expectantly.

"I know you know you shouldn't have been keeping secrets like that," I said.

"The club didn't exactly feel like the most welcoming environment at the time," Raven said. "But I know. It was stupid to go all lone wolf. I knew it was stupid when I was doing it, but I just couldn't stop myself."

He ran one hand through his hair and sighed. "It won't happen again."

"Damn right it won't," I said. "You're under my personal protection, now."

"I know that, too," Raven said.

"What?"

"Yeah. You've been lurking around nonstop. And Logan told me Priest asked you to keep an eye on me." He grimaced. "You're stuck watching over the boss's kid again, huh?"

"He didn't need to ask me. I was planning on being on duty regardless."

"Why?" Raven stared down at his shoes. "I know you don't *really* want to be around me. This is just part of your job."

I wanted to be around him every second of every day. And if I were a better man, and if Raven wasn't so bright and ambitious and on his way to something great—if I were a little less terrified of what it would mean—I'd tell him that.

"No," I said. "I want to keep you safe. Not as your sergeant. As your friend."

Raven bit his lower lip, unconvinced.

"I'm sorry about Ankh." I reached out and touched Raven's arm. "You shouldn't have had to face that alone."

"I handled it until the very end there," Raven said.

"I know you're capable," I said. "We all do. No one else in the club could've figured out as much as you did. But asking for help doesn't make you weak."

"I know that."

"Do you?"

Raven finally met my eyes.

I touched his bruised, swollen cheek.

"I miss Ankh, too," I said. "He gave me a second chance at life with this club. I just—I don't think I can provide any real assistance to your investigation beyond kicking any Viper's ass who tries to enter our territory."

Raven smiled weakly. He didn't pull away from my touch.

"But I don't want you to have to carry all that pain alone," I said.

"I didn't want to hurt anyone else," he said.

He said it so matter-of-factly, as if it were that simple. He didn't want any other members to feel the pain of confusion and betrayal that he felt. His selflessness stunned me, even when it led to such idiotic decisions. My heart clenched in my chest. I wanted suddenly and powerfully to embrace him, to wrap him in my arms and pull him close to me, and give him a safe place to release some of the pain he was so clearly keeping dammed up inside.

Our eyes met.

Raven's tongue wet his lower lip.

I stepped closer. Raven's dark blue eyes flickered shut. In the space between us, I heard his breath catch as I leaned in.

"Yo!" Blade called as he stepped back across the threshold. "Logan's heading into town to restock the med kits, and we need to talk about timelines."

I leaped backwards. Raven's cheeks turned cherry-red.

Blade stared at me, eyebrows raised, and gave me a little downward head-tilt that I knew meant he'd be grilling me later. I brushed it off, but I couldn't ignore him forever.

Taking advantage of Blade's distraction, Raven darted up the stairs.

Blade sighed and scrubbed his hand across his forehead. "Everything okay?"

"What do you mean?" I asked.

"You know what I mean."

The rush of attraction I'd felt standing so close to Raven disappeared like a flame suddenly smothered. Blade had known me for as long as I'd been in the club—he could probably read my desire for Raven on my face. I steeled my expression into an impassive stare. If I suffered from some bout of insanity and actually ever pursued a relationship with Raven, Blade's nose would forever be in my business.

"He seems to be handling it well, all things considered," I said. "Seems like he really understands why everyone was so pissed about his solo act there. Shouldn't happen again. And I know he's really struggling with learning about the murder, you know, more than the rest of us are. Which is understandable. But he's hanging in there."

Blade raised an eyebrow. "I meant between you and him."

"It's fine," I said, not suspiciously at all.

"Anything you want to talk about?"

"Yes." I crossed my arms over my chest. "Our plan for dealing with the Vipers."

Blade snorted then clapped me on the shoulder. "Fine. Just know my door's always open. But until then, I do need your professional advice: I think I'm going to ask Logan to contact Rebel."

I started. My worries about Blade catching me and Raven flew from my mind instantly as I began calculating the risks of reaching out to the Vipers. "You think that's a good idea?"

"I don't know," Blade admitted. "Honestly, I don't know where else to start. If Raven can't dig up any more leads, how the hell are we supposed to?"

He was right about that. Raven was the best investigator we had. I doubted any boots-on-the-ground investigation would outweigh whatever information Raven had been able to dig up online.

"And I just…" Blade paused and pressed his lips together in thought. "I have a feeling about Rebel. Ever since he helped us after Crave shot Logan. He doesn't seem like the rest of the Vipers. It might be worth the risk."

"You know you're biased, right? Just because he helped his brother doesn't mean he's disloyal to the Vipers. And if Logan *does* reach out to him, then the Vipers will know we're sniffing around. And they'll have the upper hand again."

Blade grimaced. "Good point."

"Don't ask Logan about it yet," I said. "Let's talk about it at church. You got the next meeting set up?"

We worked out a few more logistical details to inform the members of the upcoming meetings. Then Blade's phone went off with a message from Logan, and Blade was out the door like he had a literal viper striking at his heels.

The clubhouse was suddenly very quiet.

After the meeting that morning, the members had dispersed to attend to their own private rituals of grief: Siren and Maverick to Ankhor Works, Coop to his room, Tex and Heath to the bar. Priest to his empty home. We were usually such a noisy, rowdy bunch that the calmness was unnerving. It reminded me of the days after Ankh's funeral. And in a way, we were reliving those days now.

The kitchen island was where Ankh and Priest had sat side-by-side for so many years. I'd seen them fix coffee in the morning, share slices of cake at members' patching-ins, knock shoulders together as they pored over territory maps. To think we could've had that a little bit longer... It made my stomach churn painfully.

I'd organized my life in such a way that death was always only a few paces away. Always visible in the side mirrors of my bike or at the sharp end of my weapon. Ever since Afghanistan, I'd considered myself to be buddy-buddy with death: not seeking it out, but ready for it. Prepared.

But apparently I was only ready if death occurred on my terms. This murder—so long unknown—shook me.

Maybe that's what had me acting so recklessly. The reminder that all of this could change at any moment. Could be snuffed out. That's the life I chose, wasn't it?

And yet I really had almost kissed Raven, right in the middle of the clubhouse kitchen.

Blade's entrance should've been a rescue, a way of preventing me from making a huge mistake. But it didn't feel that way. It felt like… It felt like an interrupted moment.

I didn't kiss. And if I did, it was always an afterthought in the bedroom—like a baseball player giving a teammate a slap on the ass. A 'good game' sort of gesture after the heat of the moment. But just kissing? Kissing that didn't lead to anything else? It just didn't happen.

But I wanted it to. I wanted it with Raven.

I climbed the clubhouse stairs. I needed to rest, review my notes, and prepare the information I had for church tomorrow.

Instead, I found myself standing outside Raven's door. The same place I'd stood when he'd clocked me hard in the face a few weeks back. I grinned and rubbed my jaw at the memory.

"Raven?" I turned the doorknob and found it unlocked. I opened the door. "You there??"

The room was empty. I closed the door behind me.

Then the door to Raven's attached bathroom opened, releasing a flood of steam. Raven stepped into the bedroom with nothing but a towel hanging loose off his narrow hips. His pale skin was flushed pink with the heat from his shower, a pink glow on his chest and cheeks. He'd messily towel-dried his dark hair and it hung loose into his eyes. When our eyes met, his mouth dropped open the barest amount and his tongue wet his lower lip.

"Jeez, Gunnar," Raven said without anger. "What do you want?"

A dangerous question.

God, this was a bad idea. It was bad for me, and bad for Raven. Yet I couldn't bring myself to walk back out the door. There was something between us, something I couldn't ignore any longer. My gaze traveled slowly down his lean, muscled body, lingering on the subtle definition of his abs, his narrow fingers holding the towel, the curve of his ass, even his endearingly knobby knees.

"Gunnar," Raven said again, softly this time. He shifted his weight from foot to foot. "Say something."

Heat built low in my gut as we stood facing each other. The space between us was both unbearable and insurmountable. Raven's cheeks pinked further, and it wasn't from the heat of the shower. God, I wanted him—physically my fingers itched to wrap around his narrow hips and pull him flush against me.

But it wasn't just that. The endearing way he squirmed under my gaze like he was embarrassed or shy sent a bolt of desire through me—it was so unlike the casual, introverted confidence he usually displayed. He was such a delicious contradiction. Smart, self-sufficient, snarky—but at the same time anxious and unsure.

Or maybe it was just *me* who made him unsure.

"I'm sorry."

I hadn't meant to say it; it just spilled out. I looked away.

"For what?" Raven asked with some confusion.

Honesty, openness... Supposedly these were the things that kept the club strong. That's what we'd all told Raven, at least, as we took turns chewing him out for keeping us in the dark.

But I was just as bad. I was *worse*. Raven was brave enough to come clean, while I crept around in the shadows, hiding my own truth. Even if I'd waited too long—even if we couldn't be together, not really—it was idiotic to pretend like there wasn't anything simmering between us.

"I'm such a fucking coward," I muttered.

Raven reached out and touched my wrist. His fingers brushed gently over my racing pulse. Even the barest contact was a jolt, a spark I couldn't deny.

"I haven't been telling you the truth." I finally met his gaze, and his blue eyes were wide and curious.

"What truth?" Raven's voice was just above a whisper. He bit his lower lip.

"'Course I want you," I said. Saying it out loud released a pressure inside me and I huffed out a breath. "I've wanted you for years."

Raven stood stunned silent in front of me. His hand was still wrapped around my wrist.

"I just—you know I couldn't just—act on it. Not when I'm your sergeant. And I'm an old fucking dog," I said. I didn't mention anything about my past; I couldn't handle any questions right now. "So I had to push you away a little bit. Make sure you had your own life. I didn't want to keep you from growing up independently. I knew you had a crush on me when you were younger, but I would've sooner let Ankh shoot me than take advantage of you."

I pulled my hand away, and then traced the curve of his jawline. "I'm sorry if I hurt you. It wasn't trying to make you think you weren't... good enough, or something stupid like that. If anything, you're *too* good for someone like me. I was just trying to put the brakes on before I..."

"Did something like this?" Raven asked with a sly smile.

No, I thought, *before I admitted I—*

Wanted him? Liked him? Was attracted to him?

It was more than that, and I knew it.

But I couldn't say that word. Not even to myself.

"Yeah," I dropped my hand. "Before I did something like this."

"So you've apologized," Raven said. "What now?"

"I don't know."

"Where do you want it to go?"

"Your bed," I said without thinking.

"Horndog." Raven bit back a smile.

"Well," I said as I finally let my gaze draw down his bare chest, slow and indulgent. "How am I supposed to help it?"

Chapter 15 - Raven

Gunnar stood in front of me, nearly vibrating with nerves. I'd never seen him like this—he always wore a mask of some kind; he always had a role to play, be it sergeant or best friend or bachelor.

I'd fantasized about this moment for so long, never really thinking it would happen. In my imagination Gunnar was always straightforward and intense, the confession dramatic and passionate. It was never so honest as to be anxiety-inducing.

This was *real*.

And what was I supposed to do with it? I *could* collapse into his arms and let him ravish me. But then what?

Why this? Why now?

For years I'd watched him fix his piercing gaze on men and women at club parties, luring them close to him with an easy smile and a low, sultry laugh. It was masterful—the same moves seemed to work on everyone. Gunnar was magnetic that way. And every time I watched him take some gullible nobody's hand and lead them upstairs, it was like a piece of my heart got chipped off.

This whole time he'd known I wanted him, and he did all of that bullshit anyway, in front of me, in some backward attempt to… protect me? Anger churned in my stomach like a hangover. Possibly it was seeing me hurt that caused this change of heart. Maybe he finally realized that I had a life, too—I had plans, and ideas, and pain, too.

Well, I wasn't a kid anymore. And I wasn't going to let Gunnar call all the shots.

"Sucks to be you, but getting into my bed isn't in the cards." Suddenly very aware I was still only wearing my towel, I tightened my grip and pulled it higher on my hips.

"Right," Gunnar said. "Sorry. I—I know that."

"You can't just come in here and say a few nice things and expect me to just fall into bed with you," I said. "I'm not that easy anymore."

Gunnar's eyebrows twitched upwards. "Anymore?"

"You gave me that blowjob a few days ago, and then you just… Started avoiding me again, like it meant nothing. Same as you always have. I can't keep up with you." I pushed my hair out of my eyes with a frustrated sigh. "I never know which Gunnar I'm going to get. The one who wants me, or the one who wants me gone."

Gunnar rocked back on his heels as if he'd been struck. "You… You're right."

I started. Those were two words I was not used to hearing from Gunnar. "Sorry, what?"

"I've been trying to do right by you, and by Ankh, and by the club. And I keep fucking it up. Because I thought the right thing to do was get out of your way. But I can't. I can't keep away from you."

I cleared my throat hard, willing the lump forming there down. "It wasn't the right thing. It's not."

"I know that now. So I'm not going to try to stay away anymore."

I wanted to believe him. Seeing his face so twisted with regret pulled at my heart and part of me desperately wanted to soothe that expression away. I'd never seen him like this, open and vulnerable, like *he* needed something from *me*. He never, ever acted like he needed me.

But another part of me worried that this was just another swing of the pendulum, and he'd be back to ignoring me just as quickly. "I just don't understand what you want from me."

"I don't want anything. I'm just trying to be honest. For once."

"Just this once?"

"From now on."

"Okay." The anger started to melt just a little, and it was replaced by something warm and ominous—hope. I wanted so badly for this to be real. I'd give him a chance to prove himself, but I wasn't going to let him off the hook entirely. "I like this new Gunnar."

"Good," Gunnar said in a low voice. "Because he's not going anywhere."

I huffed a laugh and raised my eyebrows incredulously. That was a hint of the flirtatious Gunnar I'd seen scoop up people in bars. If this more honest version of Gunnar was here to stay, I'd believe it when I saw it.

"Except now," Gunnar amended. He took a step back. "I'm leaving your room. I meant more like, the general honesty. Is a thing I'm working on now. But yes, I'm physically leaving your space."

I couldn't help but laugh, shaking my head as I watched Gunnar fumble with the doorknob. I liked this awkward, endearing guy more than the smooth charmer. And despite my frustrations, I wanted to get to know him better. Wherever that may lead.

"I was just going to relax and watch television," I said. "If you wanted to. Stay. For a while."

Gunnar blinked. "I probably can't keep up with whatever high-brow drama you watch for fun."

"It's just *Bake-Off*," I said. Then slammed my mouth shut as I felt my cheeks redden. Of course I made a stink about being so mature, and then admitted I wind down with baking competition shows.

To my surprise a slow, open smile spread across Gunnar's face. I'd spent a lot of time in my life cataloging Gunnar's expressions: the sultry smirk he gave strangers at the bar, the fierce set of his jaw when handling a rival club, the relaxed attentiveness in his eyes on a casual ride. I'd never seen him smile like this before.

"Sure," he said. "I'll stay."

I nodded towards the loveseat in the corner of my room. It was a ratty old thing, its navy blue fabric overstuffed and well-worn, awkwardly positioned so I could see my computer setup from its cushy middle. In that way my desktop doubled as a television. I was nothing if not efficient.

Gunnar glanced at the couch and then back to me. "Why don't you, uh, put some pants on first."

"What if I prefer to watch *Bake-Off* in my towel?"

"Oh, is that the dress code? Bring me a towel and I'll comply." Gunnar wiggled his eyebrows, and then dropped onto the couch and kicked his feet up onto my desk chair.

"No way," I said. "B-Y-O-T. Remember that for next time."

I fished clean clothes out of my dresser and slipped into the bathroom to change as Gunnar laughed warmly.

I pulled on a soft pair of sweatpants and a thin t-shirt—one of Pops' old shirts that no longer fit in him in his old age. It had an old version of the Hell's Ankhor logo screen-printed on the front, just the anchor with the top of the ankh, no flames at the base as there were now. It had been printed by hand by Dad and Pops themselves in the earliest days of the club.

Gunnar had said he wanted me to have my own life. But didn't he know the club *was* my life? I hadn't been forced into it. I chose it, same as he did, even when I felt a little out of place or wanted to prove that I could handle things on my own.

When I was in college, I'd had plenty of opportunities to cut ties with the club. I turned down a finance tech job in New York and an IT security job in London. I'd had a handful of relationships and a wide circle of friends. I'd fit in fine, but I couldn't connect—not really. There was always a club-shaped hole in my heart. And the people I hung around with couldn't understand what it meant to be a part of a club like Hell's Ankhor. How could I explain to a citizen the brotherhood, the devotion, the intensity, and the pure wild fun of it?

Did Gunnar think I was just in the club because I didn't know any different? Or that I was simply biding my time until something "better" came along, and then I'd gleefully ditch my family?

I'd experienced life without the club, and I'd found it lacking. I'd thought that when I returned to the club, older and more experienced, Gunnar would see me as his equal. I'd hoped he'd stop pretending he didn't want me, and we could finally act on the thing that had started simmering between us before I'd left.

But he hadn't. And I'd spent years trying to get over him. And now, here he was, in my room, telling me he wanted me.

Part of me didn't believe it was real. Perhaps he'd turned on the charm like he did for all the people he'd seduced over the years. And as soon as he wasn't required to be my security detail, he'd change his mind again. If I let him get close—if I got attached, and he pulled away again—didn't know how I'd recover.

But I'd deal with that when it happened. I was a Hell's Ankhor senior member. Ankh's son. Tough as nails. Resilient as leather. And right now I was going to sit on the couch with the man I'd pined after for so long and watch television and enjoy it.

I stepped out of the bathroom and sat on the loveseat next to Gunnar. The couch was small enough that we each had to press into the arms of it to keep a small amount of space between us.

I swatted Gunnar's legs off my chair. "That's not an ottoman."

"Hey," Gunnar said, frowning at my shirt. "What's that? I've never seen gear like that."

I smoothed the shirt, the screen-printed pattern rough on my palms. "Special edition. High-ranking members only."

"Oh, I see. I'm not worthy?"

"Not yet." I turned slightly so he could see it. "It's not legit. It's one of the early versions from when Dad and Pops were still designing."

"So you're club historian now, too?" Gunnar flicked his gaze up to meet mine. "You're full of surprises."

My cheeks burned. I tore my gaze away and fiddled with my phone, pulling up the show and playing it remotely on my desktop.

"This is quite the setup," Gunnar said.

"It works," I said.

"I don't understand how."

"You don't have to."

Gunnar paused. "There's a lot about you I don't understand."

I shifted on the loveseat just enough so our thighs touched. Even through the layers of clothes, the contact thrilled me. I kept my eyes on my phone.

"You don't have to," I said again.

Gunnar hummed thoughtfully. Then the show started, the theme song blaring loud enough to rattle us out of the tense moment.

"I'm on episode three of the new season," I said. "If you were wondering."

"Oh, bread week," Gunnar said. "I'm not caught up. Have they done biscuits yet?"

I gaped at him. "Excuse me?"

"What?" Gunnar's cheeks colored slightly. "It's relaxing!"

"I'm not the only one full of surprises," I said.

The episode started. As the hour-long program continued, Gunnar relaxed minutely next to me, sinking deeper into the loveseat, our legs pressing together.

"That's over-proved," he commented at the screen as one of the contestants set their bread dough on the counter. "Gonna ruin the texture of the brioche. Rookie mistake."

Never in my life had I considered that Gunnar might know something about how long a brioche dough needed to rise. It was enough to make me wonder what else I didn't know about him—what other parts of him were performance, and what other facets of his personality I could unearth. I'd known him for so long—but did I really *know* him?

I'd forgotten to put on socks, and so I pulled my feet into the couch and tucked them under me, and leaned closer to Gunnar. He was solid and warm against me, soothing my nerves.

God, it was intoxicating. He smelled like cheap soap, unscented deodorant, and sweat—his sweat, a rich, musky scent that made me want to press my face into his nape and inhale.

Eventually, I leaned all my weight on him, awkwardly pressed against his shoulder. Gunnar shifted slightly and raised his arm, wrapping it around me so I could lean more comfortably against him.

"That okay?" he asked, super-extra-casual, which meant it wasn't casual at all.

"Yeah," I murmured. If I relaxed fully, I could probably fall asleep.

This version of Gunnar, this relaxed, warm, open guy whose attention was half on a baking competition show and half on me, was a lot better than the uptight, aggressive sergeant I'd gotten used to dealing with. He reminded more of the guy who'd been a friend to vent to in confidence when Dad and Pops were driving me crazy. Of the guy who taught me to throw a punch and disarm a knife. The guy whose steady, strong demeanor I'd been able to rely on during my craziest teen days.

Maybe I shouldn't have turned down his offer to jump into bed so quickly. This was nice—really nice—and the longer I spent pressed against him, the closer I wanted to get. I wanted to feel his bare skin on mine. I wanted to feel his muscular body pinning me down again. I hadn't been this close to Gunnar since our one night together, and I'd still been recovering then. My hands itched to touch him more now.

As the episode wound down, my gaze drifted away from the screen. Gunnar's legs were long and strong in his jeans, kicked out in front of him casually and crossed at the ankle. His t-shirt was soft and loose on his body, his breaths slow and relaxed. The tattoo of the Hell's Ankhor logo was clear but slightly faded on the side of his neck, immense and gorgeous, proof that he'd never abandon the club.

He really was strikingly handsome. Over the years I'd trained myself not to think about it, but now, with his arm around me, I let myself admire the strong, square line of his jaw and aquiline nose. His blond hair, always cropped short, had grown out just enough to reveal a slight curl above his cauliflower ears.

Gunnar fidgeted under my stare and finally met my gaze. "What are you looking at?"

I reached up and ran my forefinger gently over the shell of his ear where it was swollen and deformed. "I never noticed how bad your ears are."

"Oh, thanks," Gunnar said, low and teasing. "It's from being punched."

"Just proves you're good at your job," I said. "That you're not afraid to get your hands dirty."

Our faces were close together, close enough that Gunnar's breath was on my lips as he exhaled, his expression softening. "I get them too dirty." His brow furrowed deeply, suddenly. "I'm not—"

I cut him off with a kiss.

The world seemed to career suddenly to a stop, like slamming the brakes on my bike and skidding out. Controlled and shocking stillness.

Gunnar cradled my jaw with his free hand, his other arm still wrapped around my shoulders, guiding me to deepen the kiss. I pressed as close as I could, wrestling a confusing desire to crawl on him, over him, to get as close as physically possible. I choked off a moan—I couldn't help it. This was even better than it was in my fantasies; *everything* about Gunnar seemed to be better than it was in my fantasies. His mouth was so hot and demanding, kissing me as if he needed it more than breathing.

He hummed into the kiss, and then he pushed me backward, and I moved easily beneath him. It was awkward on the tiny loveseat, a tangle of limbs, my head on the arm of the sofa and our legs half-on and half-off the cushions. But it didn't matter. What mattered was his mouth on mine, his warm callused hand combing through my hair, his hips pushing down on me.

God, I just went to pieces beneath him. I squirmed on the loveseat because I wanted him to stop me from moving— wanted to feel his physical strength. I skated my hands across his back, and then dared to slide my hands under the hem of his shirt. I pressed my palms to the warm skin of his lower back. My fingertips dipped beneath the waistband of his jeans but went no further. He kissed me and kissed me, passion without pause.

"Fucking hell, Raven," Gunnar murmured, his voice wrecked like he'd just chain-smoked a pack of cigarettes. He pulled back enough to meet my gaze, and his expression was unreadable, shifting, and his lips were slightly swollen. He touched my hair again where it was damp from my shower and now from sweat, and his gaze darted over my face greedily like he wanted to memorize it.

I murmured his name, and then arched up to kiss him again. I shifted my body and pushed my hips up to meet his. Our legs tangled and his thigh slid between my legs, and I couldn't help but thrust forward. My cock was so hard in my sweatpants, unmistakable, and I gasped at the bolt of pleasure that shot through me. I was desperate for more—more contact, more Gunnar—and I jerked against him.

Then suddenly he was off me, across the room as fast as a dog who'd just run into an electric fence.

"Sorry." He exhaled hard. "We should slow down."

I blinked slowly at him. My brain needed a little time to catch up. He was trying to use words to communicate when all I wanted was more of his mouth and his hands. "Huh?"

Gunnar stared at me. I was lying on the loveseat, my head on the arm, one foot on the floor and one leg kicked onto the other arm. My erection was clearly visible where I was sprawled out, and Gunnar stared at it for a long moment, his mouth slightly open. Then with visible effort, he looked towards the ceiling and scrubbed his hands over his face.

"I got carried away," he said. "We should slow down. You're right. I don't want to push you."

I had said no earlier. That much was true. And if he hadn't stopped the kiss, I certainly wouldn't have. I didn't know how far we would've gone, and I didn't know if I would've regretted it. I'd wanted to wait, to make sure Gunnar wasn't just in this for the night. I wanted to be sure he was in it for the long haul.

"Okay," I said.

"Okay," Gunnar repeated, apparently mollified. "I'm going to, uh, go. To my room. And shower. Before we have to... I don't know. I think there's a meeting."

"Sure," I said. My mind still felt like it was working at half-speed. Like this was all a dream I was bound to wake up from.

Gunnar stepped forward and leaned over me, kissing me briefly, almost chastely, and then slipped out the door.

Lying on the loveseat, I lingered in a daze of confusion and arousal. On my computer screen, the *Bake-Off* credits rolled merrily as the streaming service threatened to start a new episode. I let it begin, the familiar noise soothing me as I stared at the ceiling. I had never thought of Gunnar as the type to put the brakes on. I thought he'd take what he wanted, regardless of the consequences. That was how he gave me that blowjob when I was recovering. That was how he operated with all his previous hookups, as far as I could tell.

Maybe he didn't think of this as a hookup. Maybe it was more than that.

That little spark of hope jumped in my chest again, and this time I didn't try to tamp it down.

That didn't change the fact that I was half-delirious with arousal, though. Next time. There'd be a next time. He wouldn't have left the way he did if he didn't think there'd be a next time.

Right?

I sighed and touched my lower lip, remembering the pressure of his mouth on mine and the sharp edge of teeth in his hungry kiss. Next time I'd take what my body wanted and let my heart catch up after.

Chapter 16 - Gunnar

I stumbled into my bedroom, thankfully undisturbed by any other club members. My blood felt like it had been lit aflame in my veins, and my cock was painfully hard in my tight jeans. I fell onto my bed, flat on my back, and palmed my hard-on through the denim.

God. It wasn't nearly as good as Raven's slim leg between mine. Or as good as the feeling of his erection pressing against my leg as he rutted against me unselfconsciously. He was so gorgeous beneath me, his pale skin flushed pink as he moved beneath me, constantly wiggling like he had stores and stores of pent-up energy.

And he'd kissed me.

I'd let him. I hadn't pulled away.

I'd wanted it.

Did he know how few people I'd kissed? Did he know how new this was for me? I hadn't made out like that since I was a teenager. And somehow, that clothed, juvenile make-out session had gotten me harder, more worked up, than any hookup I'd had in years.

Kissing Raven had awoken something in me. When I looked back on my hookups now, they all felt—perfunctory. I had been going through the motions for a hit of pleasure. And sure, they'd been enjoyable, fun even, but nothing like this. Nothing like this electric attraction I felt for Raven.

I ripped my jeans open just enough to get my cock out. With a sigh of relief, I fisted myself once, twice, enough to take the desperate edge off.

I'd stopped our tryst as soon as his hard cock had pressed against my leg, because I knew I only had so much willpower. Had it gone any further, I didn't trust myself to stop. The man I'd craved for years had been lying beneath me, willing and ready to give me probably whatever I wanted—honestly, I was proud of myself for stopping it when I did.

And that was the right decision for both of us. This had to be on Raven's terms, whatever it was. I wouldn't push him into anything he wasn't ready for. And I wouldn't let him push his own boundaries in an attempt to prove himself to me. We'd go slow. I was fine with that. Slow was good. I just had to keep repeating that to myself whenever I got frustrated.

In the privacy of my own room, though, I let myself imagine what might have happened if we hadn't stopped.

I jerked myself slowly, smearing precum down my shaft. I would've gathered his slim body in my arms and deposited him on the bed. He'd have laughed warmly and pulled me on top of him. I ached to hear his quiet, barely there laugh now—wanted it like a strong drink after a hard day. He'd been so focused and gloomy for so long that seeing him smile beneath me had sparked a flame deep inside me.

If we'd continued, I'd want to keep hearing it, so I'd drop kisses on his neck and collarbone, and I'd slide my hands under his shirt. (Shouldn't have told him to put on clothes before we sat down to watch *Bake-Off* together. Learned my lesson.) He'd be deliciously responsive beneath me, moaning and shifting under my hands.

I stroked my cock faster and tightened my grip. I imagined Raven spread out on the bed beneath me, naked now, all that pale skin on display, his cock hard against his belly. His cock had tasted so good in my mouth when I'd given him that blowjob, and he'd gone so crazy for it—I wanted to see how many other ways I could make him come.

In this fantasy, it was simple. It'd just be his body pressed against mine. Tangled together in the sheets, I'd kiss him deeply and thrust my bare cock against his, and the heat and pressure of it would make him moan and drag his nails down my back.

My orgasm built inside me. I pushed my heels into the mattress and thrusted my hips to meet my hand. I imagined Raven coming against me—he was so sensitive, the kissing and the intoxicating contact would be enough to drive him over the edge. He'd gasp into my mouth, a sweet sound, and tense in my arms as he came.

I exhaled hard and came harder. My orgasm bowled me over and left me exhausted, like I'd just gone a few rounds with a guy twice my size. I melted into the mattress, slowing my breaths to slow my pounding heart.

I felt like I was a decade younger than I was. Like I was discovering sex for the first time. In a way it was unnerving.

We hadn't even taken our clothes off together, and already it was better than any of the one-night stands I'd had with club hang-arounds. I hadn't known it could be this good.

If I could have something even better than this—how would I stand to let it go?

The thought swept away my post-orgasmic dreamy haze. I sat up, cleaned up, and changed out of my sweaty clothes.

No point in worrying about that now. Regardless of my personal feelings about Raven, I was still his personal protective duty until we got all this shit with the Vipers sorted out. Whatever was going on between us couldn't overshadow that.

***

Over the next three days, Raven and I didn't talk about what had happened between us—not really.

But since I was still on protective duty, we spent all our time together. It was surprisingly easy to fall into a rhythm with him. I guessed our first official make-out session had taken the edge off our relationship, in a way that the blowjob hadn't. Raven seemed calmer, more at peace—had my behavior been bothering him that much? Had the space I'd put between us really been driving him that crazy?

I didn't know, and I wasn't about to ask, but it was nice to see him smile a little more often.

But we hadn't kissed since that afternoon, either.

I wasn't going to be the one to initiate. I wasn't going to push Raven. This was operating on his terms. His safety was my first priority, and my own daily hard-ons weren't going to get in the way of that. Even though we hadn't kissed since, Raven was more receptive to a kind of casual closeness that went beyond just my sergeant-at-arms duty. When we walked into town for breakfast, he let his shoulder knock against mine. During late nights at Ballast, we sat side-by-side. Yesterday, when I'd dropped my keys, Raven had picked them up off the clubhouse floor and slipped them into my back pocket. The contact had me breathing hard like a teenager. Kid was fucking dangerous.

But I couldn't get too comfortable. That much was extremely clear as I sat down at the kitchen island for a mid-morning church meeting, our eighth in just three days. And for what, I didn't know. It's not like we'd made any more progress on Ankh's murder or who had contacted Raven with the information. The only progress we'd made on this issue was Raven's progress—the investigation he'd done behind our backs. Now that the whole club was involved, we'd fully stalled out. I was a few minutes early, and the rest of the club members were yet to arrive.

"Incoming." Raven's hand grazed across my shoulder as he leaned over to set down a mug of coffee.

The rich smell of it drove the frustration from my mind—a familiar, spicy scent. I turned towards Raven, and he bit his lip as he flushed slightly.

"Where'd you get this?" This wasn't the usual Elkhead Coffee house blend we kept around. This was my favorite coffee, a specialty bean from a roaster up in Washington State.

Raven shrugged. "From that place you like."

"Where'd you get it, really?" I asked. I knew it was out of stock, because I'd run out and had been diligently checking to reorder it.

Raven shrugged again. "I may have gone into their wholesaler from the back end and had a batch routed here."

I couldn't suppress the smile spreading across my face. I didn't even know he knew what my favorite coffee was. I was constantly underestimating how observant he was. "You hacked the coffee company?"

"It's their fault. They have really bad security." He touched my shoulder again, his fingertips brushing my bare skin at the collar of my t-shirt. "I just wanted to say thanks, I guess."

"For what?" I hadn't done anything special. I was just doing my duty as sergeant. If anything, I'd figured he'd get annoyed with me always hovering near him soon enough.

"It's been hard," Raven said. "Dealing with all this stuff with

Dad. And the past three days, I mean—it's been nice. With you. I was worried having protective detail would be a real pain in the ass. But you've made it really easy."

I took his hand off my shoulder and gripped it tightly in my own. I suddenly had the crazy urge to kiss his knuckles—the same knuckles that'd given me a shiner just a few weeks ago. But this wasn't the privacy of his room, and a kiss like that wasn't appropriate, not in church, where everyone could see and comment and judge. He needed support, real support, and not the kind of interrogation that would follow if anyone saw us together like that, or any pressure from me to turn this into more than it was.

"'Course it's easy," I said. "You're my friend."

Raven's face softened. His gaze flicked to my mouth. He squeezed my hand in return.

My stomach flipped. How did he do that? Make me feel like a teenager with just the smallest gestures?

Then the front door banged open and Raven stepped away smoothly, back into the kitchen to fix his own coffee.

Blade stomped in, his jaw set and his eyes blazing. I took a sip of my coffee. Delicious. And perfectly brewed. Blade glowered at me.

"You look happy," he said accusingly.

"It's the coffee," I said.

Blade dropped into the chair next to me. The determined set to his jaw made it clear he was getting antsy. Blade and I were similar in a lot of ways, and I could tell from the frustration radiating off him that we still hadn't made any real progress.

Nothing frustrated Blade—and me—more than talking in circles without any action.

Logan followed soon after Blade, apparently in a much less volatile mood.

"You forgot this," he said to Blade, depositing a Thermos in front of him. Logan kissed Blade's temple, more an afterthought than anything, and then drifted into the kitchen to raid the fridge. Blade visibly relaxed.

Over the next few minutes, the rest of the senior members filtered into the clubhouse, all of them worn out. The meetings were getting exhausting and repetitive without any new information to disseminate.

Coop walked in, a little more upbeat than everyone else as per usual, and shot a questioning look at Raven. Raven tilted his chin down in a little nod.

"He made me pick it up from our PO box." Coop nodded at the mug in front of me. "Can you believe that? I didn't even know we had a PO box."

"How did you not know that?" I asked.

"Enforcers don't care about mail," Coop said matter-of-factly. "If anything, Raven should be grateful I'm willing to do any favors for him after he ditched me at the pig pen."

"You're still going on about that?" Raven shouldered Coop out of the way to sit in the seat next to me.

Coop sat next to Raven on his other side. "Yes, I am, and I will continue to go on about it until I am adequately repaid."

Raven rolled his eyes.

"All right," Blade said. "Enough chit-chat."

The room settled down and the senior members of the club took their seats around the kitchen island. Priest arrived last and sat at my other side. Logan sat next to Blade and slid an airplane bottle of bourbon towards him. Blade added it to his coffee Thermos.

The meeting started as all the other meetings had—reviewing the information we'd reviewed dozens of times, looking for some missed detail or new insight.

With a sigh, Blade read the printed copies of the mysterious emails yet again. "And you don't think your brother is the one who sent this?"

Logan's face darkened. He spoke with a bitter tone that suggested he and Blade had discussed this before, probably more than once. "No. He's fully entrenched in the Vipers. Under my father's—Crave's—thumb. He didn't do a damn thing when they had me."

Blade grimaced. "He helped after you got shot."

"That's a really low bar for a Good Samaritan," Logan said. "Just because he didn't stand there and watch me bleed out doesn't mean he's not a Viper through and through."

Blade's grimace deepened.

"I haven't heard from him since then, anyway," Logan said, crossing his arms over his chest. "After everything, he just disappeared again. Like he always does. Luke—Rebel, whatever—would never care enough to betray the Vipers like that. It's someone else."

"'Like he always does'?" I asked. "Did he disappear a lot?"

Logan fidgeted. Clearly he didn't want to have this conversation. "He's sort of a mercenary. Dad lends him out to other clubs as muscle or investigation. He'd be gone for months at a time. Total radio silence."

Next to me, Raven leaned forward, propping his elbows on the kitchen island. "Hang on. So he'd go into other clubs as an open Viper member and provide backup?"

"Yeah," Logan said. "Dad always said it was part of Luke's job to go out and improve the Viper reputation. I don't know if that meant actually helping clubs or just tossing around threats. Since then, Luke was the one Dad sent if a club needed assistance. Easy way for the Vipers to make some extra money, or curry favors with other clubs."

I could almost see the gears turning in Raven's head. "That's weird," he said. "I've never heard of a club loaning members out. Has anyone else?"

Around the table, everyone shook their heads.

"And no one else in the Vipers did this? Just your brother?" Raven asked.

"Just him," Logan said. "I never thought about it, really. It just pissed me off that he was gone so much."

He didn't look pissed. He looked hurt.

"If he's out running mercenary jobs like that all the time, is there a chance he's not as entrenched in the Vipers as we think?" Raven asked carefully.

Logan pressed his lips together and said nothing.

"It's a really odd practice," Raven said. "And I don't think we should discount the fact that he did step in to help you at the risk of Viper retribution. I haven't been able to get any other leads on this. I think we should contact him."

"Absolutely not," Logan said.

Blade steepled his fingers. "And if he's not the source, the Vipers will know we're searching for their mole."

"Well, obviously we don't open with that. I'm not asking Logan to lay all his cards on the table immediately." Raven rapped his knuckles on the table, suddenly full of vibrating energy, like he always got when he was on the brink of a breakthrough. "But we have to start somewhere. Even if I don't get any intel directly from Rebel, opening a line of communication could offer other opportunities. Like tracking."

Blade looked deeply unconvinced. "Gunnar, what do you think?"

All eyes turned expectantly to me. "How would we go about contacting him? What kind of encryption?"

Raven raised his eyebrows. "Since when do you think about encryption?"

"Since people started sneaking around online instead of trying to break into clubhouses the good old-fashioned way," I grumbled.

Raven didn't laugh, but his eyes sparkled with fond humor before he turned seriously back to Logan and Blade. "If you have a way to contact your brother, a phone number or email, I can set you up with an encrypted VPN so they can't find its source. So if the message gets in the wrong hands, there won't be anything to tie it back to us."

"Other than Viper inferences," Blade said.

"But we're not sending a message to all the Vipers," I said. "Just Logan's brother."

"What do you think, Logan?" Raven asked.

Logan grabbed Blade's spiked coffee and took a long sip. "If that's our only option, I'm willing to try."

"I don't love it," Blade said. "Your encryption better be good."

Raven snorted. "Please. It's always good."

Tense but satisfied, Blade nodded and adjourned the meeting. Raven drifted up the stairs toward his room, moving distractedly as his mind was clearly five steps ahead, already working on the VPN for Logan.

I trailed behind him as was my duty. Raven didn't even seem to notice. He nearly slammed the door in my face as I followed him into his bedroom.

"Oh," he said, blinking back into the present moment. "Sorry. I'm—"

"Already coding," I said. "Get at it."

With a small, grateful smile, Raven dropped into his desk chair and spun it on its axis, one excited full rotation before he unlocked his desktop and opened one of his many complicated software programs. It was all way out of my pay grade. I stretched out on the loveseat near his workstation, leaning against one arm, my legs kicked out over the other, and folded my arms behind my head.

"Shouldn't take too long," Raven said, his attention fully on the screen. "I already have the VPN built, I just want to add in some extra security—"

I waved off his explanation. "Don't gotta explain it to me," I said. "I won't get it anyway."

"Yes, you would," Raven said. "Don't sell yourself short."

His attention returned to his desktop. Over the time we'd spent together, I'd noticed the slight changes that overtook him when he was deep in a project. As his fingers danced across the keys, his eyes darted rapidly over his code, checking and rechecking what he'd written.

He usually worked with his legs curled beneath him in the large desk chair, leaning slightly forward over the desk so his body wasn't against the backrest at all. A large stool would've served him just as well. But that was just like Raven—finding a different way of doing something, a way that might not make sense to me, but seemed to suit him just fine.

I couldn't even begin to imagine all the work Raven had put in to develop these skills. I hadn't even finished high school. As soon as I'd turned eighteen I'd left to join the armed forces. I didn't regret that choice. College was never in the cards for me, and by the time I turned sixteen, I'd figured out that if I stayed in my hometown I'd end up in some dead-end job or a dead drunk in a ditch. The Marines were my way out—and for a while, it had been okay.

Life might've worked out differently if I'd stuck with the Marines. Maybe I could've been an officer by now, climbing up the ladder and bossing around my own crew of eighteen-year-old burnouts.

But I wasn't cut out for the Marines. I had asked too many questions, and I'd had too much doubt. I didn't doubt my brothers-in-arms, but I doubted our leadership every step of the way and the intel we were receiving. These were lives on the line, theirs and ours. And that day in Afghanistan haunted me. I remembered the look on the man's face—

The small shadow in the corner—

I dispelled the memory. I forced it away and shoved it back into its box, where I'd done my best to keep it all these years.

And anyway, if I were still in the Marines, I wouldn't be here in Elkin Lake, lying on this loveseat and watching Raven chew on his lower lip as he edited his code.

Every moment I spent with Raven built up my desire more and more, like I was slowly stoking a spark into a wildfire. Part of me had known from the start that if we began a relationship of any kind, I wouldn't be able to keep it casual. That's part of why I fought it for so long. It was an almost laughable idea, since I was pretty much exclusively casual and exclusively with strangers for the majority of my life. But now I just—I wanted him. All of him. I wanted him in my bed every night and to wake up to him every morning. I wanted to protect him, take care of him, learn from him.

I wanted to be his Old Man.

I pushed that thought down. Far, far down.

It was bad enough that we'd gotten this close. I didn't need to start entertaining ridiculous fantasies like that. Raven was his own man, and as soon as he figured out I was more worn-out old road dog than the badass sergeant-at-arms he'd idealized me as, he'd undoubtedly get some sense and move on.

And that wasn't even taking into consideration what would happen if he found out—no, I couldn't even think about it.

But until then, I'd keep by his side as his protective detail. I'd give him what he wanted—I'd try to be the man I should've been since the beginning. And if Raven decided to move on... I'd figure out how to handle myself. I wouldn't make a scene. Besides, for now it was one day at a time, at least until we got to the bottom of Ankh's murder.

Raven pushed his office chair back from his desk with a heavy sigh and cracked his knuckles, a noisy series of pops from each hand.

"That sounds like it hurts," I said.

He interlaced his fingers and stretched his arms overhead. "Feels great. It's compiling now. Just gotta wait to see how many dumb errors I made."

"Closest without going over wins," I said. "I say… Nine."

"Fifteen," Raven said. "Bad bet. I have a serious advantage on you."

"You have all kinds of advantages," I said.

Raven rolled his eyes.

I sat up on the loveseat, clearing a space for Raven. "Take a break, then."

He did, sliding onto the cushion and pressing his shoulder against mine. "You think this'll work? Having Logan contact Rebel?"

"Honestly?" I tipped my head back against the back of the loveseat. "I don't see anyone else acting as a mole. Except potentially Bane."

"Bane? The Viper VP? Why would he try to feed us info?"

"To get Crave out of the picture, I suspect. Bane seems the type to try to gun for the presidency if he sees a route to it."

Raven scowled. "They really are sickening. So what happens if we contact Rebel and he isn't the mole?"

"Well, with your encryption, hopefully nothing."

"But what's the worst case?"

"Rebel will try to set up another trap," I said. "To get Logan alone. Try to use him as a bargaining chip again. That's the worst case."

"And Blade would never let that happen." Raven nodded to himself.

"Exactly," I said. "He's not a guy you can fool twice."

Raven relaxed slightly. "I hate this. I hate not knowing."

"Me too," I said. "We should start a support group. Control freaks anonymous."

With a low chuckle, Raven turned his face into my shoulder and nudged me in a shy, animal show of affection.

I wrapped my arm around him and tugged him close. "How are you holding up?"

"Better than I was," Raven said. "It still hurts—knowing Dad was killed. But it's easier now that everyone knows. And that we have some semblance of a plan. And that I—hm. Never mind."

"That you what?" I asked.

Raven paused. He exhaled hard, his warm breath rushing across my neck. "That I have you now."

My heart clenched hard in my chest, as if Raven had stuck his hands into my ribcage and squeezed it himself. I'd set the intention that I'd be following his lead, letting him set the pace and decide how far we'd take things and when—but now the painful twist in my chest overwhelmed all my logical plans. I touched his chin, guiding his face to mine, and kissed him.

It was the only way I knew how to say: *You do. You do have me.*

Raven deepened the kiss for a few delicious moments. Then he pulled away just long enough to shift on the loveseat, crawling on top of me so he was straddling my lap. I skated my hands up his back, curling my arms around him to keep him close. Raven framed my face in his palms, his gaze meeting mine like he was looking for something. I felt stripped bare under his searching expression. I moistened my lips with my tongue, and his eyes flicked down to track the movement.

Somehow having Raven in my arms, looking at me like this, felt more intimate than the blowjobs or the fevered kissing. I couldn't hold his gaze for long. I broke eye contact to kiss the soft skin of his neck. Raven sighed and scraped his nails over my scalp. I slid one hand into the dark hair at his nape and gripped there, not pulling, just keeping his head tilted back as I kissed up his neck and the line of his jaw.

"Feels like a dream sometimes," Raven murmured, more to himself than to me.

"Not a dream," I assured him.

He shivered.

Behind us, his desktop computer chimed.

"It's done compiling," Raven said.

"I don't even know what that means." I kissed the jut of his collarbone through the fabric of his t-shirt.

Raven tightened his knees around my hips. "Means I gotta go check it. Fix any errors." He didn't move.

I released my grip on his hair and slid my hands down his back, and then gripped his ass and squeezed playfully. "Go check it, then. I'm not going anywhere."

Raven kissed me quickly, but the kiss was mostly smile. Then he leaped out of my lap and back into his desk chair, his focused, quasi-confused programming expression dropping into place almost immediately. I stretched back out on the loveseat.

"There's a weird runtime error here in the sequence where it initially connects to the VPN," Raven murmured, leaning closer to the screen. Then he glanced over at me. "Mind if I use you as a sounding board?"

"Not at all. I can't help, though."

"Talking it out helps," he said.

Raven verbally walked through his code, half to me and half to himself, noting errors and logically connecting them as he went. I barely understood any of what he was saying, and eventually I tuned out the content of his words, preferring to let the sound of his low, murmuring voice wash over me.

When—if?—Raven decided to move on, it wouldn't be the sex I remembered most vividly. It'd be moments like this: Raven perched on his desk chair like a genius gargoyle, glancing between me and his code as if we were equally deserving of his attention.

Chapter 17 - Raven

Logan looked exhausted, but not bad—like he'd finished running a race and placed higher than he thought he would. He leaned heavily on the pool cue as if it were a staff. At every club party, we always seemed to gravitate towards each other. Logan was nearly as introverted as me, and we both found the club parties a little overwhelming. This gathering wasn't quite a party, though. It was more of an impromptu group wind-down. Everyone had been on edge since I revealed the contents of the emails I'd gotten, and now that we had started to move forward, even in the smallest way, we all felt like we deserved a slight break.

Logan and I were tied in our pool game, but that was only because I was working more on trick shots and difficult geometric lineups instead of winning. I'd missed a lot, but in my defense, my attention was mostly elsewhere. As was Logan's. The game was just something to do with our hands.

"How'd it go?" I asked.

"Program installed just as well as you said it would," Logan said. "Really seamless. I'll probably keep it on my phone just because it makes me feel better."

"Come on." I lined up a calculated ricochet shot, and then screwed it up completely. "You know that's not what I meant."

Logan sighed and paced a circle around the pool table, but he wasn't really looking at it.

"He didn't answer," he said finally. "I thought I wasn't expecting him to. I mean, why would he, with the number blocked and everything? But I guess part of me was still holding out hope that he'd pick up."

"But you left a message?"

"Yeah. No voicemail greeting on his phone, either. Just the robotic voice. It's weird. I really did want to hear his voice." He lined up a shot, changed his mind, paced the perimeter of the table again. "I still don't trust him, though. He's still a Viper—that hasn't changed. So I didn't leave him any details in the message, I just told him it was important, and he needs to get back to me in private as soon as he can. I doubt I'll hear back."

I shrugged. "Only one way to find out. Wait."

"I hate waiting."

"Yeah, me too. So take your damn shot."

Logan rolled his eyes then lowered his pool cue to neatly lined up corner pocket shot and sank it.

Clearly Logan was being pulled in opposite directions by his conflicting feelings: the love he had for his brother that he couldn't seem to stomp out, no matter how hard he tried, and the anger and hatred he felt for the Viper's Nest.

But I had a strange feeling that we were on the right track. Rebel would get back to us. I didn't say anything to Logan, as I didn't want to complicate his feelings any more than they already were, but if Rebel was anything like Logan, he'd know when he needed to do the right thing. There was no reason for me to feel so sure, but I couldn't shake it.

"So who's been the crazier one, with all the waiting around?" I asked. "You or Blade?"

Logan lightened at the mere mention of Blade's name. Since Logan had been patched in, the easiest way to immediately improve his mood was to talk about his Old Man.

"Definitely Blade," Logan said. "You think I'm bad without something to do? At least I'm used to it. When I was under the Vipers' control, I spent so much time standing around waiting for them to figure out what awful thing they were going to do next. Or just waiting for some gutted member to stumble through the clubhouse door."

"God, I'm glad you're rid of them."

"Tell me about it," Logan muttered. "You know Blade, he always wants to be doing something. He's been like a dog chasing his own tail the past few days. I feel like I have to physically stop him from charging into Viper territory himself."

"That's the Hell's Ankhor way, it seems."

"Yeah, apparently. Since that was your initial reaction, too." Logan picked a shot and missed, and then motioned for me to start my turn. He leaned against the table, clearly ignoring the game now. "How are you doing with everything?"

I thought about it. How was I doing, really? Dad's death still chewed at me, as if my grief were a physical animal that lived burrowed inside me: a mole working on destroying my deepest roots.

But this time, I wasn't alone.

"As good as I can be," I said.

Logan looked at me pensively, and then nodded, as if he'd decided to accept my answer. "If there's anything I can do for you, just say the word."

"I know," I said. "That's the only reason I'm hanging on, really. I know everyone in the club has my back."

The front door banged open noisily as Coop shouldered in, arms laden with grocery bags. He glanced around the room, taking in

Logan and I at the pool table; Blade, Maverick, and Gunnar at the kitchen island; and Priest, Heath, and Siren on the couch.

"Are we having a little party?" he asked, visibly betrayed. "While I'm tasked with running errands? So not fair."

One of the bags began to slip from his grip.

"Ayúdame!" Coop yelped. His Spanish only came out when he was particularly moody.

Siren ambled over and took two of the bags out of his arms. "It's not a party. We'll put these away and fix you a drink, big guy."

Tex followed Coop in, carrying even more bags and looking visibly irritated with Coop. Logan darted over to Tex to help him with his load. The groceries were quickly put away.

Logan got waylaid in the kitchen by Blade, and Coop sidled up to the pool table in his absence, with one beer in each hand, now looking much happier.

"Oh, thanks, but I have one," I said, motioning at my beer perched on the edge of the pool table.

"What? These are for me." Coop took a sip from each beer. "I'm still mad at you anyway for ditching me."

"You're so whiny," I said. "Do you want me to reset the table?"

"Sure," he said. "And now, on top of ditching me, you've gone and stolen my sergeant-at-arms, so I have to manage the enforcers all on my own."

"You're managing the enforcers?"

"Well, no, Siren is managing, but I still have to do more work."

I couldn't help but laugh. "Come on, Coop, let's shoot a little pool."

I hadn't seen much of Coop since I had ditched him at the police station, as I'd been holed up with Gunnar and hadn't been concerned about much else. Spending time with Coop always lifted my spirits, though. He had an infectious positivity like he couldn't help but see new and wild ways to have fun in less-than-ideal situations. Even if I sometimes gave him a hard time for his shenanigans, his lightness was a necessary counterweight to the often harsh reality of club life.

Plus, he was loyal as a hound and could kick serious ass when the situation called for it.

"So what's up with that?" Coop wiggled his eyebrows. "The protective detail. What's going on there?"

"It's protective detail," I said. "So I don't get offed by Vipers in my sleep."

"Pretty intense for the sergeant-at-arms to be tasked with protective detail instead of just a regular enforcer, don't you think?"

"Why, were you gunning for the position?"

"Yes," Coop said. "I wanted to spoon you every night. As the little spoon."

"There's no spooning involved."

"Ah! But he's in your bed?"

I narrowed my eyes. Then, as punishment, I sank my first three shots. "Coop. We're friends now. It's nice. I thought everyone would be happier now—it'll make group settings easier, that's for sure."

In the kitchen, Gunnar was rooting through the fridge. I couldn't help but stare at his ass.

Coop followed my sightline, and then rolled his eyes when he saw where it landed. "Right. Friends."

It wasn't that I didn't want to admit that Gunnar and I had something going on between us. I just wasn't sure what to call it. The only word we'd used to describe our relationship thus far was "friends," and to be sure, that was a big leap from the animosity we'd been working with before. "Friends with benefits" didn't sound exactly right, either—this didn't feel casual. It felt important. And I wasn't ready to talk about it yet, because I had no idea what I'd say, and I didn't want to risk knocking down this delicate house of cards Gunnar and I were building.

As Coop scoured the table for a viable shot, cursing my pool skills under his breath, I watched Gunnar crack open the bottle of ginger ale he'd pulled from the fridge and take a drink.

He leaned against the kitchen counter, casually adding a pour of the ginger ale to a highball glass of whiskey. He caught my eye as he lifted the glass to his lips and took a slow sip.

A bolt of heat shot through me.

Gunnar set the drink down and turned his attention back to Blade and Maverick, laughing at whatever conversation they were having. He casually tucked his thumbs into the waistband of his jeans, pulling them down just enough to reveal a thin strip of tan skin between his jeans and the hem of his shirt. His gaze darted towards me. My arousal was matched by a spark of fond annoyance—he was winding me up on purpose.

I stuck my tongue out quick enough so as to not get Coop's attention, but I knew Gunnar saw it.

"Your turn," Coop said with a cheeky smile. Maybe I had overestimated his inattention.

I turned my back to Gunnar and leaned over the table to line up a shot.

"Okay," Coop said. "Now you're being ridiculous. This is like watching two brainless birds do a mating dance."

"I'm just playing pool," I said mildly, and sank two more shots before I missed. I only had the eight ball left, versus Coop's six stripes on the table.

"'Just,'" Coop said. "And I'm 'just' a guy with a bike."

"Exactly," I said.

Coop missed his shot.

"Well, whatever's going on," he said, clearly resigned to his upcoming loss, "I'm happy for you."

I paused. "What?"

Coop motioned at me vaguely. "This. All of this. You look better. Happier. That makes me happy."

"I was happy before," I said.

"Not like this."

I threw him a stern look.

Coop raised his hands in surrender. "I'm not asking for details. Or confirmation. Or any of that. Just saying it's nice to see you a little more lighthearted. That's all."

I sank the eight ball. Coop gasped in faux shock. "I can't believe it, I've lost."

In the kitchen, Gunnar caught my eye as he finished the last of his drink. He flicked his eyes upwards towards the stairs, and then gave me a little shrug, as if to say, *You wanna?*

This secret conversation thrilled me. It made whatever we had between us feel a little more real—it still existed even among the other club members. Even if I didn't know how to vocalize it to the others, the attraction was there in the heated looks he pinned me with, and the subtle motions of his eyes and hands from across the room. He wanted me. He wanted me badly enough to leave the party behind.

Grinning, Coop clapped me on the shoulder then hopped over the back of the couch, scaring the shit out of Siren as he landed on the cushion beside her.

Gunnar said something to Blade and Maverick, and then wandered up the stairs. All eyes fell on me for a moment before the conversations restarted. I lasted barely a minute before I followed.

Chapter 18 - Gunnar

I left the door to my bedroom cracked open. I hadn't spent any time with Raven at the party itself; I figured he needed some time to catch up with Logan, especially with the weight of Logan's task of contacting his estranged brother hanging over him. I'd tried to give Raven space, make sure I wasn't smothering him with attention, but I couldn't keep my eyes off him.

Ever since our second kiss in his room, every motion of his body drew my attention closer like a magnet. In the ease of his grip on the pool cue, I saw his fingers running through my hair. In the curve of his smile, I felt his kiss. And when he leaned over the pool table—on purpose, little bastard—and wiggled his ass at me, I remembered how that ass had felt in my hands when he was in my lap. I almost had to adjust my jeans in the middle of the kitchen from thinking about it.

Footsteps padded gently up the stairs. Silence. For a moment I thought Raven might change his mind and go toward his own room. I waited to hear his door click closed.

Instead, my door opened.

Raven slipped inside and closed the door behind him. He leaned his back against the door, hands at his sides, and drew his lower lip in between his teeth. His gaze lingered at his feet, almost shy. The skin of his neck was a stark pale contrast to his dark sweatshirt—I was already cataloguing places I wanted to leave marks.

Then he flicked his flashing gaze to mine.

Like I'd been physically dragged forward, I closed the distance between us and pressed him against the door. I grabbed his hips roughly, slotting one foot between us so our bodies were nearly flush. I tipped my head down and pressed my forehead to his. Raven sighed like my touch was a physical relief. He wound his arms around my neck and his eyes flickered close, his long lashes dark against his pale cheek.

"Hey," I said.

Raven's bitten lips curled into a smile. "Hi."

I kissed him.

It was electric.

Raven shuddered beneath me but didn't passively give into the kiss—he kissed back hard, like he was just as hungry for it as I was.

Having him close to me changed me, turned me into a more desperate, animal version of myself. Something I'd been keeping down, locked away, far away from the daylight for many years. A weakness. A weakness in that I'd do anything he asked of me.

This was different than the family loyalty I carried for Hell's Ankhor, and not the blind obedience I'd had in the Marines. It was a terrifying, bone-deep knowledge that I'd do almost anything to ensure he was safe and happy. I'd treated him so badly in the past, and he'd had such a rough go at life—and now, I'd do anything he asked if it'd help him recover from the ordeal I'd put him through.

And that kind of power—even if he didn't realize he had it—was enough to scare me shitless. I'd be left unmoored, completely adrift, if he ever decided to let me go.

Maybe it wasn't just him I'd been protecting all these years when I was keeping my distance.

Raven slid his slim hands under the hem of my shirt and caressed my abs. His touch sent a thrilling rush of pleasure through me. He took control of the kiss without even trying, his quick-moving tongue guiding the pace, before he paused just to catch my lower lip in his sharp teeth, a bright edge of delicious pain in the overwhelming warmth of his closeness.

I ran my hands over his body. I needed him out of these clothes *now*. Watching him from across the room at the party had driven me to the brink already, and if we didn't move things along, I'd end up coming in my pants like a teenager just from rutting clothed against him.

I broke the kiss just to kiss his neck instead. Pulling the collar of his shirt side, I revealed the sharp line of his collarbone and set my mouth on it. I sucked hard, even bit a little, and the skin was red and angry when I pulled back.

I wanted him to look in the mirror tomorrow and see my work.

Raven inhaled a sharp little gasp when he realized I was doing it intentionally. He whispered my name.

I growled in response and slid the palm of my hand roughly over his crotch. His cock was already fully hard, straining against the zipper of his tight jeans. I fumbled with the button.

"Gunnar," he said again.

"Hm?"

With a huffed exhale, almost a laugh, Raven pushed my hand away from his jeans. "Gunnar. Wait."

"For what?"

"I want to talk to you."

I stepped back. The air rushed in to fill the slight space between us, and I suddenly felt cold.

Raven laughed, a real laugh this time. "You look like I just said you've got a terminal disease or something. Calm down." He grabbed my hand and tugged me towards the bed.

Raven kicked off his shoes, and then sat at the foot of my bed with his feet curled up under his body. I sat at the head, leaning against the wall, and stretched my legs out in front of me. Raven reached forward and pinched my big toe. Playfully, like he wanted to soften whatever he wanted to say. From the slight shift in his eyebrows, I could tell it was serious.

"I just wanted to be on the same page, I guess. What are we doing here? Is this—" he lifted his fist to his mouth and rapped his knuckles against his teeth, a little nervous tic he had when he really wanted to bite his nails— "Is this just sex for you?"

Raven's own words rang in my memory: *"If I needed help, it wouldn't be from the club slut."* At the time I'd thought he'd finally said what he really thought of me. That I was heartless and shallow, distracted by hookups—tarnished, somehow. Not good enough. The realization of what he'd actually been saying hit me now like it'd been dropped from a helicopter onto my head. He hadn't been judging my character.

I'd been *hurting* him.

Every time I'd brought some stranger into my bedroom, I'd only thought about what I wanted. And what I'd wanted was distraction: trying to snuff out my attraction to Raven one pointless fuck at a time. Thinking that the more I sated my physical desire, the less I'd want him. Clearly, that hadn't worked. And in the process, Raven—with his keen sense of observation—had watched me every single time. Watched me choose every person in Elkin Lake but him.

"It's not." My voice broke slightly. I coughed, clearing my throat. "It's not just sex. It's—it's more than that."

I didn't have a word to describe whatever was happening between us. But it wasn't casual.

Raven looked up and a slow smile spread across his face. He brushed a strand of dark hair from his eyes.

Of course, I loved him.

My heart vibrated in my chest like a car engine in neutral, bursting with energy but with no direction to go. I couldn't say it out loud—the words stayed trapped in my throat.

"So why?" Raven asked. Not accusingly, just curious, leaning toward me like he couldn't stay too far away. "I mean, why now? We've known each other for years. And nothing has ever happened. I mean, you fully rejected me the first night last year, I…. Well, you know. And things are moving so fast now. I just—I want to talk. I want to be on the same page."

Just another way Raven was the smart one. We should've had this conversation ages ago. But of course I was too scared to rock the boat.

"After that night," Raven said, "you started avoiding me, even more than you had been. Was it—was it because I'd tried something while you were asleep? I know it was fucked up. I shouldn't have taken advantage of you while you were asleep. Especially when you were so nice to let me crash with you. I misread the situation." He wrinkled his nose, like the memory disgusted him. "I'm sorry. I really am."

"Hey, hey," I said. "That's not why. It's not."

Shame bubbled inside me, and any resistance I'd had toward explaining my feelings to Raven crumbled in the face of his self-deprecation. Not only had I made him feel unworthy because I slept around—he'd also convinced himself *he'd* taken advantage of *me*. After I'd given him clear signals that I was interested.

God. I was such a fucking asshole.

"It took every ounce of willpower I had to stop that blowjob," I said. "I wanted it. You didn't misread that. You didn't do anything wrong."

Raven sighed with relief. How long had he been worrying about that?

"Then why'd you stop me? Why'd you start avoiding me?"

"You weren't in a good place that night," I reminded him gently. "It was the night after Ankh's funeral. If I hadn't stopped you, *I* would've been the one taking advantage. You were a wreck."

"Doesn't mean I didn't know what I was doing."

"What kind of man would I be if I let that be our first real time together?"

"But then you avoided me." Raven scooted closer and drew my feet into his lap. He traced the knobby bone on my ankle with one finger, his gaze following the touch, like he couldn't bring himself to meet my eyes again. "If that were all, something would've happened sooner."

I sighed. The truth couldn't hurt him more than I already had. "You're Ankh and Priest's son."

Raven's hand stilled.

"I can't believe I'm telling you this," I said. "Listen, I first noticed you when you were young. Still a teenager."

"How young?"

"When you were eighteen."

Raven's lips quirked into a slight smile. "Really?"

"Yeah, really. And I felt like a fucking creep for it. One day you were the kid I was teaching how to throw a proper punch in the backyard, and then the next day I wake up and you're this... man. A gorgeous one! And my first thought is, I'm a fucking creep for wanting to sleep with a guy more than ten years younger than me—who looks up to me!—and my second thought is, if Ankh and Priest find out, they're going to kick my ass and kick me out."

"That's not true," Raven said. "They wouldn't have done that."

"Maybe not," I said. "But it would've changed my relationship with them. And—Ankh was like a father to me, too, in a way. He gave me a second chance in this club. I was pretty fucked up before I found Hell's Ankhor. And I just... I didn't want to risk disappointing him. Having him think I was trying to take advantage of his only son."

"And now?"

"Now? I'm still afraid of how Priest will react. If I were in his position, and I saw some old lowlife like me circling my kid, I'd beat that guy's ass."

"What?" Raven finally looked up, his brow furrowed deeply. "What do you mean?"

"Look at me!" I gestured at myself. "I'm a beat-up old enforcer, couldn't cut it in the military, history of violence, bad-tempered, and going nowhere beyond where I've been the past decade. I didn't even finish *high school*. If I wasn't in Hell's Ankhor, I'd probably be in jail or worse. You don't need a guy like me dragging you down. I'm just gonna be here, doing this, living and working with Hell's Ankhor for as long as they'll have me. But you…"

I pulled my feet out of his lap, sat up enough so I could lean forward and touch his cheek. A deep frown appeared on his face.

"You're so fucking smart," I said. "You could do anything you want. Go anywhere. Meet people, solve problems, fix shit. You could have any guy you wanted."

Raven's eyes blazed. He shoved me backwards, and I flopped back against the wall, stunned.

"What if I want *you*, huh? What if *you're* the guy I choose?"

"Raven, listen—"

"No, you listen!" His eyes shone, but no tears fell. "You don't get to decide if you're good enough for me. *I* decide that. I'm not a fucking kid."

"I know you're not—"

"But you're sitting here trying to make my decisions for me. It's patronizing. You think I don't know who you are?"

I said nothing. Raven pinned me with his passionate, furious gaze.

"I think you're a jackass who's been jerking me around for years, making me think he liked me, and then turning around and ignoring me and fucking other people in front of me. Treating me sweet one minute and cruel the next. I think you're a guy who's been causing me a hell of a lot of emotional whiplash."

This was what I wanted, right? I'd wanted Raven to use some common sense and see that I wasn't worth any of his time. But the thought of him getting up and walking out the door cut through me so painfully it left me breathless.

"I also think you're the best fucking sergeant-at-arms a club could ever dream of having," he continued. He still looked pissed, but his voice softened the barest amount. "And I think you're loyal as fuck. You underestimate your own smarts. And you put everyone else's best interests over your own to the point of it being a fucking problem."

"Raven..."

Raven crawled over me and straddled my lap. The fury in his gaze dissipated, like a summer storm that pours then passes, and what was left was just the raw intensity.

"I don't want to leave the club. I already did, and I came back. I'm not leaving again. And I don't want anyone else. It's not..." Raven paused, pursed his lips, gathered his thoughts. "Whatever this is between us, it's not about being deserving. I'm not a prize. You don't have to prove anything."

He kissed me gently, sweetly, with none of the urgency of our kiss prior. It flattened me.

"Do you want me?" Raven asked. "Do you really want this?"

"God, yes," I said, and it felt like a confession.

"Then that's all it takes." He cupped my face in his hands and kissed me again.

We kissed slowly, passionately, and Raven's body slowly undulated against mine. I wanted to believe him. I wanted to think that simply wanting each other was enough. I'd been an idiot to think that I could really hide anything from Raven long-term—my attempts to create distance and space had been bumbling at best. And all they'd done was confuse him, hurt him, and make him doubt himself.

Was it really possible that he'd seen me to my core and still wanted this?

Part of me still doubted it—I couldn't help it. Too many years of habit and thoughts to break in just one moment, or even a few weeks.

But for now I had him in my arms.

We kissed for a few moments more, and then broke apart just long enough to pull off our shirts. I changed our positions, shifting so Raven was lying flat on his back on the bed. Beneath me, his dark hair spread out on the comforter, and his sharp eyes twinkled with joy now instead of anger.

I pressed my body against his, and his heartbeat pounded against my bare chest. The heat of his skin against mine shocked the breath from my lungs. He skated his hands down my back, and then slid his hands under the waistband of my jeans. He squeezed my ass, smiling into a kiss as he did so, and then slid his narrow fingers in between my cheeks to run across my entrance.

"I want you," he murmured in a low voice. "I want to be inside you."

I broke the kiss. I didn't move away from his touch, but I didn't encourage it, either. I'd murmured that same phrase in my partners' ears before. But I'd never been on the receiving end. Getting fucked had never appealed to me—especially not in a one-night stand context. But when Raven spoke those words, in that warm, velvety voice, it sent an unexpected spark of arousal through me.

"I've never…"

"Hm?" Raven continued stroking me, slow and steady, and my cock twitched with interest.

"I've never done that," I said. "Been on bottom."

Raven's eyes snapped open and he pulled his hand away. "Sorry," he said. "I just... I assumed... You don't have to, obviously. And it wouldn't bother me if you never want to."

I rolled off him, and Raven rolled onto his side, so we were facing each other lying on the bed.

"It requires trust, I guess." I reached up and tucked a strand of Raven's hair behind his ear. "I haven't had that with a partner before."

Raven hummed. I traced a path over the shell of his ear, then across his jawline, and finally his kiss-swollen lips.

"But I want to," I said. "With you."

His gaze met mine and his mouth dropped open slightly in surprise.

I couldn't take back all the times I'd hurt him, ignored him, or treated him badly. But we could have this experience together. Something I'd never done with anyone else—I wanted to do with Raven.

"You don't have to," Raven said.

"I know that. I want to." I kissed him and slid my hand across his torso, to his hips, and then reached between his legs to cup his cock hard. "Touch me again."

"Take your pants off, then," Raven said teasingly.

Moments later we'd kicked our jeans and shorts off and were kissing again, tangled naked on my bed. Like Raven had plucked this moment from my fantasies and made it better than I ever could've imagined. I pulled a bottle of lube from my nightstand and pressed it into Raven's hand before pulling him down for another kiss.

His lithe body pressed hot against mine, and I touched him hungrily, exploring the intimate parts of him I thought I'd never, ever get to see: the bony jut of his hips, the crease at his thigh, the backs of his knobby knees. His cock looked painfully hard, leaking precum steadily. I slotted our legs together, and sighed into his mouth as our hard cocks aligned.

Raven shivered and thrusted his hips against mine.

"Come on," I murmured. I couldn't stop kissing him wherever my lips landed. "Touch me."

"I'm gonna go slow." Raven tilted his head back and exposed his neck for more kisses. "Make it good for you. Lie back."

I did as I was told.

Without any warning, Raven scooted down the bed and sucked my cock into his mouth.

I gasped, the sudden wet heat sending a powerful thrill through me. After our first disastrous night together, I'd thought I'd never get to feel Raven's mouth on me again. This time I could rake my fingers through his hair and sink into the pleasure without guilt. Then Raven traced my entrance again, this time with a finger slick with lube. The cool, slick pressure added an edge of anticipation to the blowjob.

Raven slid his mouth off my cock with an unselfconscious wet sound. "Relax," he murmured, and pressed a kiss to my hip. His finger rubbed slowly, soothingly over me.

Our gazes met. God, the sight of him between my legs, touching me, nosing at my cock like he couldn't get enough of it even when it wasn't in his mouth—

How did I ever get so lucky?

Raven slipped his finger inside me. "There you go," he said, and then began to suck me again, his lips moving in time with his finger thrusting slowly and steadily.

With his slim, deft fingers alone Raven soon had me pliant and open beneath him. The odd sensation of his fingers in me had built into a deep, intense pleasure, rising like a tide, but it wasn't enough.

"Stop teasing me," I growled, tugging on his hair to pull him up to my eye level. "I want you in me."

Raven inhaled sharply. "Say that again."

I found the lube in the mess of covers and coated Raven's cock, jerking him slowly, getting him wet.

"I want you," I said, nothing more than a breath in his ear. "Please."

Raven kissed me hard, and then slid a pillow under my hips. He gripped his cock by the base and pressed the head to my entrance as he gazed down at me.

"You're fucking amazing," he whispered.

Slowly, slowly, he pushed inside.

I pulled him down so he was flush against me, and we touched everywhere possible. I wrapped my arms around him and cradled his head against my neck, and from his thick hair in between my fingers to the hard, full heat of his cock inside me, my nerves were on fire with sensation. He moved his hips slowly, rolling like a wave, in and out, and it was unlike any pleasure I'd felt before.

He kept that slow, relentless pace, whispering sweet nothings into my ear and saying my name. I felt drunk, lost in the sensation, swept away. I'd never wanted to give up control in bed before. But Raven made me feel like I was safe—taken care of. Adored. It was completely new, and I never wanted to lose it.

Raven lifted his head enough to press his forehead against mine. Our eyes met.

The depth of emotion I saw in his eyes terrified me, yet I wanted it, I wanted all of it.

What did he see in me?

"I'm close," Raven whispered.

I wasn't able to form words. I nodded agreement as the relentless, delicious pace of his cock inside me kept building, rushing toward me like a storm.

Then he reached between us and grabbed my cock, and the sudden, intense pleasure made my head spin. It only took a few strokes.

My orgasm crashed over me, so powerful I had to close my eyes against it, tipping my head back and clinging to Raven like I might get physically pulled away if I didn't. He groaned a drawn-out syllable that might've been my name as he followed me over the edge, and then collapsed in a sweaty heap on top of me.

I kissed his temple, and he made a snuffling noise.

"You gonna fall asleep?" I asked.

"Could," Raven murmured. "Could stay like this forever."

Forever—there was no way he meant that. But for a moment I indulged myself and imagined that he did. That we could have this forever. I squeezed him tighter.

Chapter 19 - Raven

The sun streaming in through the blinds stirred me awake. In my bleary, half-awake state, I didn't know where I was. My room had blackout curtains—sunlight cast a glare on my computer screen—and I woke every morning to a blaring alarm.

Then, with a grumble, Gunnar rolled over and draped his arm over my side. He exhaled hard against my nape before his breaths evened out in sleep again.

Warmth flooded me as memories of last night rushed back. I scooted backward, deeper into Gunnar's sleeping embrace. The hard line of his cock pressed into my lower back. In his sleep, Gunnar hummed and ground his hips against me.

I floated, awake but dozing, as if I were emerging from a dream. Last night had been unreal. Even with Gunnar holding me, I could hardly believe it had happened. I'd been imagining it for so long, but my imagination couldn't even come close to matching the reality. Gunnar's solid, muscular body had been spread out on the comforter beneath me, so open and vulnerable, so unlike the powerful, dominant guy I'd seen lurking around the bar trying to pull strangers.

Out of all the people Gunnar had slept with, none of them had seen him like that. None of them had touched him like I had.

After we'd cleaned up and tumbled back into bed, Gunnar had grabbed me and kissed me hard.

"I don't want anyone else," he'd said. "I'm not sharing you."

I'd laughed at his intensity even as my heart had pounded hard. "Pretty sure I should be the one worried about sharing *you*."

I'd used a joking tone, but I meant it—I hadn't had more than a handful of hookups since I got back from college, and they'd been discreet. And part of me had still worried that despite whatever connection we had, it would only be a matter of time before Gunnar would have a few drinks in Ballast and find some hot young woman he couldn't resist.

"You won't," Gunnar had said. "I'm done fucking around."

I still wasn't exactly sure what he'd meant. Was he done fucking around with other people? Or done fucking around with me? Or both?

I know he'd said that this wasn't casual for him, either—were we finally moving toward something *real*?

"Go back to sleep," Gunnar mumbled next to me now. "You're fidgety. Thinking too hard."

I took his hand where it was looped over my side and kissed his knuckles. "I'm gonna go put the coffee on."

That seemed to appease him. I stood up and Gunnar rolled onto his back, folding his arms behind his head. The bed's thin sheet was pushed down to his hips, and sunlight fell in stripes over his tanned body. His half-lidded, sleepy gaze tracked my movements across the room.

I pulled on my jeans, and then rooted around in Gunnar's dresser and pulled out one of the plain gray long-sleeved shirts I'd seen him wear countless times. On Gunnar it was snug, nearly skin-tight. It was looser on me, the collar wide and the sleeves ending at my knuckles.

"Looks good on you," Gunnar said in a low, possessive voice.

I inhaled Gunnar's scent from the neckline of the shirt: clean soap, leather, the barest hint of aftershave. "Smells like you."

"You like that?"

"No way," I teased. "You stink like a dog."

Gunnar grinned, and then reached out and hooked a finger in the waistband of my jeans, pulling me back towards the bed. I leaned down and kissed him, morning breath be damned.

"How do you feel?" I asked, a little hesitantly.

"Good," Gunnar said. "Maybe a bit sore."

"Oh, yeah?" A bolt of heat ran through me at the thought of Gunnar going about his day with the aching memory of what we'd done together every time he moved or sat down.

"Guess I need more practice."

"That can be arranged." I bit my lip. "Go back to sleep. It's barely eight. You've got another two hours."

"Or three." Gunnar flopped back down on the bed.

I slipped out of Gunnar's room and padded down the stairs to the clubhouse kitchen. I was usually one of the first members awake—no matter how late I stayed up, I couldn't seem to sleep past seven. I started a full pot of coffee for the house, as I did every morning.

This relationship, or whatever it was, was so different than the one I'd imagined when I first began crushing on Gunnar. I thought he'd be tough, relentless, cagey—ready to take what he wanted and bring me along for the ride. I'd underestimated the depth of his feelings: the longing, the pain, the tenderness. Every layer I peeled back only made me want him more. I was beginning to believe that perhaps I didn't have to let Gunnar take control—that maybe he didn't even want to.

Perhaps we could be equals.

The front door swung open. Logan glanced around the clubhouse, a little desperately, and when he saw me in the kitchen, he sagged with relief. "Ugh, thank God you're awake."

The coffeemaker chimed its completion. I poured Logan a mug and set it on the kitchen island. He took it gratefully. He was wearing sweatpants and one of Blade's shirts under his club leather jacket, and he looked haggard, like he hadn't slept at all.

"What's going on?" I asked. "Everything okay?"

"I don't know," Logan admitted. He took a sip of his coffee, sighed gratefully, and then stared into the mug like it had secrets to reveal to him. I waited patiently as he sorted through whatever was racing through his mind.

"He called me back," Logan said finally.

I started. "Rebel? What'd he say?"

Logan had been so sure Rebel wouldn't respond—but he had. And fast. Faster than I'd hoped.

"He agreed to meet." He said it like Rebel had agreed to this own death. "Tonight. The Vipers are heading north for a job, and Rebel's supposed to stay behind to meet a contact. After that, he's coming to us."

"Tonight? That soon?"

"I know," Logan said. "I—I wasn't ready for things to come together so quickly."

I'd assumed we'd have at least a week before we had any response from Rebel. My stomach twisted with a dark excitement. I was desperate for information about Dad's death, but if Rebel'd had anything to do with it, it wouldn't end well.

"I'm scared," Logan murmured, like he was admitting it out loud to himself.

"He's coming to us, right?"

"Yeah."

There were a few ways this could go sideways. Like if Rebel tried to bring a bunch of Vipers into our territory. Or if he admitted he'd been involved in Dad's death, and counted on his relationship with Logan to save him.

Because regardless of Rebel's familial status, he was still a Viper. And as much as I loved Logan, I wouldn't hesitate to kill Rebel myself if he was behind Dad's murder.

"Rebel's smart," I said. "He wouldn't agree if he didn't know the risks."

"I know he knows the risks. But I don't think he understands how angry Blade is." He looked up, his hazel eyes cutting through me. "And how angry you are."

I broke eye contact, fidgeting under his searching look. I couldn't deny it; I wanted vengeance. Sure, Rebel was Logan's brother, and sure, he'd called emergency services when Logan had been shot—but he'd also stood guard in that warehouse and let Logan languish alone.

He'd helped the Vipers. He *was* a Viper. And that outweighed everything else.

Logan set his coffee down and ran his hands through his hair, shaking off his nerves. "I just want to get it over with. I know Blade will make the right decision. It's been months, but I still have to remind myself that Hell's Ankhor doesn't operate like the Viper's Nest. I know everyone won't be needlessly cruel. But it's just... It's the not knowing that kills me."

"Fucking tell me about it," I said.

"But you seem less angry these days. And I've never seen you wear that shirt," Logan said. He paused, took a long sip of his coffee. "I've seen someone else wear it, though."

My cheeks heated. "I don't know what you're talking about."

Logan grinned. He hopped up onto the kitchen island like it was a stool—he was always doing that, sitting on things that weren't chairs—and peered down at me. "Come on, Raven. You've been crushing on him for as long as I've known you. Are things happening?"

I glanced towards the stairs, irrationally worried that someone—particularly Gunnar—would burst in and hear me talking all sappy. "Yeah," I admitted. "Things are happening."

Logan grinned like a cat with a cornered mouse. "What kinds of things?"

"We're working it out," I said vaguely. "It's not—I mean, last night—"

"Last night?" Logan squawked.

I waggled my hand flat in front of me in a desperate 'keep it down' motion. "Last night he told me he didn't want to share me."

"So you're exclusive."

"I guess so."

"Are you like… In a relationship?"

I grimaced. "Not officially, I guess. It's hard to talk about. Especially with everything going on in the club. It feels stupid to worry about whatever's going on with Gunnar when I should be focusing on the real problems at hand."

"I get that. But you should let yourself be happy." He paused and fixed his piercing eyes on me. "Can I say something weird?"

"Everything you say is weird," I quipped.

Logan ignored that and said softly, "I never met your dad."

I nodded, and then crossed my arms over my chest and looked away. It was still hard for me to talk openly about Dad without that chasm of grief inside me splitting open. And it was too early in the day for me to start crying yet.

"But I've heard a lot about him," Logan said. "From Blade. He talks about Ankh a lot. About how much he admired Ankh… About how he's shaped his presidency after Ankh's example. And it sounds like Ankh was a man whose goal wasn't to build a club for power or influence. That was *my* dad's goal. From what I can tell, Ankh wanted to build a home for people. Where people could build a life. Priest said it was meant to be an anchor in a storm."

I couldn't speak around the lump in my throat. But I nodded again.

"Sorry if this is presumptuous," Logan said, "but I think he'd want you to be happy. We've got to treasure any moment of happiness we get. Even when it seems to come at the wrong time. I'd say especially when it's the wrong time."

I exhaled hard and pushed the heels of my hands hard into my eyes, willing the tears away. After a few controlled breaths, I could speak again. "Gunnar thinks Priest will hate him for wanting to be with me."

"Gunnar thinks he's a big scary pit bull when in reality he's a big Labrador retriever," Logan said, rolling his eyes.

"And I treated him like shit for a little while," I admitted. "Pushing him away. Calling him names. I was lashing out like a stupid kid because he rejected me."

"Is he mad about that?"

"I mean... I don't think so."

"Then what's the problem?"

"It's just... It's taken such a long time for us to get this point, you know? He really gave me the runaround. And I gave it to him, too. And we've fought so much, and he's so anxious about how the club will respond, and I—I'm scared he's going to change his mind. It feels like he's wielding all the power. I've been crushing so hard on him for so long—he has to know I'm not going anywhere. He's got me wrapped around his finger, but it always seems like he's looking for an escape hatch. Like one wrong look from Priest or Blade, and he'll drop me like a bad habit. Like he's ashamed to want me."

"Has he been in a real relationship before?" Logan hopped off the counter and poured himself another cup of coffee.

"Not to my knowledge." I'd seen him fuck a lot of people, but never the same person more than once.

"So he's going from no relationships at all to, potentially, a meaningful relationship with the vice president's kid... I gotta be honest with you, Raven, I'd be a little nervous, too."

A brief flare of childish anger rose in my chest. "I'm more than just my father's son."

"If anyone knows that, it's me," Logan said.

That made me feel like an asshole. Of course Logan knew what it meant to be defined by your father's actions. But there wasn't any anger in his eyes, just understanding. He grabbed me by the shoulder and pulled me into a quick, tight hug. "He'll get his head on straight. And if he doesn't, we'll kick his ass."

I laughed. Despite how well I'd slept, cuddled next to Gunnar, exhaustion tugged at me. God, I was ready for all this shit to be over. Dealing with Gunnar and the Viper investigation simultaneously was draining me of every ounce of energy I had.

"Thanks, Logan." I pulled away. "Don't tell anyone, though. Please."

"I won't."

"Not even Blade?"

Logan sucked his teeth. "I won't. Mostly because I know he'd open his big mouth to Gunnar."

I laughed, and then started puttering around the kitchen, gathering the ingredients for breakfast.

"I'm happy for you, though," Logan said. "I really want this to go right."

"Yeah." I turned the stove on and watched the gas flame flicker. Maybe Logan was right. Maybe Gunnar wasn't ashamed to be seen with me—maybe he was just scared. Scared of what it meant to be with someone for real. He'd alluded to his past vaguely, like it was something he didn't want to think about— like it was something that happened to someone else. What had happened that made him so... resistant? "I want that, too."

Chapter 20 - Gunnar

The atmosphere in Ankhor Works was tense with anticipation. I shifted my weight from foot to foot, keeping myself from physically pacing the perimeter of the building, which I knew from experience would drive the rest of the club members crazy.

Inviting a Viper into our territory didn't sit right with me. But at this point, I didn't know what other options we had. Our investigation hadn't dug anything up, and Raven's had hit a dead end. This was the only lead I had. And at least if shit went south, we'd be on our turf, and hopefully we'd outnumber whoever showed up. I wouldn't put it past a Viper to say he was showing up alone, and then bring a posse with him. I'd seen it happen once before, when we'd tried to set a trap using Coop as bait, and they'd counter-trapped us. Bunch of assholes.

From his seat on the low couch in the shop waiting area, Raven caught my eye. He raised his eyebrows inquisitively, and I nodded. Everything was fine. Raven went back to looking at his phone. I had no idea what he was doing—probably something I didn't understand. Logan sat on the couch next to him, with the resigned, unhappy look of a man waiting for a root canal.

Admittedly, I didn't love having Raven on the premises for this meeting. I wanted him somewhere safe. I knew he could hold his own in a fight—he'd made that clear when he'd decked me in the hallway—but he didn't need to be a part of the violence.

If it came to that.

And part of me wanted it to come to that.

Whoever showed up, I wanted to pulverize them. My hands itched for it. After seeing all the evidence Raven had collected, it was obvious Ankh hadn't just crashed on his own.

I missed Ankh badly. We all did. This realization had reopened all our wounds, and mine was festering. Of course being a club president came with risks, but shady murder like this was beyond anything I'd ever imagined. If I imagined my own death in the club, it was usually in the form of a gunshot during a territory skirmish, or an accidental crash, or a slow death behind bars. Never something so sneaky and cruel as a staged accident.

It was fucking cowardly. Dishonorable. And I wanted to make whoever did it pay.

The rest of the club members present also radiated anticipation and tension. Siren and Tex lingered by the door, and Coop was outside. Priest was in a chair near Raven. And Blade stood at my side, flipping a knife from hand to hand. That's how I knew he was really chomping at the bit to get this started—the mindless knife tricks only made an appearance when his nervous energy was close to a breaking point.

After Ankh passed, I admittedly hadn't been sure about Blade as the next president. I trusted him with my life, of course; he was my best friend, and we'd risen through the ranks of the club together. He'd been sergeant-at-arms for years, and I'd been an enforcer. I'd known him as a friend and fighter—he'd led the enforcers well, but I hadn't known if that would translate to leading the club as a whole.

But Blade had stepped up. Ankh had left big shoes to fill, and Blade was no Ankh. He was just himself. He didn't try to be Ankh, and that's why his leadership worked. Didn't hurt that Blade had some of the same traits that had made Ankh such an effective president: loyalty, strength, and a strong sense of right and wrong—but also a strong sense of justice.

Blade would do anything for his family. His selflessness and his loyalty inspired the rest of the club to act the same way. The leadership shaped the club. And we were still shaped in Ankh's image.

"He's late," Blade growled.

"He'll show," Raven said. He caught my eye.

"What makes you so sure?" I crossed the short distance between us and sat on the armrest of the couch next to where he sat. "You tracking him?"

"I wish." His rich blue eyes blazed with frustration. "He's got encryption on his end, too."

I brushed my hand over the back of his neck tentatively, half-expecting him to pull away, since we were surrounded by the other club members. To my surprise, Raven pressed back against the touch with a contented sigh. He tipped his head forward, invitingly, and I scraped my fingers through the thick, dark hair at his nape. "You all right?"

We'd danced around the relationship conversation—I'd told him I wasn't going to sleep with anyone else, and he'd said the same, but we hadn't agreed on anything further. But the closer we got, the more that conversation loomed.

Raven had told me that all I needed to do was want him. I was trying to believe him, but I still carried the weight of all my mistakes with me, and what they would mean to Raven when he found out. But how could things not change once he found out what I'd done, what was really in my past, especially now?

I didn't want to give this up. Maybe I could prove to him—and to myself—that I was worthy of his attention, despite all the shit I'd done. I could change. Maybe I could be a good enough man for him, if he'd have me.

It felt like a lot to hope for.

"I'm good," Raven murmured.

I'd work it out. After we figured out all this shit with the Vipers and got justice for Ankh. Then I could talk to Raven and convince him to give me a shot, a real shot—a relationship and everything that came with it. Then I'd work on getting Logan to trust that I wasn't going to lead Raven on only to drop him. And then I'd tell Priest.

That was the conversation that scared me the most, even more than talking to Raven himself. How the fuck was I going to explain everything to Priest? If he had any goddamn sense, he'd strip me of my title and kick me to the curb for messing around with his son, who he'd trusted me with in his most vulnerable moments.

But now, that was a risk I was willing to take. I'd put it all on the line if it'd show Raven I was serious about this. That I wasn't going to be a defensive, stubborn asshole anymore.

"What about you?" Raven asked.

"Ready for this shit to be over," I muttered.

"Join the club," Logan said.

He and Blade shared a complicated exchange with just their eyes. I let my hand linger on Raven's nape regardless.

"Light on the horizon." Siren called. "He's here."

"Anyone else?" Blade asked.

"Just the one headlight," Tex said. "Don't let your guard down, though."

The side door to the garage swung open moments later. Rebel stepped in with Coop's grip tight on the back of his jacket.

"Company's here," Coop called, a bitter edge to his usually jovial voice. He manhandled Rebel to the center of the garage, backing him up against the grill of a muscle car currently in for repairs. I stood up, standing in front of him, and Blade moved to my side, still flipping his knife menacingly.

Rebel's gaze darted nervously around the room, cataloguing exactly how outnumbered he was. He was tense—not like he was going to try any funny business, but like he was tempted to make a break for it. His gaze lingered on Logan, who didn't meet his eyes.

The resemblance between Rebel and Logan was striking. They had the same sharp, small features and thick, fine hair, though Rebel's was a shade darker brown, and he wore it shorter and neater than Logan did. And where Logan's eyes were a shocking bright green, Rebel's were deep-set, hazel, and a little less revealing. Rebel was broader than Logan, too, and he carried himself like an enforcer even though he was wearing a plain denim jacket in lieu of his club gear.

"Weapons, Coop." I crossed my arms over my chest.

"Is that really necessary?" Rebel asked.

"Yes," I said.

Coop patted Rebel down roughly, and thoroughly—a little more thoroughly than I'd expected—moving steadily over his legs, hips, and across Rebel's torso. For all his searching, he only uncovered a single knife in Rebel's back pocket.

Coop handed the knife over. I looked down my nose at him. Coop shrugged.

Rebel twisted his mouth like the room had a foul aroma. "Unarmed. You happy?"

"No," Raven said. He stood up from the couch and fixed his gaze on me, and then Blade.

Both of us took a step to the side.

"Did you send me the messages?" Raven asked coolly. He fixed Rebel with a hard stare, barely a foot of distance between them.

"Yes." Rebel didn't shy from Raven's stare.

"Did you do it?" Raven asked, his voice low, almost dangerous, unlike any tone I'd heard him take before. "Did you kill my father?"

"No. I didn't."

"Don't fucking lie to me," Raven snapped. He grabbed a handful of Rebel's shirt and jerked him closer. "Who killed him?"

Rebel, unfazed by the manhandling, didn't break Raven's gaze. "It wasn't me. I wouldn't be here if it was. But I know who did."

Raven released him and took an unsteady step backwards. "Tell me."

"It was Dad, wasn't it?"

Logan sat at the very edge of the couch, his elbows on his knees and fingers steepled at his mouth. His eyes kept darting away from Rebel, like it physically hurt to look at his brother.

Rebel deflated. The defensiveness leeched from his body, like he'd suddenly forgotten the rest of us were present. "Hey, Logan."

"It's something he'd do," Logan said. "Fits the Vipers' MO. Rotten at the root."

"It was Bane," Rebel said.

Murmurs rippled through the shop, and then a tense silence descended.

"The vice president," Logan said. "Acting on his own?"

"Yes," Rebel said. "Independently. Trying to curry favor from Crave. It was like a gift. Ankh's murder was a big part of the reason he was promoted from enforcer to vice."

Raven clenched his fists and turned away. He took a few deep breaths before speaking. "Then why'd you send the photos? Why start this wild goose chase?"

"I owed Ankh a debt," Rebel said blandly. "And I want Bane gone. It's a win-win."

Rage ran through me. A win-win? This fucking scumbag had the audacity to call anything related to Ankh's death a win-win? I lurched forward and socked Rebel hard in the stomach. He choked, keeling forward.

Logan looked away.

"You want Bane gone. Why not just take care of it yourself?" Blade asked.

Coop grabbed Rebel roughly by the shoulder and hauled him back up to standing. Rebel cursed to himself, his face twisted into a painful grimace.

"I am a Viper," he said, glaring at me defiantly. "Bane is worthless. The club deserves better. If he's gone, I'll get his role."

"And you wouldn't if you took out Bane yourself?" Blade asked.

"Dad doesn't tolerate in-fighting," Rebel said. "Not after what happened with Logan."

"And what's this debt you owe?"

"Paid," Rebel said. "Fuck off."

I shifted my weight just to see Rebel flinch.

"If you wanna hurt me more, go ahead and get it over with," Rebel said. "I've told you all you're gonna get. Let's pick up the pace here, I need to get back to the city before the road crew returns."

The side door to the garage slammed closed as Logan left. Blade's gaze tracked his movements, but he didn't make a move to follow.

"Hell fucking no," I said. "You're staying with us."

"No, he's not," Priest said firmly. His voice was steady, his expression stony, revealing nothing. "Where can we find Bane? I know you wouldn't come here without a plan."

"We're closing a big deal," Rebel said. "And Bane, instead of being a decent fucking VP, will celebrate as he always does. He'll cross the border into Nevada and spend the night at Darlin's. I guarantee you that's where he'll be in forty-eight hours."

Priest nodded. "He'll have backup?"

"Some," Rebel said. "But not a lot. He's cocky like that."

"Anything else, Blade?" Priest asked.

"I think we've got what we need," Blade said. "Thanks for your cooperation, traitor."

"I'm not a fucking traitor." Rebel thumped his chest. "I'm a Viper. I'm putting my club first. I thought you'd understand that."

"Club members don't try to get their leaders killed." Blade motioned to Coop, and Coop tossed Rebel's knife over. "I'll be keeping this."

Blade put his own knife away and opened Rebel's then stepped close to him and pressed the edge to Rebel's throat. "And if there's any funny business tomorrow night, I'll come for you personally."

"Logan wouldn't much like that."

"Club comes first," Blade growled. He shoved Rebel at Coop. "Send him home, Coop."

"Roger." Coop dragged him out the side door.

"Church tomorrow afternoon," Blade said. "We'll finish this shit." He left without another word. From the deep furrow in his brow, I knew he had debriefing to do with Logan.

Outside, Rebel's engine revved noisily, and then faded as he tore away from the shop. I caught Raven's eye. He looked just as conflicted as I did—and about ten times as exhausted.

What was Rebel's goal? For all the big game he talked about being a Viper, he didn't carry himself like the rest of them. He seemed smarter; there had to be something else at play. His ploy to get Bane out of the picture had to be part of something bigger—maybe part of a larger plan to usurp Crave's presidency. The guy who oozed guilt and nostalgia when he saw Logan couldn't be the same guy who was okay with Crave trying to murder Logan.

Something wasn't adding up. But I'd have to wait to pull on that thread.

"You heard your president," Priest said. "Dismissed."

Chapter 21 - Raven

Elkin Inks wasn't thrumming with business yet, as it was still early in the day, and the jingling bell when I opened the door cut through the near silence of the shop. It was a small business, with just three tattoo chairs and brightly painted walls crowded with photographs and art. Pops was in the chair furthest, a young tattoo artist already hard at work on Pops' left shoulder.

"Raven," Pops said fondly. He tapped the artist's shoulder.

The kid popped a headphone out of his ear. "Everything all right, sir?"

"Yeah, no changes. All right if my son hangs out for a few minutes?"

"Sure." The kid stuck his headphone back into his ear, changed his gloves, and then returned his attention back to Pops' shoulder.

"What are you getting done?"

"Just a touch-up," Pops said. He exhaled slowly as the gun began moving across his skin. Pops had a hell of a lot of tattoos—more than anyone else in the club, I'd wager—mostly because of situations like this. Tattoos were his most reliable stress reliever. He didn't get them for fun anymore. When he really needed to blow off steam, that's when new ones appeared. That's when I knew things were starting to get to him.

The tattoo on his shoulder was a simple, early version of the Hell's Ankhor logo, same as the one on the shirt he'd given me. It was one of his first tattoos, faded with age and blurring at the edges. The tattoo artist was tasked with cleaning up the lines and brightening the ink, but not adding anything new. Just detailing what was already there.

"Raven," Pops said. "How are you feeling?"

"Tired." I sat on another artist's chair and scooted it close to the tattoo chair, so the kid and I flanked him. The kid, though, was absorbed in the touch-up, chewing gum as he worked.

"Yeah." Pops opened his palm, resting on his thigh. I reached out and grabbed it, careful not to jostle him.

This whole endeavor had begun out of an intense, almost rabid desire for revenge. Rebel's emails had filled me with so much rage, so much hate—I couldn't think about the future. All I could think about was vengeance. I hadn't cared at what cost.

"And guilty," I admitted.

"Guilty? Why?"

"I had all this energy for the investigation," I said. "All this hunger to make it right. But now I just want it to be over. Done with."

"Hate will do that." Pops squeezed my hand. "Drains you until there's nothing left."

"But I can't let go. That'd be wrong. I have to stay at it. For Dad."

"Hey," Pops said firmly. "That's not true. I think you know that's not true. The last thing your dad would want—the last thing he ever wanted—was for you to suffer. Not for him. Not for the club. Not ever."

Pops was so calm, so steady, even though I knew he was hurting, too. He'd always been like that, the reliable one, the serious one, the one who always knew what to say. Dad had been a little more impulsive and rough around the edges. Dad always wanted me to take more risks, get into shit, get my hands a little dirty. Experience things.

Pops didn't shelter me, but he recognized my potential in school and wanted me to pursue that. Pops saw that my education could be an asset to the club—or a way out, if I so chose. And Dad wanted me to follow my heart, wherever it took me, fuck the consequences. I'd never felt pulled in different directions, though. Rather they'd balanced each other out, encouraging me to take risks, follow my dreams, but to have a backup plan. A safety net.

And now Dad was gone.

"I miss him." My voice broke. "I just really miss him."

Tears spilled from my eyes, and I roughly rubbed them away.

"Sorry," I said. "I'm being a baby."

"Hey, Kenny?" Pops tapped the artist again. "Mind if we take a quick break?"

The kid shrugged. Pops thanked him and led me out the back door, onto the tiny patio behind the shop—if a gravel patch with a bench and a tiny, sad tree could be called a patio. More like a smoking section. But it was nice to be outside in the cool air.

"Let me tell you something," Pops said. "I don't ever want to hear you apologize for your grief again."

His serious tone surprised me. "What?"

"You understand me? Tears don't make you less of a man." He grabbed me by the shoulder and shook me, roughly affectionate. "They make you more of one. Men feel, and feel deeply. Don't push that down. It's what makes you who you are."

The abyss of grief inside me threatened to open up and swallow me whole. I tipped forward into Pops and pressed my forehead into his shoulder. He wrapped an arm around me.

"Ankh would be so proud of the man you've become," Pops murmured, almost to himself.

Something inside me snapped, and I stopped holding back. I let my grief wash over me, fast and powerful like a wave, and for a few minutes, I just cried. Pops rubbed my back soothingly.

And then, like a wave receding, the worst of it passed. I sat back and rubbed my eyes hard. "That just made me more tired."

"Go back to the house and get some rest before church," Pops said. "Or spend some quality time with your man."

"Pops!" Blood rushed to my face. "What the fuck are you talking about?"

"Son, I'm your father, and I'm not blind. I've seen you and Gunnar these past few weeks. Plus, he seemed to be getting pretty comfortable with you before the interrogation at the shop. And I've seen the way he looks at you."

"He doesn't look at me any sort of way," I grumbled.

Regardless of how he behaved when we were in private, our relationship was still technically unofficial. He hadn't said a word beyond not sleeping with other people. Part of me still wondered if he wanted to keep the option open to sleep with me a few times, get it out of his system, and then move on.

But if that were true, why did he touch me like that in Ankhor Works? In front of everybody? His strong hand on the back of my neck had immediately relaxed me, like he'd intuitively known exactly what I needed.

He wouldn't do things like that if this wasn't real.

I just needed him to say it.

"All right, don't hurt yourself thinking so hard," Pops said. "You really do need to get some more sleep."

"I'm fine," I groused.

Pops herded me back into the tattoo shop. "All right, Kenny, let's keep this party going."

He sat back down in the tattoo chair. Kenny blinked back into reality from where he was dozing at the front desk and walked back to start prepping the gun again.

I shoved my hands into my pockets. "But… You'd really be okay with it? If there was something between me and Gunnar?"

"Of course I would," Pops said. "In this very hypothetical situation, mind you. You deserve love. I had something really special with your dad. I want you to have that, too."

"Thanks," I muttered. "But. Like I said, nothing's going on."

"Right," Priest said, with a serious nod. "Not a thing. Now go back to the clubhouse. I have to finish this touch-up before church."

***

Church was short and to-the-point: a welcome difference from the dragging, conversational meetings we'd been having when we were poring over the same documentation over and over again, looking for any hint of information that might give us a push in the right direction.

Tonight, Blade laid out the plan on a large map of the territory. All the senior members were present and eager, Gunnar especially, chewing his lip thoughtfully as he followed the route Blade planned.

"He'll be in Nevada, outside Hawthorne. It's a six-hour haul—not too bad. We'll leave before sundown. Road crew is enforcers, Priest, Maverick, Heath, and Raven. Heath, I'm not saying this is a test, but it's not *not* a test."

Heath, newly patched-in, adjusted his leather jacket tight around his shoulders, unfazed. "Won't let you down."

Gunnar caught my eye and tilted his chin down slightly. I nodded in acknowledgment. Likely Blade hadn't wanted me to be a part of the road crew at all—I certainly wasn't part of the club muscle. Had Gunnar pushed for me to be included in the road crew?

If he had, I owed him a serious thanks. Because if Blade hadn't included me in the road crew, I would've followed them on my own, and no one needed to be distracted with that tonight. Gunnar probably figured out that much.

"Tune up your bikes," Blade said. "Get some rest. It's gonna be a long night tomorrow. But we're doing it for Ankh."

***

Later that evening, Gunnar disappeared. As sergeant-at-arms, he had much to do to prepare for tomorrow's action—and I knew he'd wait until late to work on his bike. Gunnar didn't like to work in the shop when others were doing the same. He liked the quiet.

I slipped in through the side door. As I'd expected, Gunnar was alone in the back of the shop, working under the overhead lights that cast long shadows around the shop. His low-profile

Harley waited in the center of the room as Gunnar picked through the tools on the nearest bench. The bike was immense but understated, coiled with power like a lurking predatory cat. The chrome details, the fork and exhaust, that glinted in the sunlight on other bikes, had been painted matte black. It was a gorgeous, intimidating bike.

It suited him.

Gunnar found the socket wrench he was looking for, and then turned back to his bike. He paced a circle around it, checking his work. He'd changed into one of the canvas garage jumpsuits, but had tied the top half around his waist, revealing a thin white undershirt. The fluorescent light above cast him in chiaroscuro, drawing my gaze to his deltoid muscles and the functional strength of his forearms.

I felt suddenly overdressed in my jeans and hoodie.

"Hey."

Gunnar started and turned around. Then he curled his lips into a smirk as he gave me a slow, open once-over. "Hey. You found me."

"Were you hiding?"

"No," he said. "But I hoped you'd show up."

I stepped closer and leaned against the workbench. "Ready for tomorrow?"

Gunnar ran his hand over the leather of his bike seat. "More than. Are you?"

"I'm not usually on the road crews," I said.

"This is a different situation."

"That's a very diplomatic response, sergeant."

Gunnar chuckled. He tossed the socket wrench overhand, spinning it in the air then catching it, drawing my gaze to his hands again. Something deep in my gut flared hot. I wanted those hands on me everywhere. Standing here waiting for it, hoping for it, made it even more enthralling.

"I know you want to be there. And you should be," Gunnar said. "This is all happening because of the work you did."

"Blade didn't want me to go, did he?"

"He really fuckin' didn't," Gunnar said with another low laugh.

"You convinced him?"

"No," Gunnar said. "I wouldn't say convinced. I just reminded him of the truth: that this is *your* investigation first and foremost. And that sheltering club members is not the same as defending them."

"And he didn't smack you?" I tried to keep my tone light, but my voice came out quiet. This didn't sound like the Gunnar I thought I knew. If someone had asked me just a few weeks ago, I would've said that Gunnar would lock me in my room like a princess in a tower before he'd let me join tonight's road crew.

He just kept surprising me.

"He knows when I'm talking sense. And, same as me, he knows you're an important asset to the club." Gunnar tucked the socket wrench into the pocket of his jumpsuit and wiped his hands on a rag. "How about your bike? Ready to go? Coop didn't slash the tires?"

Warmth spread through me. An asset? "Coop's still mad I ditched him?"

"No," Gunnar said. "But you know he likes to have something to guilt trip you about. Just in case."

I hummed thoughtfully, stuffing my hands into my hoodie pocket.

Gunnar approached me, slowly closing the distance between us. He stood with his feet bracketing mine and his hands on the workbench at my sides. I was boxed in with the hard edge of the table behind me and Gunnar's body solid as a cliff-face in front of me.

"So why'd you drop in?" Gunnar tucked his face very close to my ear. Nowhere did our bodies touch, only his hot breath that gusted over my ear when he spoke, the words a low vibration. The inches of space between us were electric with possibility.

I tilted my head to the side minutely to offer my neck. Gunnar nosed at the vulnerable place beneath my ear and released another hot exhale. This close, he smelled intoxicatingly of sweat and motor oil. I couldn't repress a shudder—it took effort just to remain standing, when all I wanted to do was drop to my knees and let him take control.

I'd spent so much time during this investigation—and this developing relationship—trying to prove to myself, and to others, that I was strong. Capable. Independent. And now I was fucking tired, and I wanted a break from decisions. I wanted Gunnar to take control.

"I wanted to see you," I said.

"Yeah?" Gunnar suddenly combed one strong hand hard through my hair, sending a shock through my nerves. His palm was hot against my scalp, and the dull pressure of his grip in my hair was a direct line to my cock. "What else do you want?"

"God, you smell good." I grabbed him by the belt loops and pulled him closer so our hips collided. I couldn't help but grind against him.

"Not what I asked," Gunnar said teasingly. He kissed my jawline, and then followed it with a soft bite.

I shifted my grip to his hips and squeezed. "Want you to fuck me."

"That can be arranged." He kissed me on the mouth, finally, a heavy, sloppy press of lips that sucked the breath from my lungs. He wrapped his free arm around my back and pulled me flush against him.

"I can't stop thinking about you," he murmured against my lips. "Should be focused on the job. But whenever I have a moment to breathe, you're all I think about."

I opened my eyes and found Gunnar's gaze piercing into me. "What do you think about me?"

"Your mouth." He kissed me. "Your voice." He kissed my neck. "The dimples on your lower back." He squeezed my ass. "Your dick." He cupped my hard cock.

I squirmed in his arms. "Tease."

"You asked," Gunnar retorted. He released me just long enough to tug my hoodie and shirt over my head. He sucked his lower lip in between his teeth, his gaze darting hungrily over my body. "Come here."

He led me to his bike.

"Really? On the bike, really?"

"Indulge me," Gunnar said, totally unembarrassed.

I didn't tell him that *he* was indulging *me*, in his skin-tight undershirt smelling of leather and oil. I threw my legs over his bike, straddling it, and leaned on the handlebars. "What do you think?"

Gunnar's gaze darkened. He stepped closer to the bike then tripped his hand down my bare spine, over my denim-covered ass, and then onto the leather of the seat. "Looks good."

"That's all?"

Gunnar's face did something strange, twisting into a pained, open expression I hadn't ever seen. "The things you fucking do to me."

I swung my legs to one side of the bike, sitting on it like a lady riding side-saddle. Gunnar stood between my legs and kissed me hard again. He wrenched off his undershirt and tossed it aside, revealing all of that tanned, muscular skin. I slid my hands over his chest, feeling his pleased hum reverberate through my fingers.

It was so easy to untie the arms of the jumpsuit from his bare waist. He wasn't wearing anything under the jumpsuit, which sent a sharp, unexpected thrill through me—I suddenly imagined myself working in the same garage, changing into that same canvas jumpsuit, knowing Gunnar's bare cock had rubbed against the fabric. I shoved the jumpsuit down around his hips and wrapped my hand tight around his cock without preamble.

Gunnar hissed my name into an open-mouthed kiss. I stroked him roughly.

"I'm gonna take you apart," he said in a voice more like a growl. Then he grabbed me by hips and maneuvered me, positioning me so I was bent over his bike, my legs spread. I couldn't deny how good it felt to be manhandled a little. To be reminded of exactly how strong Gunnar was.

He bent over me, his chest pressed to my bare back, his heart beating rabbit-fast, fast enough to rival my own. "That okay?" he asked gently.

"Fucking amazing." I rested my cheek on my crossed forearms. The smell of the leather seat flooded my senses.

Gunnar dropped kisses on my nape, a few with a teasing edge of teeth. The hard line of his cock pressed against my ass. The denim between us dulled the sensation enough to make me squirm, desperate for more.

"Quit teasing." I pushed back against him.

"I'm enjoying it," Gunnar countered, but he reached around to the button of my jeans and wrenched it open. He shoved my jeans down so they pooled at my ankles, exposing me, but still keeping my movement restricted.

"Don't move," Gunnar said. He stepped away, and the loss of his body against mine was so acute I actually—to my embarrassment—whined.

Moments later, he returned and smoothed his hands over my back. "Be patient." His calluses from riding, from shooting, from all the various physical tasks of his job, were rough on my skin, adding a sharp edge to the sweet sensation.

Then his hands moved to my ass, cupping my cheeks hard and squeezing.

From behind me, I heard the tell-tale click of a bottle of lube, and then he dragged a cool, wet finger down the full length of my crack, from my tailbone to my balls. I shuddered hard.

Gunnar reached around and stroked me teasingly. His grip was deliciously wet with lube.

Then he leaned down and kissed square between my shoulder blades as he pressed one finger inside.

God, it felt good. I exhaled hard into my arms, breathing through the stretch as Gunnar began to move his hands. It didn't take long until he had three fingers sliding easily in and out of my hole as lube dripped down my legs.

"Come on," I begged. "Come on, Gunnar."

At the sound of his name, Gunnar growled, fucking his fingers into me once more before pulling them out. Immediately I felt painfully empty. My body craved his, my cock hanging heavy and ridiculously hard.

Gunnar spread his hands across my lower back and I tipped my hips up towards him, a silent physical request. He slid his cock in between my ass cheeks, thrusting slowly. "God, you're gorgeous."

"You better get on with it." I turned my head enough to glower at him over my shoulder.

Gunnar grinned then leaned over me and kissed me hard on the mouth even though the angle was a little off. "Since you asked so nicely."

The head of his cock nudged at my hole. He didn't move.

But before he could thrust in, I pushed my hips backwards, taking his cock into my body. I exhaled hard into my arms, and Gunnar gasped in surprise, gripping my hips as he sunk deeper.

He leaned over me and dropped kisses over my back and neck, setting his teeth gently on my shoulder, and murmuring my name in my ear. Like he was just as overwhelmed as I was. And then he began to move.

He fucked me in deep, long strokes, his breath hot against my ear. My knees shook with the effort of holding me up, and he seemed to know, because he wrapped his arms around my middle to support me. I melted in his hold, supported by the bike and his raw strength. He grasped my cock, stroking me in time with his thrusts.

God, I was putty in his hands.

"I want to hear you come," he growled in my ear. "I want to feel you come on me."

He changed the angle of his thrusts slightly, going deeper, faster, and each stroke brushed against that sweet spot inside me that sent a jolt of pleasure through me.

"Close," I managed to say as I gripped the leather seat, gasping for breath as my orgasm built.

"Good," Gunnar said. "Let go."

It wasn't on command. But having him tell me to come did help push me over the edge. I came hard, hard enough to tense the muscles in my legs, lifting me onto my toes and writhing against the bike. It felt so fucking good, good like a strong drink or a fast ride. Pure, delicious relief.

Gunnar groaned my name. He pulled out and I felt his release land in hot, thick stripes across my lower back.

We stayed like that for a long few moments, breathing heavily. Gunnar's hands traveled over my back—the parts of it that weren't cum-stained, at least—tracing idle patterns.

"Don't move," he said. He disappeared again, and then I felt a rough rag cleaning me up.

"Oh," I said. "Thank you."

My brain felt slowed-down, foggy, like I was trying to emerge from a dream. Exhaustion weighed heavily on me, but it wasn't purely stress exhaustion now. I felt sanded down, smoothed out around the edges. I slowly lifted myself up to standing.

"Oof. Dizzy." I all but fell into Gunnar's arms.

He grinned. "Hold on to me, then."

He knelt down. I rested my hand on his shoulder for balance as he pulled my jeans back up around my hips. "There. You're decent."

"Your bike's not." I nodded at the bike. The opaque streams of my cum stood out against the matte black detailing.

"What?" Gunnar asked. "You don't like it? I think it's a nice addition."

"You're gross." I kissed him.

"I'll clean it before we leave tomorrow," Gunnar said.

Right. Reality came rushing back in. Tomorrow we had a long ride to Nevada. I leaned against Gunnar and tucked my face into the crook of his neck. What would happen after tomorrow? If we made it to Nevada with no trouble, captured Bane, and got justice for Ankh—what would happen afterwards?

Without the investigation keeping us together, would Gunnar have any reason to stay with me? We'd had to spend time together when he was my protective duty, and now, if this was the end of the investigation, would it be the end of whatever was going on between us? Sure, he didn't want to share me while he had me, but how long would he really want me *for*?

Once this job was finished, and everything was back to normal, could Gunnar really be happy in a regular, boring-ass relationship? Would he still want to spend time with me without the added excitement and responsibility of the investigation? Or would he get antsy, and start missing his freedom?

Now that I'd had this with Gunnar, I couldn't imagine my life without it. There was something between us, something more than just the sexual tension I remembered from my youth. We had a connection I couldn't have predicted. He didn't even realize the power he held over me. If he ended things with me now, my heart would be shattered. How could I ever go back to how things were now that I'd experienced this closeness?

I needed him to tell me exactly what we were doing—but I didn't know how to ask for it. And part of me, the petulant, needy part, didn't *want* to ask. I just wanted him to tell me he wanted me and only me. All of me. And if he wasn't going to do that, I needed to slow down. Just to ensure I'd survive the blow if everything dissolved.

But now wasn't the time for any of that. Now was the time to focus, to get justice for Dad and for Hell's Ankhor. All the rest would have to wait, and I'd have to push it out of my mind as best as possible.

"You all right?" Gunnar combed his fingers through my hair again, gently this time.

I closed my eyes, burning this moment into my memory. "Yeah," I said. "Tired. But good."

Chapter 22 - Gunnar

Twenty minutes south of Darlin's Brothel stood a small, empty cabin on a large plot of untamed land. The dominant club in western Nevada, the Desert Warriors, couldn't stop Bane and his crew from patronizing Darlin's. They hated the Vipers as much as we did, largely because the Vipers were often the source of the drugs that ripped like a tornado through the towns they ran, but they didn't have the manpower to do anything about it. Hell's Ankhor had a cordial relationship with the Warriors, and when I'd reached out to a contact to ask about a facility to use, they'd offered their property without hesitation.

Enemy of my enemy is my friend, and all that.

My phone lit up with a notification. "Coop and Siren have eyes on the Bane. He's got four Vipers with him as backup."

"Four's not so bad," Tex said.

Maverick nodded in agreement. "And the rest of the Vipers are still upstate?"

"According to Rebel, yes," Blade said. "If we're lucky, we can grab Bane without alerting the other Vipers present."

Raven was silent, lingering at the edge of the group. His pale face was pinched with nerves. Not fear, though. A rush of pride bloomed in my chest. He'd never been on a ride like this, but he was stoic, unafraid, and attentive: ready to do whatever the job required.

I only hoped it wouldn't require too much from him. Raven didn't need any blood on his hands. That was my job.

"All right, everyone knows their roles?" Blade asked. "Tex and Heath, you're in the truck. Tex, Heath, Mav, you'll join Siren watching the front door. Coop will join Gunnar, Priest, Raven, and me at the back door. If necessary we'll get Siren in there to try to urge him out, but ideally it won't be. Darlin's has private quarters behind the main building, and according to Rebel, Bane often partakes in those facilities."

Blade grimaced at the thought. "If our timing is right, we shouldn't have a problem. We need to be here. And we need to do this. But goddamn, I wish we didn't have to. I'd give anything to not be standing here in front of you now. I'm doing my best as your president, but we all know it wasn't my time. Ankh was taken from us."

The muscle in his jaw jumped as his clenched his teeth hard. "We can't change the past. But we can get Ankh the justice he deserves. Priest?" Blade ceded the floor.

"I got nothing to add," Priest said. "Except... Thank you. Thank you all."

"Let's get this fucker," Tex barked. "For Ankh."

"For Ankh," everyone repeated.

Raven's voice did not rise over the din. He nodded at me, a look of determination hardening his expressive features into a stony mask. Raven respected Blade as much as I did. Priest had chosen Ankh's successor well. Raven was flush with potential paths, but the club presidency was not one of them—at least not anytime soon. He hadn't wanted the position, and when Priest had offered it to Blade, Blade had balked at first, but immediately stepped up to the responsibility. With Priest as his vice president and me as his sergeant, we were doing as well as we could've hoped in the wake of a tragedy that had rocked the club to its foundation.

I hoped bringing Raven into this job wasn't a mistake. Raven wasn't naïve—he knew the reality of club life as well as I did—but he'd never delved into the violence of it. I knew he could handle himself. I just didn't want it to come to that.

Or maybe it was worse than that. Maybe I was rubbing off on him and had somehow been encouraging him to leave the smart-guy shit behind and get more and more embroiled in the violence of the club life.

If I'd learned anything in the military, it was this: For reasons good or bad, taking a life changed you irreversibly. It made you unfit for regular society. After what I'd done, I couldn't walk around in civilian life, grocery shop, chat to people at bars, and pretend to be normal. There was something inside me that regular citizens could feel emanating from me like an aura. In Hell's Ankhor, I didn't have to hide that part of myself.

But I didn't want this experience to change Raven. I didn't want him to feel cut off from a normal life. What if he changed his mind one day and wanted to leave this all behind? What if this experience—and his relationship with me—ended up being the thing that haunted him at night? The thing he wished he could undo?

The only thing worse than that, though, would be making that choice for him and not letting him come at all. I'd made that mistake too many times in the past to make it again. I had to trust him, no matter how much I'd rather just protect him from the entire world.

Dismissed, the club members filtered out of the cabin. I turned to grab my leather from where I'd tossed it carelessly against the folding chairs leaning against the wall. The space was bare of other furnishings, but it'd serve our purposes. A chair in the middle of the room was all I needed to make Bane sing.

I pulled my jacket on then turned to leave. The cabin was empty, save for Raven, leaning against the doorframe with his ankles crossed: a calculated imitation of casualness. "Everything good to go?"

"Course it is," I said. "I planned it."

His frown only deepened, but he directed it at his feet. Was he already having second thoughts? Well, it wasn't too late for him to cut out—I'd make sure that happened if he needed to.

I stepped closer. With two fingers, I touched his chin and tipped his face up towards mine. "What's wrong?"

"Nothing's wrong." The anxiety radiating off him was not assuaged. "I just…" He pressed his lips together. "Just watch yourself during this part, okay?"

His anxiety wasn't about the action itself—it was for *me*. He was worried I'd get hurt during the takedown. Warmth flooded me, and I couldn't resist gripping the collar of his leather jacket and pulling him in for a kiss. Only weeks ago he'd been cursing me out, avoiding me, punching me in the face. And now, due to some insane stroke of luck I certainly wasn't worthy of, he was pressed against me, worrying about my safety in a job I'd done for nearly two decades.

"Don't worry about me." I cradled his face in my hands. "It's gonna go fine, and it's gonna be over quickly. You'll get to see the master at work."

"Oh, the master?" Raven bit back a smile. "Master of what, staring at people threateningly?"

"In fact, that's exactly what I'm the master of." I kissed him again, a quick promise for later. "Let's do this. It'll be over before you know it."

That only seemed to ratchet Raven's anxiety up again. He turned to walk out the door and I took the opportunity to slip my hand into his back pocket and squeeze his ass. "You better watch your ass, too."

Raven squawked and swatted at me, but it seemed to have lifted his mood again, so I counted it as a victory.

Outside the cabin, the rest of the road crew was waiting, engines idling. Blade nodded at me, and I took my place in the lineup at his right.

We covered the distance between the cabin and the brothel and moved into our positions as Blade had instructed.

Darlin's was a squat cinderblock building in the middle of a scrubby patch of land just off the highway. Its immense neon sign advertised all the things a patron could obtain in the facility: SLOTS, FULL SERVICE BAR, GIRLS, GIRLS, GIRLS. Behind the main building, tiny square cabin-like structures stood in rows as if the bar was a campground.

"Private rooms," Blade said, motioning at the buildings.

"Bet it cuts down on hearing the guy in the room over," Coop said with a grimace.

I had a bad feeling about this place. I'd seen my fair share of brothels and bars in Nevada and LA alike, but this one was a little rundown, a little grimy, a little quiet. And any place frequented by Vipers likely had a sour history.

My phone lit up, and I skimmed Siren's message. "All clear at the front door. She says he's still inside."

"Time?"

"Just before three," I said.

"We'll give him until three-thirty, and then we'll send in Siren," Blade said.

Time passed painfully slowly in the dull expanse of desert. The brothel was well-lit inside and silent outside.

Moments before I was about to contact Siren, the back door opened. Bane staggered onto the back patio, hanging onto a slim woman who looked cold as soon as she stepped into the night.

I was a good enforcer, and a better sergeant, because I had the ability to pack my emotions away in a little box and set them aside to address after the job. Enforcing wasn't just brute-force violence: it was planning, risk assessment, and on-the-fly decision-making. Emotion-based thinking, rash thinking, was an easy way to endanger the club. I prided myself on my cool head in high-stress situations.

And yet as soon as I saw Bane, a cold bolt of rage sliced through me. We weren't hidden from view, that was impossible in the desert, but we were shadowed by the small cabins. I almost leaped into Bane's path to take him out myself. Only Blade's hand on my shoulder stopped me.

Raven looked like he might throw up.

With an exhale, I reined myself in. First and foremost this was just another job. Same as any other. Excess emotion would simply complicate things.

Bane managed to make his way away from the main building and toward one of the small standalone buildings. He tried to stuff the key into the lock, missing it repeatedly, and the girl laughed as she hung off his shoulder. It was a hollow, fake sound.

"Bane." Blade stepped out of the shadows. Priest, Coop, and I followed, with Raven close at my back.

Bane dropped his key, and then turned around with a slow grin breaking across his flat bulldog face. He gripped the girl by her waist and tugged her close to him.

"Blade," Bane said. "Nice to see you outside of your little home base. And you brought your friends."

"I've got some questions for you," Blade said. "Why don't you come with us?"

Bane pulled the girl in even tighter so she was halfway in front of him. Like a human shield. That fucking asshole. I clenched my fists.

"Now's not a great time." Bane's toothy grin was still plastered on his face. "Why don't you meet me in the city tomorrow and we'll talk like grown-ups?"

"Thanks for the offer, but I've got a better idea." Blade reached into his pocket.

"Watch it." Bane nodded at the girl.

With catlike speed, Blade pulled a knife from his pocket and threw it, perfectly accurate, into Bane's thigh. Bane barked in pain, lurching forward, and the girl pulled away.

I caught her by the arm as she tried to leave. "Can't let you go inside. Not yet."

The girl looked young, way too young, her wide brown eyes red-rimmed with pinprick pupils. Stimulants, probably. "I won't say anything."

"Gunnar. Let me." Raven took the girl by the upper arm and led her back to the main building. I let her walk. She relaxed minutely, and I saw her speaking to Raven as they stood by the back door.

Bane pressed on the wound, stabilizing the knife as blood oozed between his fingers. He snarled something unintelligible, likely a curse, and reached into his jacket.

Gun. I darted forward, slamming bodily into Bane before he could wrest the gun from its holster. I knocked into the knife, causing the blade to shift in the wound, and Bane grunted in pain. Then I gripped his wrist and pulled his empty hand from his jacket. After a few moments' struggle I had him restrained, my front to his back, his wrists restrained in my hands.

"Weapons," I said to Coop.

With a nod, Coop stepped forward and stripped Bane of his weapons—the handgun from his side and the knife from his pocket.

"You think you scare me?" Bane hissed. "You think it's a show of power to show up five-on-one? Cowardly fuckers, all of you."

Bane knocked his head back, and the back of his skull collided with my mouth. I must've bitten my tongue, as all my teeth were intact, but the coppery taste of blood still filled my mouth.

"Watch it, asshole," Coop said. He twisted the knife in Bane's leg.

Bane howled.

"That's enough," Priest said.

Coop stepped aside.

"Gunnar, let him go."

"Priest—"

"I said let him go!"

Priest's sharp tone shocked me into compliance. Against my better judgment, I released my grip on Bane.

He staggered forward a step. Bane laughed and straightened up and opened his mouth to speak. Then Priest threw one elegant, well-aimed punch. His knuckles connected with Bane's temple with a dull thud, and Bane dropped to the ground like a heap of roadkill.

"I won't hit a man who doesn't have the chance to hit back," Priest said.

Blade nodded, impressed. "Tie him up, Coop."

Once Bane's hands and wrists were zip-tied together, we threw him in the bed of the truck. No words were spoken. We all knew what was about to happen.

I caught Raven's eye. He just shook his head. His expression was stony and flat. Justice was close, yet Raven didn't look eager. He looked resigned. Ready. In silence, we rode side-by-side back to the secluded cabin.

Chapter 23 - Raven

Bane came back into consciousness with a gurgling groan. An immense bruise was blossoming on the side of his face, and Blade's knife was still embedded in his leg. I refused to risk removing it and having him lose too much blood before I could question him properly.

"You motherfuckers." Bane's voice was thick, like his mouth was full of cotton. "Fucking pansy club. You just wait."

"Wait for what?" I asked. "No one's coming to save you."

Bane said nothing. His eyes flickered around the room. There was nothing in the cabin except for the chair Bane was fastened to and my Hell's Ankhor family surrounding him.

He was afraid. A rich rush of satisfaction filled me at the sight. This was the man who'd killed my father. Who'd left him to bleed out alone on the asphalt of the town he loved. This was the man who'd taken the leader from our club and wounded us all. And finally, after all this time, I had him weak and helpless in front of me.

Staring down at Bane, an unfamiliar feeling gripped me, pinning my feet to the floor. It was beyond anger, beyond fear, beyond bloodthirsty revenge. Different than the anger that'd cut through me upon receiving the emails. Different than anything I'd ever felt before. It was isolating and intense, an icy sensation that coursed through me, wrapping cold tendrils around my heart and paralyzing any trace of empathy.

Hatred. It was pure, undiluted, and intoxicating; it sharpened my senses and muted my mind. I wanted Bane to suffer, and I wanted to be the one to cause it.

I backhanded Bane hard across the face. My knuckles connected with his jaw with a satisfying crunch. Bane grunted in pain. I followed it with a punch. His nose collapsed. Blood poured from his nostrils. I struck him in the face again, and again. His blood stained my hands. His face swelled and bruised, like I was an artist and his face my canvas. But my relentless assault did nothing to mitigate the icy cold hatred inside me—if anything, it started to thaw into an all-consuming rage.

"You killed him," I said.

Bane spit blood on the floor at my feet and said nothing.

I struck him once more and Bane's head lolled back before dipping forward, his eyes dazed.

"Raven." Someone behind me said my name. I barely heard it.

I moved to strike Bane again, but a hand caught my arm and pulled me away.

"Raven!" Gunnar pulled me backward. "That's enough."

"*Why*?" I struggled against Gunnar's grip on my shoulders. I felt wildly out of control, and I wasn't done with Bane. He needed to hurt as much as I did—to suffer as Dad had suffered. "Why did you kill my father?"

Bane stared at me for a long moment, his brow furrowed, and then realization dawned slowly on his face.

And he had the audacity to chuckle. "Is that what this is all about? You're Ankh's boy."

"You keep my father's name out of your mouth."

"So you're letting the kids come out and play with the road crews, huh, Blade?"

"Watch your tongue," Blade growled, "or I'll cut it out myself."

"He was weak. A fool," Bane said. "A stain on the reps of West Coast clubs. Not that you're any better, Blade, but no one knows who you are. I did you all a favor."

My stomach fell to my feet as if I'd suddenly been dropped from a great height.

This was really real. This was the man who had killed my father. And part of me had thought once I had him in front of me, once I'd been able to learn why it'd happened, and enact some sort of revenge, I'd feel better. But this monster didn't even care. And no amount of pain inflicted would bring Dad back. I'd known that, intellectually, but my heart hadn't known it.

Blade kicked Bane hard in his thigh, just inches away from where the knife was embedded. Bane groaned. He leaned forward and blood dripped from his broken nose onto the floor.

It didn't matter. It didn't matter how much Bane suffered, it didn't matter what information I learned. None of it fucking mattered. At the end of the day, Dad was still dead. I began to shake.

Gunnar tightened his grip on my shoulders. "You should wait outside."

I wrenched out of his hold. "What?"

He pulled me a few steps away from Bane, toward the door. The rest of the club's attention flicked between us and Bane. Gunnar caught Coop's eye. "Coop, you and Raven can step out for this part."

"What the fuck are you saying?" I shoved Gunnar in the chest hard, and he stumbled back a step. "You're trying to kick me out? I'm part of this road crew. And I need to be here for all of it."

"You don't." Gunnar stepped close again, undeterred. "You shouldn't. This—you're not an enforcer, Raven. It changes you."

"You think I can't handle it? You think I need you to tell me what I can and can't do?"

"No—that's not—"

"I don't need you to shelter me. I'm not a fucking kid. I thought, after everything, that you'd finally figured that out."

"It's not about that." Gunnar grimaced deeply. "You know it's not."

"Do I? Can you read my fucking mind some more? Tell me my own feelings?" I turned away. The anger inside me was burning, boiling, overwhelming everything else. "There's not a single other person in this room you'd ask to leave. You don't get to have it both ways. You can't treat me like this—like we're together—when we're not."

Gunnar glanced around the cabin. I could feel the rest of the club's eyes watching us.

My anger and hurt turned my stomach, making me nauseous. "Nothing's changed, huh? Still trying to play this off like it's nothing unless you need me to do something that will benefit you somehow. I'm sick of it. I'm sick of your games."

Suddenly, Gunnar grabbed me by my jacket and tugged me close to him, silencing me with a hard, possessive kiss. For a moment my body betrayed me, the kiss a balm on the angry wound inside me, and I melted against him.

Then my mind caught up, and I jerked away from Gunnar's touch. The cabin was silent, even with the club members around us, save for Bane's wet, half-conscious breathing. My anger stuttered into confusion. Why would he do that?

"Look at me." Gunnar's voice was low and sweet.

I met his gaze. The honesty I saw there hit me as hard as the kiss had.

"This isn't a game to me. I'm not fucking around. What I feel for you—it's—" his gaze searched my face like he'd find the words he needed— "It's real. I'll prove it every day for the next fifty years if I have to. But I'm not going anywhere."

Stunned, I could only remain frozen.

"Please don't do this," he said. "Don't be a part of this. It won't help."

I said nothing.

"I made my choice years ago." Gunnar gripped the back of my neck and squeezed, a rough, affectionate gesture. "You did your part. You found him. Your investigation is over. We all have a role in the club—let me play mine."

My breath came fast and shallow. My gaze flickered between Bane and the door. I wanted to believe Gunnar, but I was anxious, exhausted, and wild with anger. I still wanted to be part of Bane's punishment. Gunnar hadn't gotten to be sergeant on brawn alone—he knew how to be persuasive, strategic, and maybe he was just using my feelings toward him to get me out of the room. After all, he hadn't seemed to be in any rush to make our relationship public knowledge before now.

With a sigh, Pops stepped closer, nudging his shoulder against mine. "Gunnar's right," he said. "Your dad wouldn't want this for you. Wait outside. Let the enforcers do their job as well as you did yours."

I couldn't fight Pops. Not now. If he agreed, there must be some truth to what Gunnar was saying. I nodded, hugged Pops briefly but with as much force as I could muster, and slipped out the door.

* * *

Gunnar

Even with Raven gone, tension still simmered in the room. Blade looked to Priest for next steps, and once Blade did, I did as well. It was Priest's right to lead the interrogation.

The pain was clear in Priest's eyes, but the pain did nothing to crack the foundation of strength there. I knew seeing Raven in pain had gutted Priest. But his control over his emotions was unshakeable. If I was lucky, and worked my ass off, I hoped to one day be half the man Priest was.

But today, I'd make Bane suffer. Not just for Ankh, and not just for me. For Priest, and for all of the Hell's Ankhor members who had suffered from Ankh's loss.

And for Raven.

Even though Raven had been raised in the club, and was in some ways more immersed in it than anyone else, he was still distanced from the real brutality of it. And I wanted to keep it that way. Raven's reaction when he'd seen Bane had scared me—he'd gone cold, flat, so unlike the warm, snarky man I'd fallen in love with. His anger was warranted, but it'd consumed him quickly and powerfully like a wildfire. If he wanted to start enforcing, that was one thing—there were ways to do that, a process to ease him in. But he didn't need to start like this. And I knew it wasn't what he really wanted; he didn't have that kind of violence in him.

Killing had changed me. The years after Afghanistan had been some of the hardest of my life. I'd learned to do it well, though, and I'd eventually regained my sense of self, but it hadn't been easy. Even if Raven was angry at me, it was worth it to prevent him from killing Bane. I'd never say it to his face, but Raven was sensitive. He felt deeply and passionately, and in the throes of anger it was clear he thought killing Bane would lessen his pain. He had no way of knowing killing would only make it worse.

Even if Raven wanted nothing to do with me after this, it was worth it, to keep his hands clean of Bane's death.

And I didn't regret the kiss. I knew once this was all over, I'd have some explaining to do, especially to Blade. But Raven had to know I wasn't fucking around, and that I had his best interests in mind now—truly, not like I'd pretended to before. Raven knowing that I was in his corner was all what mattered.

"Blade." Priest's voice was low and dangerous. "Two knives."

Blade pulled two knives from his person—he always seemed to have about five more than I expected—and handed them to Priest.

Priest gripped the first gleaming knife by its handle. "This one's for me. And this one—" he passed the other to me "—is for Raven."

My heart flipped in my chest. It wasn't quite approval, but it was close. I accepted the knife with a nod.

I slapped Bane hard across the chest, open-handed, and he blinked back into reality. Once he realized where he was, fear bloomed on his face. The dark, hungry part of me loved the sight. I stood behind him and tilted his head up towards Priest. I pressed the sharp edge of my knife into Bane's throat.

"I'm going to need some information from you," Priest said. "We can do it the easy way, or the hard way."

"I'm not telling you fucking pansies anything," Bane growled. "You'll pay for this."

"Hard way, then."

I pressed the blade harder into Bane's throat, slicing a long, shallow cut into his flesh. His breath quickened.

"Why'd you kill Ankh?" Priest asked in a mild, bored tone. That level of control was almost spooky.

Bane spit at him.

The bloody wad of mucus landed on Priest's jeans with a wet splat. Priest sighed. "Come on, Bane. Don't be childish."

Instead of adding a fresh cut to Bane's body, he simply reached down to the knife still embedded in Bane's thigh and twisted it hard.

Bane howled, thrashing in the chair, and my knife cut deeper into his neck. He gasped and stilled. "Fuck! Jesus fucking Christ! You think it was something fucking complicated, you moron? Crave hated Ankh. He was always ranting about your pansy-ass president and your pansy-ass club, and how he wanted them out of the way. I wanted the VP position, and guess what, I got it!"

Priest's expression was stony, but the furious pain in his eyes was clear.

"Your president was just a pawn in the Vipers' game. Same as your new president's fuck toy." Bane shot a bloody grin towards Blade.

Blade was nearly vibrating with restrained anger, but he didn't move. He wouldn't, not until Priest was finished.

"Don't worry," Priest said. "We have plenty more questions for you."

He nodded at me, and we switched places.

I stood in front of Bane and flipped my knife in my hand a few times. "I'm not as nice as my boss. So I'm not going to give you an option."

I grabbed his wrists, still zip-tied together, and pressed the tip of the knife under his thumbnail. It wasn't enough to hurt, it was just a little edge of pressure. "Why don't you tell me why you've got a traitor in your ranks communicating with us?"

"There ain't any traitors," Bane snapped. "Vipers are loyal."

"Vipers don't know a fucking thing about loyalty." I pushed the knife under his thumbnail.

Bane screamed.

I kept my grip tight on his wrist as Bane thrashed and howled. Then I took his forefinger in hand and placed the tip of the knife beneath the nail.

"I've got nine more," I said. "Then I'll move to your toes."

"Crave's losing his fucking marbles," Bane said, the words coming in a rush. "That's it."

"That's it? If Crave's unreliable, why do the Vipers want our territory so badly?" I pushed the knife in slowly, sliding it under the nail, and Bane screamed again.

"Trafficking!" Bane howled. "It's for the trafficking! Fuck! Fucking hell. That's where the bulk of our money comes from. Getting girls for the brothels. Elkin Lake is the hub we need between LA, San Francisco, and Vegas. If we have Elkin Lake, we can triple our operation and get fucking rich. And once Crave's gone, and I'm president, the Vipers will have real fucking leadership."

"Disgusting." I looked to Priest. He shook his head.

"We have what we need," Priest said.

I stepped back, and to my surprise, Priest did as well. He nodded at Blade, and then returned the knife to Blade's hand.

Blade hesitated. "Priest."

"Finish it," Priest said. "For Ankh."

Bane thrashed in the chair. "No—I told you everything—you'll pay for this. The Vipers will come for you."

"They can try." Blade lifted his knife. It gleamed in the moonlight.

Chapter 24 - Gunnar

I braced my hands against the wall of the shower and tilted my head forward. The water sluiced down my back, hot enough to redden my skin. The water swirled pink and grimy down the drain.

Bane's blood swirling down the drain would be the last I ever saw of him. The sun would be rising soon, and I'd have a few hours to sleep off the stress of the job. The familiar unnerving exhaustion was creeping over me, stalking forward like a predator.

After the deed was done, Raven had been still and quiet, like he was in a trance. He'd hardly looked at me as I'd left the cabin, and he hadn't spoken to me as we'd ridden home. I'd tried once or twice to get close, hoping to comfort him, but he'd stepped briskly away each time, and when I'd tried to pull my bike up next to his to offer silent solidarity, he'd gunned ahead, leaving me behind.

Had I finally pushed him too far? I didn't regret asking him to leave the cabin, but had I refused Raven his agency? Did Raven think I'd kept him from his vengeance, that I was still treating him like a little kid who couldn't handle club life, instead of trying to make sure the man I loved didn't make a horrible mistake that he'd regret?

Or had finally realized who I was? Did he finally see the capability for violence inside me and decided it was too much, too dirty, too broken? The ease with which I'd tortured Bane... It'd turn any sane person away.

Before I could fully work myself into a panic, a cool draft ran over my back as the shower curtain opened. I didn't move. The touch sliding over my back was so familiar now, and the tenderness of the touch set my knees shaking. Raven folded his body over mine, his chest to my back, and kissed my neck.

"Raven." My voice was slightly strangled. I didn't regret the ways I'd hurt Bane—I didn't even regret the ways I'd enjoyed it. But it didn't feel right to be close like *this* with Raven so soon afterward. Like there was still some monstrous part of me I had to pack away before I was deserving of his touch.

"I'm sorry," Raven murmured into my neck.

"What for?" The heat of the water and the heat of his body combined had me nearly melting against him.

"I'm sorry I said those things about you. I was just—I was so angry. I wanted to hurt him. Part of me still wishes I had."

I shifted, standing straight up and turning around. "Before you left, I told you it'd change you. The killing."

I'd spent so many years hiding from Raven and pushing him away. But I knew that I wanted this—I wanted to be with him. And maybe what I'd done in my past made me unworthy of his love. For as long as I'd known Raven, I'd been trying to make choices that did right by him, even when he was just a goofy kid looking up to one of the older guys in the club, but my past had hung over me like a shadow.

So now, I had to tell him the truth, and let him decide what was right. If the awful things I'd done turned him away from me—so be it. But no more games, no more hiding. I'd offer him the darkest part of myself. And if he rejected me... At least I could say I'd finally been honest. At least I'd know that it wasn't just my fears holding us back.

I leaned against the cool tile of the shower and pulled Raven into my arms, embracing him, so the water hit both of us. And so I didn't have to see his face when I spoke.

"I said it changes you because it *does*. You know I was in the Marines before I joined the club."

Raven nodded. His wet hair brushed against my jaw.

"When I was deployed, I..."

I flexed my fingers against his back. This might be the hardest thing I'd ever done—definitely the scariest. But if Raven wanted to be with me, he deserved to know what I'd done. All this time I'd been waiting for him to come to his senses and find a guy as smart, kind, and strong as he was.

Now I could finally admit I wanted that guy to be me—but this ugliness was part of me, too. And we couldn't get around that.

"I had this CO," I started again. "He was—a loose cannon. Itchy trigger finger. And I was just a kid. Couldn't even drink yet. My squadron was ordered to move to another base. No one knew what the fuck was going on, no one ever did. Our route took us right through this small town."

Raven was still, still leaning against me. The pounding of the water kept me grounded, kept me from drifting too deep into my memories and ending up back in the hot desert sand of Afghanistan.

"So we're in the Humvee driving through the town when all these bullets come flying in from everywhere. Like they're coming from every building. It's chaos immediately. My comms guy gets shot next to me. Boom, dead. I get grazed in the arm. Once it lets up, my CO is on the radio going insane. He says he's got eyes on the shooter. So now I'm out of the Humvee, my CO is still screaming orders. And I follow orders, so I go into the house he directs me to, and there's a guy in there."

After all these years, his face was still burned in my memory. His wide-eyed fear.

"So I shot him."

His body, crumpled on the floor.

"And there was a kid there." Suddenly I couldn't stand to have Raven close to me.

I pushed him away and climbed out of the shower. I grabbed a towel and wrapped it around my waist and stood on the bathmat, breathless and awkward, not sure if I should leave, or stay, or forget this ever happened. But the least I could do was finish what I'd started.

"Couldn't be older than ten. And he saw me do it. Shot his dad right in front of him." I exhaled hard. "Later, my CO said they'd caught the shooters. I don't know—I don't know if this guy was one of them. I never will. He could've just been a civilian. An innocent. Either way, I killed him. And his son watched."

I thought I might fall over, the grief and pain and fear weighing me down. "I've only ever told your dad this before."

"Gunnar," Raven murmured. "Get back in here."

"How can you—*I'm no better than Bane.* I stood there and acted all high and mighty tonight, like I was enacting justice, when I deserve the same treatment. I did the *same exact thing* to that poor kid that the bastard did to you."

"Gunnar!" Raven barked. It should've been ridiculous, Raven acting all snippy and commanding while still standing naked in the running shower, but his serious gaze knocked the wind out of me. "I said get back in here."

I dropped the towel and did as I was told.

Raven lathered the soap in his hands. He took my hands in his and washed them meticulously, focusing on the joints and my nails where the dirt and blood had caked into grime.

"You are nothing like Bane," he said after a while, with an edge of anger. "You were a soldier. And now you're my sergeant. And you never were, and never could be, a murderer."

I couldn't meet his eyes.

"What happened in Afghanistan—that's on your CO. It's not on you. You were just a kid. You were trying to do what was right."

"You make it sound so simple."

"It is." Raven's gentle touch moved up my arms to my shoulders. The suds eased his touch, and he kneaded the knots in my shoulders. Tension bled from my body. He skated his skillful hands down my chest, washing me with care. Then he slowly lowered himself to his knees and delicately washed my feet, and then my calves.

In all my years I'd never been touched like this. Never with such care and tenderness. I didn't think I deserved it now. But Raven knew all of me now, and I was done pushing him away.

Raven tipped his head forward and rested his forehead against my hip. He moved his hands up my outer thighs, half-washing, half-massaging.

"I get it now," he said. "Even without knowing about Afghanistan. I get why you didn't want me to be there."

I carded my fingers through Raven's wet hair. I was dizzy from the relief of telling him the truth, and that he was still here.

"I was so blinded by my own anger," Raven said. "Even with the whole club behind me, I got it in my head that I had to do everything. That I wouldn't have really avenged Dad if I wasn't the one to kill Bane—that it was all on me. But me killing Bane won't bring Dad back."

"I'm—really glad you realized that. But I'm sorry it didn't make it better."

"And *I'm* sorry about those things I said in the cabin," Raven said.

"You don't have to be sorry."

"But I am." Raven kissed my hip. "You meant it? You're serious about this? About us?"

I reached down to touch his cheek, guiding his gaze to mine. "I mean it. If you'll have me, I'm yours. All of me. And if you don't want this—I won't hold you back."

"Of course I want this," Raven said. "I want you. I've wanted you for almost as long as I can remember. I just—I'm still insecure."

"That's my fault."

"It's not."

"It is."

Raven laughed, the bright sound surprising me and making me grin. "It doesn't matter. I just wanted to tell you, because it might be hard for me to accept love sometimes." He paled slightly. "Or. You know. A relationship."

"You had it right the first time."

He blinked those deep blue eyes up at me. All it took was one look from Raven to drag these truths from me.

"I love you," I said.

His breath caught. "I love you, too." He dropped more kisses on my hips, nuzzling me affectionately.

"I'm sure I'll fuck up a lot," I said. "But I'm not going anywhere. Not ever."

"Gunnar," Raven murmured. "Let me blow you."

Raven's low voice sparked desire deep inside me. I leaned back against the shower wall, the cool tile supporting me as my knees weakened under his touch.

"You can do whatever you want with me," I said.

The grin he shot at me was mischievous and playful—a side of Raven I felt like I hadn't seen since all this began. That smile felt like coming home.

Raven hummed and kissed my abs, exploring the divots of the muscles with his tongue and teeth. His small, slim hands wrapped around my cock and began to jerk me off slowly and steadily, until I was fully hard. Then Raven ran his tongue up the length of my cock, sending a white-hot rush of pleasure through me.

I groaned and wound both my hands into his wet hair. Raven slid one hand around to my ass and squeezed hard. With the other hand, he gripped my cock hard by its base and kissed the tip teasingly. I sucked in a breath. A bead of my precum caught on his lower lip and his pink tongue darted out to taste it.

"You'll be the fucking death of me." My head knocked back against the tile. If I kept watching the show Raven was putting on, I'd come before he even got his mouth on me.

"That's not the idea," Raven joked. Then, to my immense relief, he wrapped his lips around my cock and sucked hard.

The pleasure was rich, immediate, and it washed away my anxieties far better than the hot shower. Raven sucked my cock down as far as he could, and then hummed in pleasure, the vibration of the sound a shocking sensation that made me gasp and grip his hair tightly.

Then he began to move, slowly and steadily sucking me down, his hand jerking whatever he couldn't fit in his mouth.

Pleasure roared through me. And it was different this time. Different because I wasn't plagued with thoughts of Raven leaving, or worse, me ruining him.

This was the start of something, instead of the end.

I tugged him off my cock and dragged him to his feet. The water was beginning to cool down. I kissed him hard on the mouth, licking the taste of myself from his mouth, and Raven moaned into the kiss.

"Bed," I demanded.

We clambered out of the shower and I took a few delicious moments to towel Raven off, wiping the droplets of water from his pale, angular shoulders, the divots of his lower back, and his long, elegant legs. His dark hair wet and slicked back made his rich blue eyes stand out starkly. His cock hung heavy between his legs, but I didn't touch it, not yet.

"Go lie down," I said. "Face down."

Raven grinned and kissed me, quick and happy, before darting out of the bathroom into my bedroom.

I dried off and took a moment to gaze in the mirror.

How did a beat-up old dog like me ever get so lucky? After everything I'd done, all the blood on my hands, all the mistakes and the fuckups... I still somehow, against all odds, found love. Just experiencing love from a distance would've been enough. It would've been enough to watch Raven grow and blossom and leave and find love with someone else. I'd been ready for that. I'd been more than happy to accept that as more than I deserved.

And by some fucking miracle he wanted to be with *me*. I wouldn't ever take it for granted. I'd be worthy of his love. I'd work for it every day.

In the bedroom Raven was sprawled on his front like I'd instructed, his cheek pillowed on his folded forearms. He peered over his shoulder at me, grinned, and then dropped his cheek back down.

"Hey there, gorgeous." I crawled onto the bed and straddled his thighs then skated my hands down his back and over the curve of his ass.

Raven hummed in pleasure and wriggled beneath me. "Don't tease me. Not now."

"But I love teasing you." I leaned down and kissed his shoulder.

"I know you do," Raven said, craning his neck towards me. I took the hint and kissed him hard on the mouth. "But don't you also love fucking me?"

"Fuck, Raven," I murmured into the kiss. "The mouth on you."

"You didn't answer the question."

"I love you," I said. "And I love fucking you."

Raven laughed and wriggled harder. "Touch me."

Warmth flooded me. Is this what sex could be? Passionate, loving—and fun? As silly and mischievous as Raven himself? I leaned over to my nightstand and fished out my lube.

I worked Raven open with my fingers until he was gasping and sighing into the sheets as he pushed his hips back against my hand.

"Come on, Gunnar," he murmured. "I want you. Please."

I couldn't resist him, not when his voice was so breathy and desperate. I stroked myself a few times, just enough to get my hard cock slick, and then pressed the head of my cock to his hole.

I slid into him slowly, steadily, one long push until I was buried inside him. As I did so, I stretched out on top of him, my chest to his back, my mouth on his neck, breathing hard against his sweat-slick skin. The full-body contact was delicious—every hitch of his breath resonated through me, every moan and gasp, every clench of his muscles vibrated all the way to my bones.

I moved inside him, pulling out just enough to thrust back in deep and hard, and Raven pushed his hips backwards to take me deeper. He cried my name as he matched my thrusts, his cock grinding into the mattress.

I kissed him again over his shoulder, awkward and messy, and fucked into that sweet, tight heat harder and faster. The pleasure built fast and sudden, and it only took a few more strokes until I was coming hard inside him.

"Oh, God," Raven moaned at the sensation of my cum inside him, squirming against me like he couldn't get enough. "Please, Gunnar, I'm so close."

I pulled out and slid my fingers back inside Raven, so easy and smooth after how hard I'd fucked him. He gasped as I found the place inside him that made his whole body tense with pleasure.

"That's right, baby," I murmured into his ear. "Come for me."

Raven came hard. His back arched beautifully as he spilled onto the sheets, and then collapsed boneless.

I pulled out gently, and Raven shuddered at the sensation. I kissed my way down his back, finishing with a little bite at the swell of his ass.

Raven groaned wordlessly, sinking into the mattress. "I need another shower now."

I tugged him into my arms and kissed him hard. Raven clung to me, melting into the embrace.

"In a hurry?" I asked.

"No way."

Our eyes met and the depth of feeling I saw in Raven's dark blue eyes made my head spin.

"I love you." I was addicted to saying it—it felt as good as holding Raven in my arms. "Raven, baby, I love you."

"I love you, too," Raven said. "Now get up. I'm in the wet spot."

Chapter 25 - Raven

Raucous laughter echoed through Ballast.

"Eventually," Pops said through his own laughter, "we were able to drag his bike out of the ravine, and the kid helped us. Ankh wasn't even mad! The kid was, like, thirteen, and he'd managed to hotwire the thing! Honestly, I think Ankh was impressed and had to try really hard not to recruit him on the spot."

Pops sighed and shook his head good-naturedly. "That damn kid is a Desert Warrior now."

"No fucking way. Who?" Blade asked.

"Oh, hell no. That information is confidential."

I laughed, knocking my shoulder against Gunnar's. We were leaning against Ballast's bar, with the rest of the club members lounging at tables or at the bar as well. We'd spent the evening sharing stories and memories of Dad; some were funny, some were sad, but all were as welcome and comforting as an embrace.

We'd had a funeral for Dad after his death, but this memorial felt like a completion. Dad would've wanted it to be like this: a celebration of his life, not a mournful affair. It'd been painful, but the club had carried me through. It hadn't fixed anything, but it helped to know that Bane had paid for his crimes. But the Vipers were still out there, and now we knew for sure they were engaged in human trafficking. I took a sip of my beer.

"Hey," Gunnar said. "You all right?"

"Yeah," I said. "Just... I'm ready to get back to work. Bane's out of the picture, but that doesn't mean the Vipers are any less dangerous."

"I know." Gunnar took my hand and tugged me to the edge of the crowd, leaning against the far wall for a modicum of privacy. "There's more on your mind, though, I can tell."

"The girl Bane was with, at Darlin's? Before she went back inside, she asked what we were going to do with Bane. I told her not to worry about it. She almost started crying right there, Gunnar, she was so grateful. She said she'd gotten into trouble with some dealers in Reno and had ended up working at Darlin's in order to pay off a debt."

"He was using his own trafficking victims," Gunnar said darkly. "That fucking bastard."

"Yeah," I said. "I'd bet most of the girls at the brothel are trafficked. Who knows how many other places have trafficked workers? And as long as Crave is in control, it's going to keep happening."

"I know," Gunnar said. "This isn't over. When we're done, there won't be any Vipers left. It's not just personal anymore, it's a matter of right and wrong. We're going to war."

Gunnar looked so serious, so sure of our victory, that I couldn't help but believe him. We'd wipe the Vipers clean off the map. Bane was just the beginning.

With human trafficking involved, the rules had changed. If it came to light that Rebel was involved in the trafficking, he was doomed. Regardless of how he'd helped us, and regardless of his connection to Logan, I couldn't shake the feeling that Rebel was playing us, somehow. He was hiding something, and if we were going to continue using his information, I had to figure out what it was.

"All right, all right, I'm not going to give a big speech," Blade said in his booming voice. "Just a quick one."

Gunnar and I moved back toward the group. Blade was standing on a chair with a pint in his hand. Behind me, Gunnar wrapped his arm around me and pulled me close. With his solid body behind mine and his arms around me, I knew whatever cruel endeavors the Vipers had in the works, Hell's Ankhor could stop them.

"Brothers, sisters. Thanks for being here. I know you all miss Ankh." Blade paused for the murmurs of agreement. "God knows I do. But he'd be fucking proud of us. Proud of each and every one of you. Our enforcers didn't just get vengeance—they got justice. And in the course of this investigation, we've found the rotten truth of what the Vipers are involved in. Ankh wouldn't want this happening on our doorstep, and we won't let it happen. As a club, our first and most important goal now is to bring an end to the Vipers' trafficking.

"But for tonight, let's celebrate. Here's to Ankh. Our president."

Blade raised his glass and the rest of the club followed. Gunnar and I both raised our glasses before taking a sip, Gunnar keeping his arm tight around me.

Blade hopped off the chair and immediately slung his arm around Logan's shoulder, tugging him close to his side. They ambled up to us.

"Gone soft, huh, Gunnar?"

"You're one to talk," Gunnar said warmly.

"I'm happy for you," Logan said.

"See?" Gunnar said. "That's how to be nice. Take notes, Blade."

"Logan's nice enough for both of us."

"That's true," Logan and I said simultaneously.

Pops walked up next to Blade and took a long sip of his beer while gazing at Gunnar. Behind me, Gunnar stiffened, but didn't unwind his arm from around my waist.

"I take it you boys have sorted things out? Is this the way of things now?"

"Yessir," Gunnar said. "If that's all right with you?"

An amused smirk spread across Pops' face, his bright eyes sparkling. "Are you asking for permission to date my son?"

"Wha—" Gunnar's hand covered my mouth before I could even get out a full word. I rolled my eyes.

"Yes, sir," Gunnar said. "That's what I'm asking."

Pops nodded, clearly happy with Gunnar's respectful request.

"You don't need it," he said. "As I'm sure Raven was about to tell you. But you have it—I've been proud to call you my son for years. This will just make it more official."

I licked Gunnar's hand.

"Raven! Gross!" He shoved me towards Logan. Laughing, I straightened up and grinned at Pops and Gunnar.

Pops burst into laughter. "I was going to shake your hand, but I think I'll pass."

Instead, Pops pulled Gunnar into a brief, hard hug, thumping him on the back. As they broke apart, Pops glanced between us both. "Your Dad would be so fucking happy."

***

Later that night, back at the clubhouse, Gunnar followed me into my room and pushed me up against my bedroom door.

"I can't believe your Pops approves of us," he said, still half-shocked.

"You really thought he wouldn't?"

"I guess so," Gunnar said. "I guess I keep expecting to wake up from this dream."

"You're a better man than you think you are."

"You make me want to be better. You make me feel like I have a future."

I shivered. "You do. We both do. Together."

Gunnar cradled my face in his hands and shook his head slightly, like he couldn't believe I was real. He kissed me slowly; it was a long, lingering kiss, one that left me melting against him. I wrapped my arms around him and skated my hands down his muscled back to squeeze his ass through his tight jeans. Gunnar groaned into the kiss.

I slid my hands under his shirt and caressed his lower back. I'd never get enough of this—Gunnar shuddering under my touch and murmuring my name into our kisses.

We broke apart just long enough to shed our clothes, and then Gunnar pulled me onto the bed. I landed with a surprised laugh half on the bed and half on his chest.

He hummed and pulled me close. With his hard, muscled body against me, I couldn't help but push closer and closer until the hard line of his cock pressed into my hip.

Our kisses were so messy they were really closer to shared breathing. I reached between us and gripped Gunnar's cock, stroking it a few times, until Gunnar caught my wrist.

His eyes flicked open and his gaze met mine. He guided my hand lower, and lower, and opened his legs for me.

"Yeah? What do you want?" I wanted to hear him say it. I'd never get sick of it.

"I want you to fuck me," he murmured, comfortable and unselfconscious, punctuated with a kiss.

I leaned back enough to watch myself slide my fingers, slick with lube, slowly into Gunnar's tight heat. He grimaced against the intrusion at first, and I continued to drop kisses along his jaw, neck, and shoulder, my free hand stroking circles idly on his hip. It didn't take long before his face softened into an open expression of pleasure, his mouth open for his sweet gasping breaths, and his hands clasped in the sheets.

No one else got to see him like this—ever. These moments were for us alone.

"Quit stalling," he demanded.

"Only since you asked nicely."

I pulled my fingers out of him, and he sighed deeply at the loss. Then I pushed at his broad shoulders, until he got the hint and rolled onto his side. I pressed against him, my back to his chest, and the contact was intoxicating. I stifled a moan as the head of my cock pressed against his hole.

"That's right," Gunnar groaned, reaching his arm back to snag in my hair and tug me close. "Good boy. Come on."

I set my teeth in his shoulder gently. The pet name sent a little thrill through me. Then with a slow exhale, I pressed into him, slowly and steadily, until my cock was buried inside him.

I wrapped my arms around him like I could sink even deeper. Then I began to shift my hips, just a little, and Gunnar growled in approval and shifted his hips to meet mine.

Soon I was fucking him in slow, deep strokes; it was a luxurious, all-the-time-in-the-world kind of sex, the kind that made sweat drip down my nape, the kind that made Gunnar exhale hard every time my cock slid over that sweet spot inside him. My orgasm built slowly, and I let it stay slow, keeping the pace steady and teasing until Gunnar was pressing hard against me, begging for more.

"Me first," I murmured into his shoulder, and something about that made Gunnar shiver.

"Then do it," Gunnar said. His grip tightened in my hair. "Come in me."

Knowing Gunnar wanted it was enough to push me over the edge. A few deep, powerful strokes was all it took before I fell into my orgasm, gasping his name as I came inside him. Then, without pulling out, I reached for his cock and stroked him hard and firm. His orgasm followed soon after mine, the power of it making him toss his head back hard, like he'd been punched. I jerked him slowly through the aftershocks, until he pushed my hands away, and then I settled for rubbing the slick streaks of cum into his chest.

Once I caught my breath, I cleaned us up just enough to sleep in peace.

Gunnar lay flat on his back on the bed, his arms folded behind his head, so deeply content he was already dozing off.

I snuggled up against him. The fact that we were here together—sharing this moment after so many years spent pushing each other away and trying to pull each other back in—

was incredible to me. I couldn't get enough of him, of how safe and right and taken care of I felt with him.

"You're my home, Gunnar," I murmured, and kissed the side of his neck, right at the center of his Hell's Ankhor tattoo. "I would've been lost in all this mess without you. You're—you're my anchor."

Gunnar kissed me back, half asleep. He didn't need to speak for me to know he felt the same.

Chapter 26 - Rebel

Somehow I found myself yet again standing on the cold concrete floor of Ankhor Works. This was really getting fucking stupid. I had to figure out a way to get the Hell's Ankhor inner circle to meet with me on neutral territory—eventually someone back in the Nest would catch on to my trips to Elkin Lake.

It'd been a week since Bane went missing. I should've known killing Bane wouldn't have been enough to appease Hell's Ankhor. Blade and his cronies were still committed to war. And I couldn't really blame them—if I were in Blade's shoes, I'd likely do the same thing.

"Just listen to me," I said, holding out my arms like I was trying to placate an angry dog. "You can't wage war yet."

Blade glanced around at his inner circle. It was a smaller group than last time—just Blade, his sergeant-at-arms, two other enforcers (the woman, and the guy who'd stolen my knife last time), and my brother.

"How about you go fuck yourself?" the woman asked casually.

"Siren has a point," Blade said. "Instead of telling us what to do, how about you eat shit?"

I wiped my hand down my face. I was fucking exhausted. I looked at Logan and found nothing but contempt on his face.

I'd always thought I'd been doing the right thing. Over the years, I'd done my best to draw our father's attention away from Logan and onto myself: taking the brunt of the beatings when I could, and acting as Dad's heir in the club so Logan could escape into a new life. When I'd convinced Dad to let Logan leave for nursing school, I'd thought Logan would finally be free.

I should've known Dad had his own motivations, though. Once Logan had nursing experience, Dad was more interested in using his skills to patch up Vipers than letting Logan have his own life. So instead of Logan getting out, he got pulled deeper into the club.

But even if Logan hated me, at least he was safe now, and far away from Dad.

"This is bigger than our little rivalry," I said. I was nearing a breakthrough, and I really didn't need a club war to start complicating things further. "There's more at stake."

"Like what?" The guy speaking was the guy who'd patted me down last time. He was tall and broad-shouldered, with dark skin and eyes so dark they were almost black.

This was the other complication I wasn't happy about—this Hell's Ankhor enforcer whose eyes seemed to burn holes into my chest. The memory of his immense hands patting me down roughly, moving up my inner thighs, was one I'd returned to more than a few times when I was alone.

"Like a nationwide trafficking ring," I admitted. These guys had their hearts set on justice. Maybe if they realized standing down for a little while would lead to an even bigger takedown, they'd do it.

"Why the fuck do you care about that?" the sergeant-at-arms asked.

The enforcer barked a laugh. He crossed his arms over his chest, and I couldn't help but notice his biceps, and the lean muscle standing out in his forearms. He was intimidating, but I was used to club guys trying to scare me. That dark, serious gaze sparked something in my gut, and it certainly wasn't fear.

"Because he's a cop," the enforcer said.

My stomach suddenly dropped to my feet. How the fuck had this guy figured it out? I'd been so careful all these years—ingratiating my way deep into the club while simultaneously working with the local law enforcement, balancing everything so carefully that Dad didn't suspect a thing.

This guy had only just met me. Yet he threw that out like it was obvious.

"What? Coop, what are you talking about?" Blade's stunned gaze darted between me and the enforcer.

The enforcer—Coop—shrugged. "Sorry, is it not fucking obvious? Why else would he be telling us this?"

"Luke." Logan's voice was very small. All the color had drained from his face. "Is it true? You're a *cop*?"

I couldn't risk this job. If I didn't admit the truth, there was a possibility that Hell's Ankhor would start running their mouths about their suspicions, and word would filter back to the Vipers. My only option was to get them to agree to keep their mouths shut so I could bring the Vipers down from within.

"Look—I'm getting really close on this job. I just need a little more time to collect the evidence that ties the Vipers to the other clubs across the country that are trafficking. If I do, I can put them away for a long time—all of them. But you can't go to war, not yet. If they're killed before I get what I need, I won't be able to bag the other traffickers."

"Oh my god," Logan said. He staggered backwards, and Blade caught him, steadying him on his feet. "All this time. All this time I thought I was alone. And this entire time, you were the *law*."

The look of betrayal on Logan's face felt like a punch in the chest. "Logan, I—"

"Don't fucking talk to me," Logan said. "Don't try to explain it. Just don't."

"Nothing's more important than the job, right, Rebel?" Coop's voice was thick with vitriol. His tone seemed to shock the other enforcers. "There's only one thing worse than a rotten club— and that's a dirty pig. Disloyal, lying, and cruel to the core. Just like a corrupt cop to let his family suffer in the name of the job."

I said nothing. I wouldn't fight them on this. I'd let the club lay into me as much as they wanted, as long as they agreed to back off on the war.

"Blade. Just give me a little more time," I said.

Blade rubbed his temples.

"All right," he said, after a long, considering pause. "Just to connect the Vipers to the larger trafficking rings. Once you have your evidence, or whatever the fuck, I'm raining hell on that club."

The rage in Blade's eyes made it clear I might be included in that. But it was a risk I had to take. If everything went well, they'd see they'd made the right decision. And I was counting on Hell's Ankhor's righteous foundation to save my life when the time came. They didn't kill innocents.

Crave found that to be a weakness—it kept Hell's Ankhor from expanding as rapidly as other clubs. But it gave them a powerful reputation in other ways, and a sturdy foundation to build upon. Their moral base was their strength—and there was no weakness in the vengeance they'd brought to Bane.

I nodded and left Ankhor Works in a hurry, with the weight of all the club members' eyes on me. Now that I had Blade's word that they'd hold off on the war, I could proceed with the next step of my plan.

I had the photos of Bane's body, courtesy of the police department. I'd tell Crave that Bane was the rat, and that I'd killed him as retribution for his disloyalty. Dad respected a man with initiative, and since Logan had betrayed the Vipers, he was desperate for me to be his heir. I knew he'd immediately promote me to VP. It was only fair.

I'd been working on gaining the role of vice president for years. Soon I'd have all the access I needed to Viper's Nest's contacts so that I could gain enough evidence to bring down the trafficking rings—and bring down Crave along with them.

But now that Hell's Ankhor knew I was undercover, things were a little more complicated.

Coop followed me outside, his arms still crossed over his chest. Apparently his trust didn't even extend this far. "You better go straight back to the Vipers. No funny business."

I stood next to my bike and nodded. "I'm not letting this go south—I'm taking this trafficking ring down. Whatever it takes."

The enforcer rolled his eyes. "Whatever it takes, sure. No matter who gets steamrolled in the process, right?"

He stepped closer, uncrossing his arms, and his hands flexed at his side like he wanted to grab me, or punch me, or something.

I didn't back down. Our gazes met. The enforcer's pupils dilated, and his gaze flicked down to my mouth, and then back up to meet my eyes.

What was this guy playing at? Was this his way of trying to gain the upper hand? I placed my hand on his chest and gently pushed him backwards. God, was he built.

To my surprise, Coop stepped back, and then snorted a condescending laugh. "Get out of here before I change my mind."

"Straight back to the Vipers," I said, repeating his words. "No funny business."

I revved my engine and took off, riding north back to El Acantilado to report back to Crave. Somehow the ride back felt even worse tonight than it usually did, the memories of Coop and his anger weighing heavy on my mind. I wouldn't inform my boss at the police station about the enforcer who'd figured it out. I'd manage it on my own. I was so fucking close.

I could only hope I wasn't overplaying my hand. A lot of things had to go right in order for this to work out—and now it wasn't just me in the know. I had to worry about Hell's Ankhor keeping up their end of the deal, too.

I could only hope the rest of the job went quickly, because being vice president of the Viper's Nest?

That was my worst nightmare.

Printed in Great Britain
by Amazon